THE DRAGON

"I'm at a loss for words here, since I have no idea how to fully convey how much I loved *The Dragon Conspiracy* . . . With Makenna's typical sarcastic narration, nearly nonstop action, and plot twists which completely surprised me, *The Dragon Conspiracy* left me aching for more."

—All Things Urban Fantasy

"[Shearin's] skillful ability to combine scary and heart-stopping chills with laugh-out-loud humor is part of what makes her books such addictive gems." —*RT Book Reviews*

"With *The Dragon Conspiracy*, Lisa Shearin has gotten even more awesome! . . . [It] contains all of Shearin's trademarks: witty dialogue, a winning protagonist, and a plot that doesn't quit. I can't recommend Shearin's work enough."

—Tynga's Reviews

"A fantastic ensemble . . . A fun and thrilling urban fantasy adventure with characters I'd love to go out and have a drink with." —Bea's Book Nook

"Lisa Shearin has painted a wonderful picture of New York and all of its supernatural inhabitants . . . A fast-paced, fun read with all kinds of supernatural goodness and great world-building." —Wicked Little Pixie

"Funny, frightening, fast-paced . . . Imminent disaster has never been more fun." —38 Caliber Reviews

"A fast-paced urban fantasy, pack[ed] with action and interesting characters and surprises in most every turn." —Ami's Hoard

continued . . .

THE
BRIMSTONE
DECEPTION

A SPI Files Novel

LISA SHEARIN

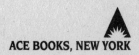
ACE BOOKS, NEW YORK

ACE

An imprint of Penguin Random House LLC
375 Hudson Street, New York, New York 10014

THE BRIMSTONE DECEPTION

An Ace Book / published by arrangement with the author

ISBN: 978-0-425-26693-9

PUBLISHING HISTORY
Ace mass-market edition / February 2016

PRINTED IN THE UNITED STATES OF AMERICA

10 9 8 7 6 5 4 3 2

Cover illustration by Julie Dillon.
Cover design by Judith Lagerman.
Interior text design by Kelly Lipovich.

Penguin
Random
House

I wasn't sure this qualified as a first date.

Yes, I was having lunch with one of the richest and most eligible bachelors of not only Manhattan but also another dimension. We were in a trendy new restaurant in Tribeca, with a celebrity chef in the kitchen. Two nights ago, I'd played a big part—along with said inter-dimensional bachelor—in saving the lives of the supernatural citizens of the tristate area.

That was three causes for celebration: hot guy, great food, still alive. Yay, me.

The fly in my fancy soup du jour, so to speak, was twofold.

First, on the other side of the restaurant, and unfortunately with a clear view of our table, was my partner, Ian Byrne. My name is Makenna Fraser. Ian and I work together at a worldwide organization fighting the forces of supernatural evil. Ian thought that my date, Rake Danescu, deserved a spot near the top of our most wanted list.

Second, I was still considered a newbie and my partner

was the protective type. Actually, that was part of his job. Protecting me, that is. Right now, those protective urges were getting on my last nerve. I'd had more than one near-death experience during the last few days, and was way overdue for some R&R. Having Ian only taking his eyes off of me long enough to stare crosshairs onto Rake's forehead was taking the rest right out of my relaxation. We'd recently ~~decided that a healthy mentor/mentee relationship shouldn't~~ also be a romantic relationship. I had to admit that took a lot of the tension—sexual and otherwise—out of our workday, which was good for focusing on the bad guys and not my partner's mighty fine backside. But right now, Ian was putting plenty of tension right back in. He wasn't jealous—at least I didn't think he was. I think he was being protective of his still relatively new partner.

"I knew you were reluctant to accept my invitation," Rake murmured, "but I assure you a bodyguard wasn't necessary."

I sighed. "I didn't tell him." It was a coincidence that we were all here at the same time. A really unpleasant and awkward coincidence.

Rake smiled slowly. "You didn't tell him? Oh, I like this devious side of you."

"I'm not being devious. My personal life isn't anyone's business but my own."

"I don't think he agrees with you."

"Doesn't appear that way, does it?"

Rake peered around a waiter to see who my partner was having lunch with, and to provoke Ian even more, he made a leisurely show of appreciating the view. I thought I heard Ian growl all the way from our table. Kylie gave Rake a smile and finger wave.

They knew each other.

Of course they did. They were both breathtakingly beautiful supernaturals.

Rake Danescu was a goblin. Kylie O'Hara was a dryad.

Kylie was a friend and coworker. Different department, same secret organization.

Interspecies dating wasn't frowned on by most supernaturals. Heck, dryads didn't have much of a choice. All dryads were female, and they all came from trees, so their intraspecies dating pool was more of a puddle. Unless they were lesbians or had a thing for botanicals, dryads had to hunt elsewhere when looking for love. Kylie had dark hair, green eyes, was five foot nothing, and like her sisters down through history, could probably get any man she wanted with the crook of one dainty digit.

Ian had had a crush on Kylie since she started at SPI. Though "crush" sounded like something out of high school. Let's say he admired her from afar, because getting close would violate one of the personal rules my stoic partner wouldn't allow himself to break—no workplace romance. I'd told him numerous times to just ask her out already. But in the end, it wasn't my doing that resulted in them being here together, it was the same near-death experience that had gotten me here with Rake. When Death does heavy breathing on the back of your neck, you reexamine your life. My partner decided that life was too uncertain to throw away potential happiness.

I smiled. The rule of "no workplace romance" was presently being bent until it squealed in Café Mina's corner booth. I wondered which of his "thou shalt nots" my partner would take out for a reexamining look-see next.

"Kylie O'Hara, a lovely girl," Rake said. "Though I always thought she had more discerning taste."

I gave him a look.

"What?" The goblin was all innocence, which was no mean feat for any goblin, let alone Rake.

"You know very well what. Ian doesn't trust you as far as he can throw you." I stopped and thought a moment. "Actually less than that. Night before last, the two of you were at each other's throats, and now here you are having lunch with his partner and making goo-goo eyes at his date."

"Goo-goo? That must be a droll, human term that I'm unfamiliar with. But if its meaning bears any resemblance to how it sounds, I assure you I have never made 'goo-goo eyes' in my life."

"It sounded better than undressing her with your eyes."

Rake lowered his voice to a soft rumble. "Do I detect a hint of jealousy?"

"In your dreams."

"You and Miss O'Hara battling, with me as the prize for the winner . . ." His dark eyes turned from teasing to full smolder. "That would be a dream worth remembering. I assure you, dearest Makenna, you are the only woman I am interested in undressing."

I took my napkin out of my lap and calmly placed it on the table.

"Are you required to check in with Agent Byrne every hour?" Rake asked, as I scooted my chair back to stand.

I didn't even need to glance at him to know he was smiling and enjoying himself immensely. But I did need to look at him to make sure he completely understood what I was about to say.

"You know I don't. Now wipe that grin off your face."

He actually batted his eyelashes at me. "What grin?"

"The grin that's telling Ian, 'I'm up to no good with your partner, and there's nothing you can do about it.' 'Cause I can guarantee you he *will* do something about it. Then I'll have to do something about the two of you, and no one here wants to see that."

"On the contrary, everyone here would *love* to see that, myself included. And now you've piqued my curiosity. We goblins are rather like your domestic cats in that regard. Once aroused, our curiosity must be satisfied." The gleam in his dark eyes said that satisfying his arousal in regard to me had nothing to do with curiosity.

That was Ian's problem.

Tall, dark, sleek, and seemingly made for sex, goblins had a reputation for . . . let's just say they had a reputation. A well-deserved one. Add to that Rake being the owner of Bacchanalia, Manhattan's most exclusive sex club, and Ian's concerns were justified, as Rake hadn't even tried to hide his interest in me. In fact, I think Rake had turned teasing me and antagonizing Ian about teasing me into his newest hobby.

I pushed my chair back and stood. Rake, playing at being the perfect gentleman, stood with me.

Ian needed to understand that I was a big girl and as such was totally aware of who Rake was and what he wanted. And he wasn't getting any of it until when—or if—I decided I wanted it, too. Not that it was any of Ian's business, which was another thing he needed to get through his head.

"I'll be back in a minute."

Rake smiled fully as he took his seat. Anyone watching saw an unwholesomely handsome man giving his date a dazzling smile. I saw all of that plus a pair of fangs. I was a seer. It was a rare ability that enabled me to see through wards, spells, shields, and glamours that supernaturals used to disguise themselves from the humans around them. Only about half the people in Café Mina were human; the rest were a mix of supernatural races.

So I knew exactly what Rake Danescu was, in more ways than one.

"I shall eagerly await your return," Rake all but purred.

I sighed. "Yeah."

I started across the restaurant, to the accompaniment of Rake's low chuckle.

Ian's date glanced up from her menu with a quick grin that, in the language of girlfriends everywhere, said: "I'm so happy for you!" Or if expressed in a single sound—"Squee!"

Ian was not happy—for me or anyone else—and he most certainly was not fighting back an urge to squee. The only urges Ian was fighting were violent ones, and he didn't appear to be fighting very hard.

"Stop it," I told him.

Two words. One directive. I didn't believe in beating around the bush.

"I haven't done anything," he said. The "yet" was unspoken.

"Neither has Rake."

"He wants to."

I resisted rolling my eyes. "So does every other red-blooded man with any woman they're attracted to." I left "yourself included" unsaid. I paused. Goblins had red blood, didn't they? For the sake of my argument I'd go with yes.

"Every other red-blooded man hasn't enthralled you," Ian noted.

Kylie did a combo groan and face palm.

"*Enthralled?* I'd ask you to please tell me you're kidding, but I know you're not."

"Rake Danescu is a dark mage, one of the best."

"And I'm a hick from the North Carolina mountains ripe for the pickin'."

"I did not say that."

"Oh yes, you did."

My first night on the job, Rake had magicked himself a look inside my mind. It hadn't been personal, merely business. Okay, maybe it had been a little personal. From what I understood, it'd be easier the next time. I'd been with SPI for well over a year now, and Rake hadn't tried it again.

The combativeness went out of Ian. "Mac, I'm simply worried that—"

A man screamed.

An immaculately groomed guy in a really nice suit who'd just come back from the men's room was staring in total and complete horror at his waiter. The guy was human; his waiter was not.

I could see that. The man shouldn't have been able to.

The two other suit-clad men across the table from him were staring at this guy like he'd lost his mind. They looked like a trio out for a business lunch. The screaming guy had a tablet next to him on the table. Yep, business lunch. If those were his clients, the screamer wasn't making a good impression.

Everyone else in the restaurant saw the waiter as what he wanted them to see—a hot-beyond-belief, twentysome-thing, out-of-work actor waiting tables to pay the rent. I saw what he really was—an incubus.

Somehow the businessman, who'd now progressed from screaming to babbling, saw what I was seeing.

The incubus's features were vaguely humanoid, but more closely resembled a creature out of a bad 1950s horror movie, with translucent skin and a slit suction cup for lips.

The man stood so quickly his thighs hit the table, nearly knocking it over on the two men with him, who scooted back to keep from taking soup in the lap. One guy wasn't so lucky with his drink, shouting a word people generally tried not to say at a polite business lunch as he grabbed a napkin and blotted the front of his pants.

The hysterically babbling man didn't notice.

I noticed his right hand was clenching a steak knife.

"He can see them," I whispered quickly to Ian.

Ian didn't answer. He didn't need to. He knew what I meant.

The man spun, taking in the supernaturals all around him, both diners and restaurant staff.

Then he spotted the one closest to him.

Rake.

Oh no.

Before Ian could stop me, I sprinted the short distance back to our table, stopping in front of Rake, trying to block the man's view. Fat lot of good that did since the goblin was now on his feet, ready to defend himself if necessary. Rake was a head taller than me, and other than the gray skin visible on his hands, from the neck up was everything that said "goblin" to anyone who could see past Rake's human glamour. To me, and any other supernatural or enlightened human with a pulse who could see past that glamour, Rake was gorgeous. But I could see where silvery skin, pointed ears, and fangs could be disconcerting.

The man's eyes widened in disbelief. "What . . . what are you?"

Ian stepped up like the former cop he was, his voice low and calm. "Sir, I need you to put down the knife."

The man quickly turned and saw the reassuringly human Ian.

"Do you see them?" His words came in a rush. "Can—"

"I see that you have a weapon, and you need to put it on the table next to you and step away."

Kylie was on her phone, no doubt calling headquarters.

The man spotted a couple sitting at the table behind us. Kelpies. Everyone else saw a nice, middle-age couple. He saw vaguely human creatures with green skin, gills, and a mouthful of sharp teeth.

"Monsters!" he shrieked.

He staggered back, stumbling and catching himself on a bananas Foster serving cart. He stayed upright, the cart didn't. Flames ignited the closest tablecloth, and were fed by the spilled rum.

People screamed, shouted, and ran for the exits as the sprinkler system went off.

I heard a siren outside. Someone must have already called the police. Now we needed the fire department, too.

Rake stepped up close behind me, his lips at my ear. "I promised you'd never be bored on a date with me."

"This wasn't what I had in mind."

All signs of playfulness were gone. "Neither did I."

With his hand at the small of my back, Rake steered me toward the restaurant's kitchen, away from the fire and the crowd surging toward the front doors. In a panic, people tended to go with the obvious, even if it wasn't the closest or safest. Leave it to Rake to know the back way out of a building he'd never been in before.

Ian and Kylie were right behind us.

I turned my head toward Ian. "Where—"

"He dropped the knife and ran out the front," Ian told me. "First one out. Right into the waiting arms of my former brothers in blue."

"In addition to his freedom," Kylie said, "I think it's safe to say he just lost his clients *and* the account."

GOBLINS, elves, vampires, werewolves, fairies, trolls, dwarves, and anything else you've read about in fairy tales or your favorite fantasy novel series.

They're all real.

It used to be known, confirmed, and accepted fact that all of those and more existed. Then humans went and got themselves civilized and educated. The smarter humans thought they were, and the more they thought they knew, the less they believed in things that went bump in the night.

Their disbelief didn't make any of those things any less real—or deadly.

In a world where supernaturals lived alongside humans, what you couldn't see could kill you. Some of them could even bring you back from the dead and kill you again.

Magic exists, monsters are real, and fighting the forces of evil is a full-time job. At least there's hazard pay.

Humans, being human, merely thought up more explanations for what monsters were, and excuses for what they couldn't possibly be.

To tell you the truth, our job was a lot easier when John and Suzie Q. Public didn't know they were lucky to make it to the office every morning without getting pecked to pieces. Though that was only during the Werepigeon Infestation of 2003. Before my time, but definitely one for the agency history books.

New Yorkers pride themselves on not even batting an eye when they walk past the weird, the wacky, and the otherworldly.

I've got news; if they saw someone change into a werewolf right in front of them, their blasé would go bye-bye, probably along with the contents of their bladder. Heck, the sound effects alone—bones popping, sinews stretching, muzzle elongating and sprouting fangs—would be enough to send them screaming into the night.

We battle the creatures of the night and keep humans in the dark.

We're the agents of Supernatural Protection & Investigations. SPI is a worldwide organization, but New York is home to the U.S. and world headquarters.

There are two New Yorks. As if there isn't enough traffic in one.

There's the New York that millions of people see, hear, touch, smell, and in the summer when the wind's right and the garbage barges are ripe, taste. Then there's the New York that's home to the world's largest concentration of supernatural beings—unseen, unheard, unknown. And it's SPI's job to keep it that way.

I was one of the agency's five seers. Since the beginning of crime, some bad guys—human or otherwise—have depended on disguises to elude capture. While humans were limited to wigs, makeup, and the ever popular but terribly ineffective sunglasses, supernaturals could tap into their magic or buy an amulet that would enable them to alter their appearance, or even hide their entire body with a cloaking spell.

It didn't matter what they used, or how good it was, I could see right through any and all of it.

So seers were downright handy in an organization like SPI.

I pointed out the bad guys, and our agents or commando teams brought them in.

Ian was our top agent.

Kylie was our director of media and public relations.

And Rake pretty much had a permanent spot on our suspects list.

Right now the four of us were sharing a booth in a coffee shop around the corner from the restaurant. The police had taken it as their interviewing room since Café Mina was presently a smoke-filled ruin. One of the cops had recognized Ian from their time together in the NYPD, and one of the staff had told them that Ian had tried to disarm the hallucinating crazy guy. Since the three of us were with him, they wanted our statements as well.

Lucky us.

Ian and Rake had declared an unspoken temporary truce. I knew it wasn't due to any newfound camaraderie, but rather that it wouldn't go over well to beat the crap out of each other in front of the cops. For the moment, they could pretend to make nice.

The officer who'd taken our statements was an elf. He knew who we were and who we worked for—or at least he knew who Ian and Kylie were, and everyone knew who Rake was. The elf couldn't see through Rake's glamour, but he knew what Rake's human glamour looked like. The elf didn't know me from Adam's house cat, and I was fine with that. It's never been a goal of mine to be recognized on sight by the police force of any city.

From what the guy had been screaming while being taken

into custody, it was apparent that he could see the supernaturals in the restaurant with him for what they really were. The young elven officer knew that but he couldn't exactly put that in his report. I felt bad for him, but in a place like New York, with its huge supernatural population, being able to work a case while keeping the city's biggest secret was a required talent. If he couldn't juggle, he'd better learn fast.

"The gentleman began behaving strangely after coming out of the men's room," Rake said. "While you were arguing," he added with an amiable smile, looking right at Ian, "I was observing."

"Arguing?" the elf cop asked Ian.

"A personal matter, Officer."

Ian's face was a perfect mask of neutrality; however, from Rake's pained hiss, Ian had just introduced the heel of his boot to the top of Rake's foot. Then Ian grunted as Kylie did the same to him, except with a stiletto heel.

I rolled my eyes.

"So you're implying that he may have taken a drug?" the officer asked.

"Well, he wasn't screaming about monsters *before* he went to the head," drawled a familiar voice from behind me.

Our day was finally looking up.

Lieutenant Frederick Ash was a detective with the NYPD's drug enforcement unit and, like the elven officer, was clued in to SPI and the supernatural community. Unlike the young elf, Fred was an elf/human hybrid. While he had enough elven blood running through his veins to use minor magic, his physical appearance lacked the jewel-tone eyes, pale skin, and pointed ears that marked the elven race, so no glamour was needed.

Fred was plainspoken and said it like he saw it.

I liked him.

I liked it even better that he was here.

Ian liked it enough that he and Fred did the bro-hug thing. Though they'd worked closely together during Ian's time with the NYPD, his leaving the force to come work for SPI hadn't weakened that bond. Not to mention, it helped us to have people inside the NYPD, and the reverse was true for them. A lot of crime in the city crossed the human/supernatural barrier, which sometimes wasn't so much a barrier as a chalk outline on a sidewalk, an outline drawn around human and supernatural alike.

Kylie's eyes went to the street outside. I turned to look.

Oh crap.

Two news trucks complete with satellite dishes. For now it was probably to cover the destruction of the city's newest trendy restaurant, but all it would take would be talking to any of the patrons, most of whom would love to be on TV, to root out the cause of the fire. A previously upstanding businessman suddenly seeing monsters, who was probably cooling his heels in a padded observation room by now, would spark the sensation and ratings seeker that was in the heart of every TV journalist.

"Officer, do you have any more questions for me?" Kylie asked.

"No, ma'am."

She nodded in the direction of the news trucks. "Then if you all would excuse me, it's time I went to work."

She scooted out of the booth and headed for the door, heels clicking on the tile with sharp purpose.

Media and Public Relations is SPI's largest and sometimes most critical department. Kylie and her team were hands-down the best at what they did—neutralizing a supernatural exposure problem *before* it became a publicly visible crisis. In addition, Kylie's "secret identity" was a world-renowned debunker of the supernatural, and the ultimate mistress of misinformation. She put herself front and center on TV and radio talk shows, and was accepted by respected journalists as an expert on the exposé.

Kylie was the best at spinning a supernatural news story the way she—and SPI—needed it to go.

Fred jerked his head in the direction of a back table. "A word with you, Ian?"

"Sure."

The boys went off to chat, leaving me and Rake alone.

An immaculately groomed man with a microphone and cameraman in tow met Kylie at the door. Though "met" was a little mild. "Ambushed" was a more accurate description.

There could've been hurricane-force winds out there and not one hair on Baxter Clayton's head would've moved.

Baxter was an investigative reporter for a local TV station and an all-round asshat. I didn't envy Kylie her job right now. Actually, I'd never envied Kylie's job. I was a horrible liar and even worse at hiding how I felt when around people I didn't like, and Baxter Clayton definitely qualified.

Rake swore.

"What?"

"Baxter Clayton."

"Yeah, I don't like him, either. I don't think anyone does. That's probably why they keep him around. The guy everyone loves to hate. Hate equals high ratings."

"He hasn't been trying to get you on camera for a story on New York's upper-class sex industry," Rake muttered.

I bit back a snort.

"It's not funny."

Baxter Clayton was in earnest conversation with a professionally poised and smiling Kylie.

"It looks like Kylie's taking one for the team then. You owe her."

"Yes, Miss O'Hara will have my eternal gratitude *if* I can get out of here without being seen."

Rake was ruffled. It was a rare sight, so I was going to enjoy it while it lasted. "You do a lot of ducking out back doors, don't you?" I asked with a smile.

"Enough that I've become quite adept at it."

With that, he scooped my hand off the table and brought it to his lips.

His voice softened. "And by the way, this lunch didn't count. A maniac setting fire to the table next to ours doesn't qualify as a successful date."

"Define successful," I managed.

The goblin gently turned my hand and placed a lingering kiss on the palm, sending a tingle of sensation to other places.

"No dinner," I said, trying for firm and uncompromising—and probably failing miserably.

Rake's eyes glittered. "Breakfast then?"

"You don't give up, do you?"

"Not anytime soon."

"How about another lunch?" I suggested.

"How about tomorrow?"

"I'll check and get back to you."

"If you don't, I will."

Giving the back of my fingers a parting brush of his lips, Rake quickly escaped out the back door.

I snuck a glance over at Ian and Fred. Thankfully, my partner had his back to me.

Fred did not.

From the sly wink he just gave me, I'd say he saw Rake's Cyrano de Bergerac exit. Then he gestured me over to join them.

Oh boy.

"I was just telling your partner what your knife-wielding businessman had likely snorted."

"So it was a drug," I said.

Fred nodded. "A new one. High-end designer."

Ian glanced back at the now empty booth.

"Rake had to leave," I told him before he could ask any questions that I'd completely blow answering.

Fred, bless him, didn't say a word.

Kylie wasn't the only one who'd taken one for the team. It looked like I might owe Fred one, too.

"I was telling Ian that from what I've heard about Brimstone, your boy was one of the latest customers."

"Brimstone?"

Fred shrugged. "That's what they're calling it. It can be smoked or snorted. We haven't gotten our hands on any yet for the lab to play with, and the latest customer didn't have any more on him. One of our sources told us it's lava colored. We're assuming that's the source of the name. And from the reactions of the three people who've taken it while in public . . ." Fred lowered his voice. "One of the side effects is that they can see supernaturals."

"Through glamours," I said, likewise keeping my voice down.

"Through anything."

Glamours, shields, wards, and cloaks.

"Well, there goes my job security," I said.

"Hardly," Fred replied. "The humans who've gotten hold of the stuff freak out like you just saw."

"How about supernaturals?" Ian asked.

"Unknown. We've had no reports of a supernatural under the influence of Brimstone. We didn't find out about the stuff until a couple days ago. But if supernaturals were taking it, they wouldn't exactly scream about seeing monsters."

"How long do the effects last?" Ian asked.

"They start to come down after a couple of hours." He paused. "Good part is that they don't remember what they saw, just that it was the mother of all bad trips."

"Great," I said. "At least if they got the crap scared out of them, they won't be lining up to buy more."

"Wish people had that much sense," Fred said. "When I heard we might have another customer, I wanted to get some fresh eyewitness accounts." He grinned. "Imagine my surprise to find you two among the witnesses."

"It wasn't exactly how we intended our lunch hour to go," I said.

"I got that impression." His blue eyes twinkled.

Fred didn't need to elaborate. Ian and Fred were beer and steak kinds of guys. Café Mina was hardly where either one would go—or could afford to go—to grab a quick bite for lunch. Fred simply eyed Ian's sports jacket and tie, glanced out at Kylie, grinned, and gave my partner a congratulatory smack on the shoulder.

Detective Fred Ash. Master of deduction and masculine nonverbal communication.

"Know where the supply is coming from?" Ian asked. My partner was the master at ignoring questions, direct or implied.

"That's the reason I'm glad to run into you two here," Fred replied. "We'll continue to investigate, but let's just say we'll only be able to get so far."

Ian swore mildly, like a man who knew he wasn't going to have time for more fancy lunches anytime soon.

Fred nodded. "Yeah. I'd bet my next paycheck that Brimstone came from out of town."

_____▲ **3**

WHEN you worked for SPI or were clued in to the supernatural world, "out of town" didn't mean Hoboken.

A supernatural criminal entrepreneur was cutting him- or herself a slice of New York's drug-dealing pie. The highly profitable, upper-crust part. That wasn't going to make the city's established drug lords and ladies very happy. And when they weren't happy, and that much money was involved, blood would start flowing.

What lunch I'd managed to eat hadn't even had a chance to settle before we got the call.

The goblin manager of an upscale apartment building had received a tenant complaint of heat and a really bad smell coming from the apartment next door. Suspecting a fire of some sort, he'd quickly knocked, and when no one answered, he used his master key to open the door.

He saw what was inside and promptly closed it.

He then called SPI, not the NYPD.

There was a dead body, it was a supernatural, and the stink was sulfur.

Sulfur could mean one of two things: demons or a black-magic-spawned portal. Or both. None of the above signaled fun times ahead for us.

Sulfur was another name for brimstone.

Coincidence?

I wasn't gonna hold my breath on that one. Especially when we learned who the dearly departed was.

Sar Gedeon.

Elf, exiled aristocrat, and drug lord, who was most definitely from out of town, just like the new designer drug.

The apartment building was only two blocks from Café Mina.

We were there within minutes.

Normally Ian and I weren't part of an initial response team unless the investigation required the services of a seer, but we were the closest agents. Our job was to secure the scene from mortal authorities until SPI's crime scene investigators could get there.

Like humans, supernaturals died every day in New York, and everywhere else for that matter. There was a problem when supernatural deaths involved a crime. Crime meant police, and police meant the potential for exposure.

Literally.

Supernaturals who didn't look human needed a glamour to disguise themselves. Any glamour, regardless of the power of the spells that held it in place, faded within one hour after death. In a murder investigation, that meant that the victim would go through a quick and rather startling transformation, either before the police arrived or while they—and the body—were still on the scene. Those were the tough ones.

Each major city had its own supernatural medical examiner's office that reported suspicious deaths to the regional SPI office.

Supernatural families also notified SPI in the case of any

unusual deaths, and our investigators and medical examiners responded. Humans have local morticians and funeral homes, and so do supernaturals. Each race has cultural or religious beliefs that dictate what is done with a body after death—without attracting the attention of mortal authorities. But when supernaturals made themselves a part of human society—or were inconsiderate enough to get themselves murdered in public—things could get dicey.

That was the situation we were dealing with now.

Ian discreetly showed his badge to the doorman at the Murwood.

The man glanced down at the ID and at Ian's face without moving anything except a pair of cool gray eyes. He wore the double-breasted, quasi-military style of long coat and hat that seemed to be the uniform of doormen at uppercrusty apartment and condo buildings citywide. His bearing said ex-military or police, loud and clear. Then his face took on the neutral and faraway expression that signaled someone was speaking to him on his Bluetooth earpiece. Either that, or he was having an out-of-body experience.

"Mr. Nadisu is expecting you." Not taking his eyes off either us or anyone else on the street nearby—which was a nifty trick—he reached back and opened the door for us.

The lobby of my apartment building was more of a foyer with mailboxes against one wall. It was almost impossible to squeeze past anyone checking their mail without way too much intimate contact with a neighbor whose name you didn't know.

At least a dozen of my lobbies would have fit in the Murwood's.

The goblin who met us there looked like his day was going worse than ours.

Goblins liked being in control of themselves and everyone and everything around them. You'd never see a goblin frazzled, at least not in public, and definitely not in front of strangers. This guy was frazzled. He wanted to be cool and collected, but today just wasn't his day to get what he wanted.

As Ian and I could attest, there was a lot of that going around.

There was no one else in the posh lobby, but Ian still kept his voice down as he introduced us, even though Jesin Nadisu knew who we were. Official protocol had to be observed.

Anyone else, Ian included, would see a human man, in his mid-thirties, impeccably dressed in a suit that probably made him fit right in with the building's wealthy tenants. He wouldn't want to offend his tenants' sensibilities by wearing anything that came off the rack. Other than that, there wasn't anything that made him particularly noticeable.

Brown hair, brown eyes, medium height. Like his suit, Jesin Nadisu had gone out of his way to blend in.

With my seer vision, I saw a surprisingly young and unsurprisingly handsome goblin in his early twenties (or whatever the goblin age equivalent was) with sleek, shoulder-length, blue-black hair pulled back in a tight ponytail at the nape of his neck, with large dark eyes. Elves and goblins age slower than humans, and do a better job of it while they do; no plastic surgery or Botox shots needed.

The goblin gestured. "This way, please."

We took one of the elevators to the seventh floor.

"How long has Mr. Gedeon lived in the apartment?" Ian asked.

"Mr. Gedeon owns . . . *owned* the apartment," the goblin said, "but he didn't live there. He visited once or sometimes twice a week. He kept the place for a lady friend."

"The name of the tenant?" Ian asked.

"Mara Lorenz. She went out of town two days ago."

"Then why was Mr. Gedeon here?"

Jesin Nadisu's professional reserve cracked and he smiled slightly. "The same reason he was always here. To get away from his wife."

When we got to the seventh floor, the stench of sulfur smacked us all in the face.

The goblin unlocked the apartment door, but made no move to open it.

I didn't blame him. He'd been there, done that, got the trauma.

Ian broke the silence. "Mr. Nadisu, I need you to return to the lobby and wait for our lab team."

The goblin nodded with no small measure of relief and turned toward the elevator.

"And don't let anyone in unless they live in the building or are from Sarkowski Plumbing," my partner added. "They're our lab team."

"I wouldn't anyway. This is a secure building." The young goblin winced. "At least it was." He swallowed in an audible gulp. "And on my watch." He paused. "Would your non-admittance request include any of Mr. Gedeon's business associates?"

"It would. And do not discuss what you have seen with anyone."

"My discretion and that of the Murwood is assured for *all* of our tenants."

"Good. Keep it that way."

I noticed he never said he wouldn't tell anyone, just that his discretion was assured. With goblins, you had to watch for the small print. Many of the top lawyers in the city were goblins—and more than a few of the politicians. I was sure Ian had noticed; he chose not to try to wrangle a promise out of him. A goblin could find ways to get around those, too.

But I still felt sorry for him. Contrary to what Ian had told him, he'd have to tell the owner of the building what had happened. I was sure we could count on their discretion as well. No landlord wanted to spread around that a murder had occurred in one of their buildings.

"Have any of the other tenants been asking questions?" Ian asked.

"No, just from the apartment one floor below, and the couple next door. They've since left for a luncheon engagement. I've called and told them that I've looked into it, and there's no cause for concern."

Goblins could spin a lie as easily as breathing. Like I said, they were great lawyers and politicians.

In my book, your next-door neighbor getting himself murdered was plenty cause for concern. Though if Sar Gedeon had been specifically targeted—considering what he did for a living, that scenario was highly likely—there really wasn't any need for the neighbors to worry for their own safety. That is, unless they stuck their noses where they didn't belong and the killer got wind of it. So, when you looked at it like that, the manager's lie might have saved their lives. See? He lied and it was for their own good. It was all in how you spun it.

As soon as the elevator doors closed, Ian drew his gun, which was loaded with silver-infused hollow points.

"Stay here," he told me.

"I can do that."

Not only could I do that, I was glad to do that. Running underneath the sulfur stink was an odor I could only describe as burned beef brisket. I wasn't a math whiz, but the smell of burned meat coming from a room with a dead body? Those added up to a cause of death I was in no hurry to confirm for myself.

Ian opened the door and slipped into the apartment.

I had the smell of sulfur and burned flesh to keep me company while I waited in the hall. I didn't know which one was worse; but since they were both here, I didn't have to choose. Lucky me.

I was familiar with the smell of brimstone. I'd gotten a snootful of the stuff only once before, and that was one time too many.

My SPI training had included a class in what was generously called "Aroma Identification." When tracking a supernatural suspect, let's just say that sometimes visual contact didn't come first.

One of the aromas covered in class was brimstone. Our instructor kept samples in airtight containers of substances we needed to immediately know when we caught a whiff of it.

Brimstone was the biggie.

Its presence at a crime scene or while in pursuit of a suspect indicated two things that set my survival instinct to twitching: demons and black-magic-spawned portals.

Neither were things you wanted catching you by surprise.

Two minutes and no shots fired later, Ian opened the door and I stepped in just far enough for him to close the door behind me.

4

WHEN a supernatural dies, any glamour they might have been using to disguise their true appearance fades within the first hour after death. A supernatural creature manifesting on a slab in the city morgue in front of a screaming technician was one of those awkward moments it was part of our job to prevent. The scene inside that apartment was bad, but wasn't the worst I'd ever seen. Believe me, you haven't seen a murder scene until you've busted into a room after a grendel has had ten seconds to rip arms, legs, and head off some poor sot, and dangle his intestines from an overhead light fixture like a party streamer.

I thought that had to be the apex of disgusting, and as far as the ick meter went.

This came close. What the building manager had found beyond that apartment door jumped right over awkward and landed smack dab on bizarre.

Sar Gedeon had gotten away from his wife. Too bad he hadn't had similar success with his murderer.

And it was most definitely a murder.

The dead elf was shirtless, as if the killer wanted to show off his work. Though at least he still had his pants on. His killer had apparently decided to confine his work to above the waist.

Gedeon's hands were clenched into claws, and the palms and insides of the fingers had been burned black. So much for the source of the burned brisket smell. The other burned body part was the skin over and around the breastbone. It had been branded with a single hoofprint. Though considering the presence of the sulfur smell, I figured we weren't dealing with a homicidal cow.

The brand was either a signature by the demon that had done the burning, or the way it had held down the elf while it—or a partner in crime—had caused what looked to me, a non-medical professional, as the likely cause of death.

A gaping hole in Sar Gedeon's chest.

Ian approached the body, careful not to step on any stain or splatter, squatted down next to the chest, and looked inside.

His brow creased. "That's interesting."

Only a man who'd spent five years as a homicide detective in the NYPD and the seven years before that doing something in the military that he wouldn't (or couldn't) talk about would describe the inside of a man's open chest as "interesting." Made me wonder what it'd take to make my partner regret eating lunch, which made me know I didn't want to find out.

However, being the curious type, I found Ian's description irresistible.

I went to where Ian squatted, leaned over his shoulder, and took a peek.

And regretted it.

Curiosity wouldn't kill a cat, but getting a gander of this could make it hork up one heck of a hairball. Right now, I was about to do something similar.

I'd heard our folks who dealt with bodies as part of their

jobs carried a little jar of Vicks with them. Constantly. On duty or off. With SPI, you never knew when off duty could turn to very much on duty.

Back in North Carolina's pollen-filled spring and fall seasons, Vicks was my best friend. Some nights I was so stuffy I couldn't get to sleep without a swipe of that wondrous eucalyptus-scented goop under my nose. Since coming to New York, my allergies were gone. My Vicks was buried in the dark recesses of the cabinet under my bathroom sink. When I got home, I was going spelunking.

I already carried Dramamine and Tums. Now I was adding Vicks. I'd only been on the job a year and I was already carrying around my own starter pharmacy.

Ian had his phone out. The pick up on the other end was quick. Ian's communication was even faster. "We've got a demon, Class Five or higher."

That'd send the folks at headquarters scrambling. Classes of demons went up to twelve. In my opinion, five was bad enough. Anything higher wasn't known for having a light enough touch to leave a brand. We wouldn't have found a hole in the victim's chest; we'd have found a hole where the vic had been squashed into the floor.

Not all demons had cloven hooves, but no other supernatural did—except for satyrs and minotaurs, and neither one of those could radiate heat through their bodies to burn hands and brand a chest.

"You're sure it wasn't a branding iron?" I didn't think it was, but it never hurt to hope.

"The burns on Gedeon's hands weren't made by grabbing a branding iron," Ian said. "The fingers are spread the same width apart and burned in the same places. Our vic was grabbing a demon's leg. The span of his hands indicates a larger demon, at least Class Five. The cloven hoof was holding him down while the demon's partner cut his chest open and ripped his heart out."

My lip curled. "That looks a bit jagged for a knife. Maybe a claw?"

Ian looked closer at the inside of the elf's ruined chest. "A possibility. Good catch."

My lip twisted further. "Thanks."

"Do you see any other evidence to support that?"

Only my partner would turn a gruesome murder scene into a pop quiz.

"The lack of blood and dark edging around the entry wound suggests cauterization." I managed a swallow, though it was more of a gulp to keep from gagging. "And what blood is there is blackened." I gulped again, any attempt at cool and casual be damned. "Like it was heated."

Ian nodded approvingly. "Nice."

None of this was nice . . . not sight, nor smell, nor oily feel on my skin from the brimstone and burned flesh.

It'd take me a while before I'd be able to eat barbeque again. And for a Southern girl, that was a crime in itself.

The NYPD knew Sar Gedeon as a human drug lord. If they'd come in here now, they would have found him dead, sporting Spock ears, a cauterized hole in his torso, no heart, and a hoofprint branded into his chest. I'd like to be a fly on the wall for that investigation.

"So what would your precinct buddies have to say about this one?" I asked, putting a couple steps distance between me and the elf brisket.

"From a human viewpoint, we've got cosplay with the ears, possible devil worship with the brand, and apparent human sacrifice. This case would drive them crazy, but they'd love the challenge. I never thought I'd say anything like this, but knowing elves and demons are real can certainly simplify an investigation." One side of his mouth quirked in a quick grin. "Makes me damned glad I came over to the dark side."

I nodded. "And we have cookies."

"The locked door and no sign of entrance or exit would

have thrown them for a loop. We know that brimstone could very well be from the leftovers of a gate. Demons aren't exactly known for walking in through the front door. With a gate, they're in, rip out a heart, they're out. Nice and neat."

I wasn't seeing anything nice or neat.

"Why would a class-five demon kill a drug lord?" I asked. "Would one of his business rivals hire demons for a professional hit?"

"Never heard of demons hiring out their services." Ian paused. "Unless the guy doing the hiring was interested in offering his soul for the low, low price of one murder."

I raised one brow.

"Demons don't accept cash," Ian explained.

"Not even credit cards? With the interest rates some of those things have, I wouldn't be surprised to find Satan himself in the big office." Then I remembered about the heat the other tenants had complained about. It felt fine in here to me. "So was the heat coming from the body or the demon?"

Ian shook his head. "Neither. It would have been from the portal the demon used to get in."

"That makes sense. That Jesin Nadisu guy seems to be on the ball. I couldn't see him missing a pair of demons strolling through his lobby."

"The area near the wall around the corner felt warmer," Ian told me. "Since there aren't any vents nearby, that'd be the most likely portal location."

I went to take a look.

Unless a portal was standing open it couldn't be seen. If Ian hadn't seen the portal, that meant it was closed. Closed equaled safe. A portal could only be used by the being that created it, or someone the creator had keyed to that specific portal. It was security at its finest.

I stepped into a short hallway. . .

And simply stared.

The wall was glowing. Orange. Not the entire wall, just a section, a seam running from the floor to a few feet from the ceiling. The seam was closed, but that didn't keep the glow from spilling onto the hardwood floor at my feet.

The light didn't come from the wall itself. It came from what lay beyond, and I didn't mean in the next room.

It was the portal, complete with sulfuric heat coming from it in waves.

A shadow from the other side eclipsed the light.

I took a step back, eyes locked on the opening.

There was something just on the other side.

Watching me.

It knew I could see it and the portal.

Terror put my gun in my hand, even though I knew that whatever was on the other side would laugh at my puny mortal weapon. I slowly backed away, my gun held low in a two-handed grip, trying to stop my hands from shaking.

My terror made it past my lips with one word.

"Ian." I could barely hear myself.

No response from the front room.

I swallowed hard and tried again.

"Ian."

An instant later, Ian was beside me, gun drawn.

The shadow retreated.

Ian looked where I was looking, body tense and ready for anything.

He saw nothing.

"Mac, we're looking at a wall."

"And it's not all there."

My partner looked like he was thinking the same thing about me.

"There's a big glowing gash down the middle," I said.

"Describe it." His voice immediately went tight with apprehension.

Now we were getting somewhere.

"It's a gash in the middle of the wall," I told him, trying to be the analytical professional I was supposed to be. "It starts at the floor and goes up about six feet. The gash is closed, so it's more like a seam, and where it comes together is . . ." I made a face. "Squishy. Like glowing orange Jell-O."

"Orange?"

"Jell-O."

"And you can see it."

"I could also see the shadow of a thing on the other side."

"The other side?" Ian adjusted the hold on his gun.

I suddenly needed a place to sit down, but I'd only be doing that after I ran all the way down to the lobby, probably to the accompaniment of my own screams.

"Uh-huh. But I can't see portals."

"That appears to no longer be the case."

I took another step back. "How?"

"Don't know."

We both looked at the wall: me at the portal, Ian at where I'd told him the portal was.

"I take it the color means something?" I asked.

"Oh, yes."

Ian had his phone out again, eyes still on the wall as if he expected something to jump out of it at any second. That made both of us.

I waited for someone at headquarters to pick up. I had no doubt Ian was calling headquarters again, just as I had no doubt that orange wasn't a good color for a portal.

Sulfur stink plus hoofprint brand equaled a portal that in all likelihood went to a place I had no desire to go.

And something in that undesirable place had seen me see it.

Oh crap.

5

SPI'S lab team arrived, and so far demons hadn't poured out of the wall.

Both were good things.

The seam had also stopped glowing and the wall appeared more solid.

Good things number three and four. We were on a roll.

Ian had left a voicemail for Vivienne Sagadraco telling her about me and the portal.

He'd told me not to tell anyone what I'd seen until the boss gave the okay. I had absolutely no problem with that. I didn't want to think about it, let alone get chatty with anyone.

Just to be on the safe side, Ian had requested backup of the demon-fighting variety, and until they arrived, we stayed.

I was happy to say that our wait was blissfully uneventful.

I didn't hold out the same hope for our investigation. When you were dealing with demons, you were guaranteed to get "eventful" by the bucket load.

However, I knew that one thing would go right. When investigating a murder, SPI had one huge advantage over the NYPD.

We had a necromancer on staff.

Once we got Sar Gedeon back to headquarters, Bert could just ask the elf who killed him.

I didn't think Sar Gedeon's body could look worse.

I was wrong.

I was convinced that morgues had the same lighting as department store dressing rooms. One made you look dead; the other made you look so fat you wished you were dead. Neither even tried to be flattering.

I looked at the elf. He didn't look like he'd gained any weight, just lost more blood, or maybe it'd just pooled in his back and butt like I'd seen on *CSI*. Now if we could solve a murder in an hour like they did.

I wondered briefly about putting "flattering morgue lighting" on my end-of-life request list.

I'd be gone and wouldn't care, but I'd rather no one see me on a stainless steel table looking anywhere near that bad. Though hopefully, some of me wouldn't have been partially cooked, and I wouldn't have had a sadistic killer rip his way into my chest and cut out my heart while his demon buddy held me down with his big ol' cow hoof. I didn't care who you were, no one looked good after that.

We were six stories below Manhattan's Washington Square Park in the lab of SPI's world headquarters complex. Nearly as big as the park itself, the complex was centered around what we called the bull pen, which was where most of the field agents had their offices. Above were five stories of steel catwalks connecting labs, more offices, and conference rooms.

We were in the morgue section of the lab. It was my first time here and I really wouldn't have minded it being my last.

Everything was white tile and stainless steel, and totally

pristine—except for the burned brisket of a mutilated elf on the table. A table with troughs and drains.

Normally when I felt this queasy, I went straight for the ginger ale and saltines.

Our resident necromancer, Bertram Ferguson, looked like somebody's grandpa. That is, if their grandpa was Santa Claus.

Even though it was only the first week of November, Bert knew better than to wear anything red. The belt loop on his jeans had long since turned over their challenging job to suspenders. Today's suspenders were navy, the plaid shirt dark green, making him look less like Santa Claus and more like an understated lumberjack. Bert was big, not in an excess of fat, but bigness of big.

The necromancer's strength and speed were equally notable. Bert attended a crime scene only if there was a dead body, but that didn't mean there couldn't still be living perpetrators lurking around. For all his size, the necromancer could outsprint most SPI field agents to reach the safety of his armored van, though it was more like a laboratory on wheels. Not being eaten by the monster du jour was a powerful motivator.

Outside the morgue lab, Bert had met me with his usual bear hug. And as usual, I'd had to stand on tippy toes to even try to get my arms over his shoulders to hug his neck. I and everyone else at SPI loved Bert Ferguson.

He regarded me with his bright blue eyes. And yes, like Santa's, they did twinkle.

"I understand you had unexpected company at lunch," he said.

"Ian or the guy having the bad trip?"

"Yes. Which one ruined your date more?"

I blinked. "You knew about my date?"

"Everyone knew. So which one was it?"

"I'll have to think about that and get back to you."

Bert chuckled. "Take it easy on him, he's—"

I waved a hand. "I know. He's just doing his job."

"That, too. You don't have any big brothers, do you?"

"No brothers, period. No sisters, either."

Bert gently patted me on the shoulder with one big paw. "You've got a brother now. And he's going to take care of you whether you like it or not."

"I'm getting that impression."

The morgue tech stuck her head out the door. "Whenever you're ready, Bert."

DETECTIVE Fred Ash had asked to be present for the pre-autopsy questioning. Before starting work at SPI, those were two words I never thought I'd hear together.

A few supernatural members of the NYPD enjoyed SPI headquarters privileges. Fred was one of them. When crimes involved supernatural perps or victims, shared information between SPI and select members of the NYPD had brought criminals to justice many times. It was a working relationship we all valued.

Ian and I were in the morgue because with me able to see the portal the killers had used to enter and leave the scene of the crime, this case was going to land on our desks with a resounding thud.

I'd called my manager, Alain Moreau, about what I'd seen. He hadn't been in his office, so I'd left a voicemail. My being able to see portals was the earth-shattering equivalent of a documented visitation from the Almighty himself, so I expected my vampire manager to come crashing through the morgue door any moment now.

The tech left to give Bert more privacy to work, so it was just the four of us. Five, if you counted the corpse we were about to have a conversation with.

Bert sure wasn't creepy and neither was questioning the victim of a violent crime. But when said victim hadn't survived the perpetration of said violent crime . . . if that didn't say creepy loud and clear, I didn't know what did.

One heaping helping of nightmare fodder, coming up.

I'd seen Bert communicate with the soul of a newly dead person once before—one that hadn't been murdered. A silvery mist had risen from the body and stopped to hover directly above it. The form was vaguely the size and shape of the body it'd arisen from. There was no face, no features, and of course, nothing that could be used to speak. The investigating agent asked the questions; Bert spoke for the dead person.

Anyone who didn't know Bert or was unfamiliar with how a necromancer worked would consider this an arrangement ripe for fraud. Though I'd like to hear their explanation for the body-sized and -shaped mist, and the details that only the victim would have known that came from Bert's mouth.

Not only was Bert legit, he was considered one of the best at his craft, period.

The process itself was quite simple and relied solely on the power of Bert's necromantic magic, which was considerable.

"Sar Gedeon."

The boom of Bert's deep and resonate voice filled the morgue's tiled walls and then some. I jumped in spite of myself. His voice and the power behind it didn't ask the dead elf to come and talk to us, it commanded him.

Nothing happened.

At least that was the way it looked. How it felt was like I'd been turned into one of those long, skinny balloons that clowns used at kids' birthday parties, and Bert's magic was hell-bent on twisting me into a poodle. Ian and Fred looked equally uncomfortable.

I swear I heard my joints pop. I sure as hell felt it. You didn't have to be a sensitive to feel magic on the level of Bert's.

I sucked in as much air as my lungs could pull in. I knew I was going to need it. Not that I minded not breathing in a room dedicated to cutting open and examining dead people who, like Sar Gedeon here, had met their ends in less than peaceful circumstances. However, there was only so long living people could stay that way without air. Mouth breathing was preferred, but morgue air had a taste, too.

Or maybe it was just me.

In the interest of being able to eat at some point today—and keep it down—I kept my breathing shallow.

Tiny drops of sweat beaded on Bert's forehead and upper lip. He could chat with the dead in his sleep—and he had. It wasn't hot in here. SPI's medical team kept it cold for obvious reasons.

The necromancer was having a problem.

I hoped it was the necromagic equivalent of technical difficulties and not a certain elf corpse fighting back.

But when Bert's brow creased in a scowl, I knew it wasn't heat or overactive sweat glands.

Neither Ian nor I said a word or even moved. Heck, I already was barely breathing.

"Damn," he said simply.

The pressure in the room, and on my body, immediately vanished.

"No luck?" I asked. Way to go, Captain Obvious.

Bert shook his head. "No soul."

Ian made his own four-letter contribution. "We waited too long."

"The soul didn't leave," Bert told us.

"But you said—"

"It was torn out."

Ouch.

"A drug lord with no heart or soul," Fred drawled. "Anyone else love the irony?"

Stereotypically speaking, I knew that demons had a thing for souls, but I thought they tasted sweeter or something when the owner signed it over voluntarily. Delayed gratification and all that.

"How do you even *do* that?" I asked.

Bert drew a breath. "Well, first the—"

I waved my hands. "No, no, that was rhetorical. I'm sure that's one of those things I'm better off not hearing about."

I'd discovered there were a lot of those in our line of work. Too often I'd been told details that'd ended up with a supporting role in my nightmares. In our profession, I had plenty of those, too.

Ian looked likewise reluctant to receive enlightenment. Considering what my partner's past careers were, that said a lot.

"I can explain without offending," Bert assured us.

"Will it help us find the demons that did this?" Fred asked.

"No, but—"

The detective held up a hand. "Then I'm ignorant, too, and happy about it."

"Expanding one's knowledge is good."

"So is me being able to eat lunch," I said. "Fill us with knowledge when we're not standing over the visual aid."

"Where's your curiosity?"

"Hiding behind the remains of my appetite."

"Very well." Bert stepped forward so that his ample belly was right against the side of the stainless steel table. "If you don't want to hear how Mr. Gedeon's soul was removed, you certainly will not like remaining in the room for what I'll need to do now, since there's no soul to communicate with."

My stomach dropped. Being a science type, Bert had never been one for exaggeration.

"If you say we're not gonna like this, I'm thinking I should leave right now. We're here because we need to hear his testimony. We have tape recorders for that kind of thing, right?"

Bert nodded. "There is a video and audio record of every interaction."

Fred snorted. "Meaning if you barf on the body, kid, it'll be playing on the break room TV within the hour."

"Bert wouldn't do that."

Fred grinned evilly. "No, but I would."

Ian gave us both a look that said he was the adult and we were twelve. "You were saying, Bert?"

"A warning, though," the necromancer said. "Depending on the level of residual energy remaining, the body could . . ." He hesitated. "Let's see how to put this delicately."

Fred shifted uneasily. "Just say it, Doc."

"Move."

"What?"

"Move. The corpse could move."

I stood utterly still. "Could you be more specific?"

"Jerk, spasm, flail. I've even had one punch me." Bert grinned. "Packed quite a wallop, too. Impressive for a deceased."

If a corpse sat up and took a swipe at me, I'd be using a lot of words, but "impressive" wouldn't be one of them.

Then without any warning, Bert placed his bare-naked hands right on the corpse's face.

Ick didn't even begin to cover it.

This wasn't a doctor examining a corpse; this was a necromancer about to do some seriously spooky shit.

Maybe this was his way of getting back at us for not letting him expand our horizons with a treatise on soul ripping.

Bert lifted the fingers of his left hand slightly and repositioned them. None of us could miss the dimples left behind by the pressure of his fingers.

Just like Play-Doh.

Please don't move your hand again, I said silently.

Thankfully, he didn't. But that image had been branded into my brain, like that cloven hoofprint on the dead elf's chest, and it wasn't going anywhere anytime soon.

"I'll be able to see what his eyes saw in his final seconds of life—hopefully including his killers. It works like an imprinting. If any images remain, they would be in the eyes."

Bert settled his fingers around the orbital bones surrounding the corpse's eyes.

Then he did what you couldn't pay me any amount of money to do . . . Okay, I'd probably do it for *some* amount of money, but it'd have to be absurdly huge.

Bert leaned over the table, putting his face close enough to kiss the corpse, his eyes less than two inches from Sar Gedeon's.

There was nothing Bert Ferguson wouldn't do in the name of science.

Unlike before, there was no joint popping, no chest constricting, and I could breathe in all the air I wanted to, though considering that it still smelled like roasted elf, I only took in what I needed to keep from passing out.

No one moved, including the dead elf. I was sure I wasn't the only one grateful for that.

Bert was breathing in and out, the breaths growing loud and labored, the speed increasing until they were short gasps. His hands and face were whiter than the tile behind him.

I didn't know what to expect; but to me, it looked like Bert was in trouble.

I shot a sharp glance at Ian. His face bore signs of worry bordering on alarm.

Fred spat a silent curse.

We all knew the cardinal rule—do *not* disturb a practitioner in the middle of a magical link or incantation. I didn't know the reason behind it, but every ounce of common sense told me that snapping a link of any kind between a living person and the spirit, soul, energy, whatever of a violently murdered person couldn't be anything but bad.

But for Bert's sake, not breaking that link would be worse.

If we did nothing, I had a feeling there'd soon be two corpses in SPI's morgue and no one left to talk to either one of them.

Ian got his arm between Bert and the corpse, wrapping his big hand around the necromancer's shoulder, and leveraged his weight against Bert's chest to pull him off the corpse. Fred did the same from the other side.

Bert didn't—or couldn't—budge.

A keening cry came from Sar Gedeon's now open mouth.

Normally spirits spoke through Bert. I had no idea who or what this was.

Fred blanched and swore. Bracing his feet on the floor, the elf detective twisted his body and pulled harder.

Nothing.

It was as if Bert was fused to the body.

The keening grew louder and more frantic.

Veins were bulging on the sides of Bert's neck.

Dammit, he was going to have a heart attack.

Bert's eyes were locked on the open and lifeless ones of Sar Gedeon. His hands might as well have been superglued to the dead elf's face.

Brute force wasn't working.

There was just enough room between Bert and where his face was almost touching the corpse.

Human contact. Calm, warm human contact. I wouldn't be touching the corpse, I'd be touching Bert.

I quickly moved to the head of the table and slipped my hands over Bert's eyes, breaking the visual contact between him and the dead elf.

"Bert, it's Mac." I tried to keep my voice calm. "Come back to us." Moments passed. "Bert, can you hear me? You can do this. Whatever it is, you're stronger. Fight it, Bert. Kick its ass."

Bert drew a breath that I swear must have shuddered clear down to his toes.

Good thing Ian's and Fred's arms were supporting him, or Bert would have collapsed on the corpse.

They eased him back onto the floor. There was another steel table next to the one the elf's body was on, but thankfully the guys chose the floor. Bert was a necromancer and was comfortable around dead people, but waking up on a morgue slab would scare the crap out of anyone. I knew what my reaction would have been, and nobody's ears could've withstood that much screaming.

Fred ran out into the hall to get help for Bert.

Bert's breathing was still shallow, but it wasn't as labored. I didn't know if he was unconscious, but his eyes remained closed. I didn't blame him one bit. If I'd damned near gotten sucked into the great beyond through a corpse's eyes—or whatever had happened to him—I'd have kept my eyes closed, too.

Bert might need to hear that, or at least some reassurance.

"Bert," I said quietly, taking one of his big hands in both of mine. It was way too cold. "It's over. You're safe now. You're safe."

Ian relaxed his grip so that it qualified more as a hug than a wrestling hold. I'd been on the receiving end of an Ian hug more than once. It'd sure made me feel better.

A medical team arrived and Ian and I relinquished our holds on Bert.

I looked up on the table at Sar Gedeon. Whatever had reanimated—or possessed—his body was gone now, but it'd left a calling card.

Sar Gedeon's dead lips were curled in a smile.

After our medical folks had taken charge of Bert, Ian and I were alone in the hall outside of the morgue.

Sar Gedeon's body was back in its refrigerated steel drawer where it couldn't channel demons at anyone else, securely under lock and key. The smile was gone. I was the only one who'd seen it. The tech explained it as a postmortem spasm.

Right.

Ian slipped an arm around my shoulders, and I wearily leaned into it.

"It was smiling," I said.

"I believe you." Ian gave my shoulders a squeeze. "Good work in there."

I knew he wasn't talking about seeing a corpse grin.

"I just did what I'd want if I'd gotten myself locked in a stare-off with a corpse—someone to hold my hand and tell me it was going to be okay." I felt myself start to tear up. What the hell?

Ian gave me another squeeze.

I smiled a little and sniffed twice. Yep, Ian's hugs always did the trick.

"You did the right thing." He went quiet for a moment. "Need something to eat?"

I would've thought that with all I'd seen and smelled, food would be the last thing I'd want to be in the same room with, let alone actually eat it. Surprisingly, I was starving.

"Come on, let's get you fed."

7

FOR SPI agents on duty—or who wanted to be nearby when a coworker regained consciousness after being psychically attacked by a demon-possessed corpse—our new onsite cafeteria was the place to get a quick bite. Though calling it a cafeteria didn't come close to describing the gastronomic delights available to hungry and stressed agents.

It's said that you can accomplish pretty much anything if you throw enough money at it. And our agency founder and director, Vivienne Sagadraco, certainly had enough wealth to throw around to ensure that her agents were well fed and happy around the clock. There were plenty of hot-shot supernaturals and clued-in human chefs available in a city known for its world-class restaurants. The boss simply waved some more money in front of them, got them to sign one hell of a non-disclosure agreement, and we had a kitchen staff that rivaled anything New York City had to offer. Our head of HSR (Human and Supernatural Resources) was a voodoo high priestess. SPI's non-disclosure agreements for new employees were signed in her office and in their blood. It didn't matter who or what you did or didn't worship, nobody messed with voodoo. No one had ever even thought about blabbing about the agency to the press or anyone else. Once signed, our secret was safe.

As to food in our cafeteria, you could get anything you wanted at any time. Human, goblin, elf, troll, gnome, vampire, werewolf, were-anything—if you had a craving, the boys and girls in the kitchens would whip it up—or procure it—for you. It was nothing short of culinary heaven.

Best of all, they kept me in iced tea sweet enough to stand a spoon in. Ask any Southerner; you couldn't get decent sweet tea above the Mason-Dixon Line. That is, if you could even find sweet tea at all. Thanks to the generosity of Vivienne Sagadraco, there was no beverage homesickness for me. I'd even managed to score numerous converts.

In case Bert came around quickly, I just went with a turkey and provolone sandwich. It sounded simple, but all bread was made on-site. I'd had enough contact with red meat for one day. On second thought, make that for the next week.

I could tell Ian wanted to ask me something, but he kept it to himself until I'd finished eating. He was having an open-faced roast beef, piled high with meat and drowning in gravy. I tried not to look at it. It didn't matter what my partner had just seen, smelled, or even touched, he could eat anything, anywhere, anytime. Even though his and Kylie's lunch reservation at Café Mina had been half an hour before mine and Rake's, and he'd had time to eat, he was hungry again. Ian was about six two and solid. It took a lot of fuel to run that.

"It's not Café Mina," Ian noted, when I polished off the last bite of my sandwich.

I sat back with a contented sigh. "You can read minds now?"

"Nope. It was obvious that you were hungry."

I nodded toward his empty plate. Even the gravy had been mopped up. "Likewise."

Ian shrugged. "Mina's was good, but it's kind of . . ."

"Froufrou?"

"Yeah."

"I know. You're a bar, beer, and burger kind of guy. Does Kylie know that?"

Ian smiled slightly. "She does. For our first time out, she said she wanted to take me somewhere nice."

"Aww. Sorry, couldn't help myself. That's just so sweet. Does she know you want actual food, not decorative squiggles on a plate?"

He nodded. "She does. Next time, I pick the place."

"And?"

"I was thinking about Franco's."

Italian. Low light. Romantic ambiance. Best of all, good food and lots of it. A carb-loading, meat-lover's paradise. "Good choice."

"Really?"

"You wouldn't know it to look at her, but that girl can put away some food. She can flat out load some carbs. I've had lunch with her enough to know. She'll love Franco's."

Ian took a breath and looked down at his plate. He could probably see his reflection in the thing. "I'm sorry about what I said today at lunch about you and Rake Danescu."

I smiled and gave him a little nudge under the table with the toe of my boot. "No, you're not."

He glanced up, his lips twitching at the corners. "You're right. I'm not. He asked you out again."

"Yep, lunch tomorrow. He . . . Wait, that wasn't a question. Unless you sprouted eyes in the back of your head, how did—"

"There was a framed print on the wall of the coffee shop behind Fred. I could see your reflection. Danescu must have been hungry, too. I thought he was going to eat your hand."

"Just because I haven't been out before with a goblin millionaire—"

"Billionaire."

I raised an eyebrow. "Well, dang." I shrugged. "Okay, all that means is there's a couple of extra zeros in his bankbook. And yeah, he's hot, but money and looks don't impress me."

"Then why would—"

"He's interesting," I said simply. "Intriguing, even. I want to know what makes him tick. That he's easy on the eyes while I'm trying to find that out is just a side benefit."

"The stereotypical mystery man."

"Hey, I'm not embarrassed to admit it."

"And if you actually find out what makes Rake Danescu tick?"

"*That* just might be the reason to keep seeing him—or send me screaming in the other direction."

Ian's expression went grim. "That's part of what worries me. He's a dark mage."

"I've known dark mages, back home and here. Heck, I'm even related to a few. My family's thick with seers, but that's not the only magical flavor in the family casserole. A lot of families have colorful relatives in their metaphorical attic. We Southerners take ours out and show 'em off. Dark doesn't mean evil. Now the big question would be why is he interested in me? I mean, I clean up good, but I'm no beauty."

Ian started to speak. I held up a hand. "Thank you, but don't bother. I'm good with how I look, and I don't need any empty compliments to boost my self-esteem. It's quite healthy."

"Any compliment I pay you wouldn't be empty."

"Thank you again." I smiled slightly. "The only reason I can come up with is that I'm probably the only woman who's ever told him no. And if it turns out that's his only reason, I'm not interested."

"There's your magic. He tried to hire you away from SPI your first night on the job."

"And he hasn't tried again since then."

"Goblins can be patient."

"Good, because I'm gonna be trying the heck out of his

patience, regardless of his reasons for chasing after me. If you're worried about my safety, don't be. Ms. Sagadraco knows all about today's lunch."

"She does?"

I nodded. "Since Rake's on the perpetual suspect list, I thought it might be prudent to check in with the boss first."

"And?"

"She told me to go and have fun. If Ms. Sagadraco isn't worried, then you shouldn't be, either. Rake's not gonna do anything without my say so, and if he's serious about trying, he's gonna have to answer to me. He's well aware that he doesn't want to piss off the boss." I gave him a quick grin. "Or my partner."

"Damn right, he doesn't."

"See? All settled."

"I wouldn't call it settled."

"Of course you wouldn't."

"But I feel better hearing your side of it."

"I can assure you, it takes a lot to turn my head—and I have yet to lose it, over anyone."

"Just know that if he ever hurts you—"

"Honey, you're gonna have to get in line behind me. Though we both might have to get in line after Vivienne Sagadraco, and once she's through with him, there might not be enough left to bother with."

Ian's grin was ferocious. "I'd gladly relinquish my place in line *and* pay to see that. Speaking of our bosses, have you heard back from Alain Moreau?"

"Not yet."

"Maybe you should go straight to the Dragon Lady. It's not every day one of her agents can see a portal."

"I just saw *one*. That doesn't mean I'll be able to see any more."

"But it makes it highly likely."

"You're squashing my hope here."

"Have you felt any different since Saturday night?"

"I had a couple of dizzy spells, but I chalked that up to getting sucked inside Viktor Kain's head for a stroll down his World War II Memory Lane. Though the trip inside Kain's head felt more like going over Niagara Falls in a barrel."

"Can anyone in your family see portals?"

"No. At least not that I'm aware of. I can see through wards and glamours on living things. To the best of my knowledge, portals aren't living things." I thought back to the pulsing wall—and what had stood waiting on the other side. "Or are they?"

"No, they're not. And what keeps anyone—except the person who created it—from seeing a portal isn't a ward, it's the nature of portals. The magic used in their creation is specific to that person on a DNA level. Otherwise they couldn't pass through."

"And I can't create portals, so there's no good reason that I should be able to see one."

"Creating one takes a level of magical skill and training that you haven't had. That being said, there aren't many people who took a direct hit from a ley line convergence."

I knew about ley lines. We had one running through the mountain near where I grew up.

Ley lines were narrow, intersecting energy streams that magnified magical and paranormal powers. There were a number of them near Manhattan. One ley line ran north and south roughly along the East River. Another ran more east to west. The east/west ley line ran directly beneath the SPI complex. It was one of the reasons why Vivienne Sagadraco chose this location for SPI's world headquarters.

Those possessing earth magic could tap a microscopic amount of power from ley lines, but they would be unable to use the lines to magnify and spread their magic. Diamonds, like ley lines, are of and from the earth. Rare diamonds—like the Dragon Eggs from our most recent big case last Saturday night—that are imbued with power can tap directly into ley lines to carry and spread the power they contain like an underground river.

The results of that connection had nearly been catastrophic.

I'd been woozy, dizzy, and faintly nauseated after experiencing just a fraction of that power, though I'd chalked it up to an involuntary psychic link to a psychotic Russian dragon/crime lord.

Maybe my dizziness then had more to do with coming so close to a convergence of major ley lines that'd been kicked awake by the power of the activated Dragon Eggs.

No one else had picked up any additional mojo.

Or had they?

Caera Filarion didn't have any magical talent to speak of. Was that still the case?

And Ben Sadler probably wouldn't know if he had picked up any extra power. He was still getting used to his gem mage powers waking up.

Crap.

What about Rake Danescu?

He wouldn't tell us how he was involved in what we were standing knee deep in. Why would I think he'd tell us he'd picked up an extra magical talent or two that night?

"Ian?"

"Yes?"

"If my being able to see portals is somehow connected to what happened on North Brother Island . . . I wasn't even touching the Dragon Eggs, and now I can see portals. What about Ben and Caera?" I paused. "And what about Rake?"

Ian ran his hand over his face.

"Yeah," I agreed. "And fat chance of his telling us if he did pick up a 'little something extra.' Ben and possibly even Caera could have gotten a boost. Though if Rake did get one of his talents supersized, at least he'd know how to control and use it. That could be good, or it could be cause for a whole mess of concern."

"You got it."

The cafeteria doors opened, and there stood Vivienne Sagadraco and Alain Moreau.

Our quiet meal was about to turn into a serious meeting.

8

WHEN SPI's top necromancer tried to link with a murder victim and got zapped with a demonic booby trap, you knew there was gonna be a meeting. If it was strong enough to put Bert in a psychic headlock, it was serious enough to earn a visit from the occupants of the fifth floor—SPI's executive suite.

And when one of the agents who witnessed said zapping had also developed an inexplicable talent for seeing portals, the bigwigs would quickly bring that meeting to you.

Entirely too many of my cases ended up with me explaining myself to Vivienne Sagadraco. Only once had I been in real trouble, but that time hadn't been my fault. A doppelganger had been impersonating me to plant grendel eggs in headquarters with the intent of slaughtering—and eating—as many of our agents as they could. When I'd seen me on that surveillance camera, for a minute there, I'd almost believed I was guilty, too.

Ian and cookies had saved me from a fate worse than

firing. My doppelganger had been dressed exactly like me. My distinguishing characteristic that day had been powdered sugar sprinkled down the front of my sweater. I'd been eating cookies that a coworker had brought in and left in the break room.

My doppelganger had not. No cookies consumed. No powdered sugar to show for it.

Saved by my sweet tooth.

My sweet tooth wasn't going to help any of us today.

Vivienne Sagadraco stood five foot and some change. Back when she was born—actually hatched—that had probably been quite tall. That had been a little over two thousand years ago. The founder and CEO of SPI was a dragon—a three-story-tall, iridescent blue and green dragon. In her human form, she reminded me of 007's M as played by Judi Dench.

Alain Moreau was a tall, slender, and impeccably well-dressed vampire. I didn't know when he'd been turned, but company rumor had it that he was at least three hundred years old. He didn't look a day over thirty-five with the silver-fox-Anderson-Cooper look he had going on.

"Agents Byrne and Fraser," the boss said.

"Ma'am," we said in unison.

"Sir," I added with a nod to Alain Moreau.

"You weren't at your desk," my manager noted coolly. "And neither of you are answering your phones."

Ian and I exchanged a baffled look and reached for our phones.

"Shit!" I jerked my hand away. "Excuse me, ma'am, but damn that thing's hot." I winced. "Excuse me, again."

Ian managed to get his hand on his phone and tossed it on the table. I could swear I saw smoke coming from it. He flipped his phone over with the back of one finger and peered at the display. "Fried."

Deep fried. The Gorilla Glass was even broken.

I wrapped my hand in a cloth napkin and extracted mine from its holster. Dead as a doornail. Even more baffling was that we hadn't felt the heat until we'd actually touched the phones.

"I called you when we got back from the Murwood," I told Moreau. "It was working fine then."

"That was before both of us grabbed Bert," Ian reminded me.

And after Bert had his brain grabbed by a demon-possessed corpse.

"Sir, may I borrow your phone?" Ian asked Moreau. "Fred Ash was with us."

"He won't be able to answer if his phone got zapped, too," I pointed out.

Moreau handed Ian his phone, and my partner started entering Fred's number. "Yes, but we'd get an 'out of service' message. That would clinch it." He waited as the phone tried to call Fred. After about thirty seconds he hung up and passed the phone back to Moreau. "Thank you. Fred's number is disconnected or is no longer in service."

Looked like touching a necromancer under attack by a possessed corpse was bad for phone health, too.

Vivienne Sagadraco settled herself into one of the cafeteria's chairs. "Considering the number of encounters you've had today, I think you'd both better start at the beginning."

Ian and I took turns, starting with our interrupted lunch.

Alain Moreau had a raised eyebrow at the identity of my lunch date, but Ms. Sagadraco didn't bat an eye. While Moreau was my manager, Vivienne Sagadraco was boss lady to both of us. She'd told me to go and have fun. Her blessing overruled one raised eyebrow. Besides, I wasn't the one dating the world's oldest gorgon, Helena Thanos. Though she *was* the boss's BFF, and was *not* on SPI's perpetual suspect list. Neither could be said of Rake.

We recounted what we'd found at the scene of Sar Gedeon's murder: the unique and grisly cause of death, and most critical—at least to me—how the killers had gotten into and out of the apartment. In order to describe precisely what I had seen, I had to recall every detail, which I wasn't too keen to do, but if I wanted to find out why I could suddenly see portals, I had a sinking feeling I'd be telling it more than once. I'd better not only be good at it, but also get used to it.

"This is a new skill," Vivienne Sagadraco said when I'd finished. She didn't ask it as a question. She knew what I could do, and until today, what I could do didn't include seeing portals.

"Agent Byrne and I believe it may have something to do with the ley line convergence," I said. "I *was* right on top of it."

"So were Ben Sadler and Agent Filarion," Ms. Sagadraco said.

"And Rake Danescu," Ian added.

"Interesting," she murmured. "Alain, would you check with Mr. Sadler and Agent Filarion to see if they are experiencing any unusual aftereffects due to contact with the Dragon Eggs?"

The vampire nodded. "As soon as we're finished here."

"Is it possible?" I asked. "I didn't actually touch any of the Dragon Eggs, but could exposure to a magnified ley line nexus do something like that?"

"Prior to Viktor Kain collecting those seven diamonds, they had never been together, let alone activated by a gem mage of Mr. Sadler's skill. Add to that the fact that they were activated above the convergence of two major ley lines . . . I feel safe in saying that we are treading new ground."

Holy crap. Vivienne Sagadraco was two millennia old. Alain Moreau was at least three centuries. They'd been around the block a couple thousand times. If they'd never heard of it happening, it'd never happened.

"I've never aspired to be a trailblazer, ma'am."

She almost smiled. "Those who are, seldom do."

"Could there be another explanation?"

"There is, but it is one that you would find distasteful."

"I've already got a bad taste in my mouth from all of this."

"You were briefly connected to the mind of Viktor Kain.

That combined with your proximity to the nexus and activated Dragon Eggs may be what is responsible for your new talent."

"I'm trying real hard *not* to think Viktor Kain might have something to do with this."

"Nevertheless, it must be considered as a possibility."

"I don't feel like I'm being influenced by evil forces."

"I wasn't implying that you were, merely that all possibilities must be considered. And as we recently experienced with Mr. Sadler, abilities previously dormant can emerge in startling ways."

"Seeing a demonic portal was startling all right."

"No doubt."

"Ma'am, do you think it'll be possible to find out what caused it?"

"Rest assured, if the answer can be found, we will find it."

I knew for a fact that Vivienne Sagadraco could read minds—and emotions. She knew I was scared. She'd hired the best and brightest minds she could lure away from both the government and private sector. What she said was what she meant: if the reason could be found, SPI would find it. I couldn't ask for better odds than that.

"Thank you, ma'am."

"For now we'll assume that Mac seeing the portal at the murder scene wasn't an isolated incident," Alain Moreau said. "Who knows about this?" he asked me and Ian.

I shifted uneasily. "Aside from whatever was watching me on the other side of that portal, just the four of us."

"There's nothing we can do about the one; but on this side, it doesn't leave this table for now. We'll bring others in on a strictly need-to-know basis."

We all knew the reason why.

As the only seer in SPI's New York office, and one of only five worldwide, I made it more difficult for supernatural criminals to magically disappear into a crowd. My three predecessors at headquarters had met untimely—and highly suspicious—ends. One death could've been an accident; two would've been bad luck. But three? In a row? That was foul play of the premeditated kind. For whatever reason, someone out there didn't want SPI New York to have a seer.

Now I could see portals.

Portals weren't exactly common. It took specialized and expensive talent to create them. Well-connected criminals used portals as escape routes. Powerful and highly placed elves and goblins used them to travel between the dimensions—most notably ours—undetected. For someone in law enforcement to be able to see them? Well, that'd make me the most popular girl on any number of hit lists.

My mouth went dry at the thought, and I downed the last of my sweet tea. "I already have a target on my back by being a seer; now I've got the magic equivalent of a red laser dot between my eyes."

Silence.

"Isn't anyone going to tell me I'm wrong?"

"I make it a point never to lie to my agents," Ms. Sagadraco said.

"Ma'am, I wouldn't mind the occasional happy, fluffy, white one."

She turned toward Moreau. "I want to bring Martin DiMatteo in on this."

Oh boy.

That confirmed that demons were going to be a big part of my immediate future; though as long as I didn't end up like Sar Gedeon, I could deal with it.

Martin DiMatteo was SPI's expert on all things demonic. We'd been introduced during my first week when, as a new employee, I felt like I'd been introduced to every person who worked at SPI and their intern. No one really expected newbies to remember all the names and faces thrown at them, but I'd had no trouble remembering Mr. DiMatteo. If SPI had business cards, Martin DiMatteo's would've said

"Director of Demonology." When we'd been introduced, he'd had pink scorch marks where his eyebrows should have been. That earned him a special place in my memory.

The eyebrows hadn't grown back.

A couple of weeks later, what hair he had on his head had disappeared as well—though I think the hair was a personal style choice rather than another work-related mishap.

Martin DiMatteo was probably a nice enough guy once you got to know him, but let's just say I'd always hoped our caseloads would never intersect on the agency meeting calendar.

Sounded like my luck was about to run out; but like I said, if I didn't end up on a slab in the morgue, it was all good.

"When we leave here, I'll be going to see Bertram," Ms. Sagadraco said. "I would like to be there when he regains consciousness. I don't want to tax his strength having him tell me what happened."

"Whereas we were there and *didn't* get walloped by a demon," I said.

"Exactly."

I let Ian do the honors. He'd had much more experience giving detailed reports.

"Detective Ash and I couldn't get Dr. Ferguson to let go of the corpse, though I think it was more like the corpse wouldn't let go of Dr. Ferguson. It was Agent Fraser who was able to help break whatever had hold of Bert's mind."

"May I ask how?" Ms. Sagadraco asked.

"You can ask, ma'am," I said, "but I honestly don't know. I just blocked Bert's visual contact with Sar Gedeon. I think Bert did all the work. I just let him know we were there and he wasn't alone."

"Sometimes the reassuring touch of another being is more effective than any magic."

"What attacked him?" Moreau asked.

"That we won't know for sure until Bert wakes up and tells us," Ian said, "but I think it was a trap, deliberately set for a necromancer attempting a postmortem contact. In this case, the soul had been taken and the trap left in its place."

Moreau leaned forward. "Taken?"

"The heart had been removed in addition to the soul."

"I'm unfamiliar with any demonic significance of those acts," Moreau said. "Madam?"

"Likewise. Another reason why Martin's insights could prove invaluable."

"Fred Ash is one of the NYPD's investigators assigned to Brimstone," Ian said. "We'll share information as needed. Even though we don't have a solid and proven connection between Sar Gedeon's killers and the drug, it's a coincidence we can't ignore. Fred said that as far as they know, Gedeon wasn't connected to Brimstone manufacturing and sales, but it's possible he could be a link in the chain."

"What effect is it supposed to have?" Ms. Sagadraco asked.

"Unknown," Ian replied. "Fred said they haven't been able to get a sample for analysis."

"Then that should be our first priority. If it is a drug that is not of this dimension, we are most qualified to locate a supply and track down its source. Our lab facilities and technicians are better qualified to analyze a drug of extra-dimensional origin, and determine what effects it has on mortal, immortal, and supernatural alike. That being said, our colleagues of the NYPD could ascertain the reason for its popularity as well as we could. I can't imagine anyone paying any amount— exorbitant or not—to be scared out of their wits."

"I don't know, ma'am," I said. "We humans can be a pretty flaky lot."

She almost smiled. "I have observed this on occasion. The same can also be said of immortals and supernaturals. Alain, have our agents with connections in the city's drug industry find out what they know about this Brimstone. Have any new underworld elements recently arrived here? And by underworld, I mean criminal or demonic—or both. If this drug is of extra-dimensional origin, it is bothersome to me that mortal law enforcement discovered its existence before we did. In the light of a possible connection between this drug and today's murder, I would like to know why."

"I will take care of it, madam."

"Thank you, Alain."

I gave a silent whistle. I was glad I wasn't on narcotics detail. For their sakes, I hoped they had a good reason why the NYPD had beat them on this one.

SPI had detectives and investigators the same as any mortal police department, and those who had contacts in New York's drug industry would be set on Brimstone's trail.

We didn't have enough evidence to connect Brimstone with the murder of Sar Gedeon, but someone involved in that murder, whether or not it was the actual killer, had set a trap for any necromancer who tried to have a chat with their victim.

Bertram Ferguson was SPI New York's only necromancer.

The murder was committed in New York.

Therefore, Bert had been targeted.

Again, we had no evidence to turn my hypothesis into a fact, but my friend nearly died—or worse—and I was fully prepared to take that personally. So I was going to investigate anything that might lead me to the asshole responsible.

I had a source. And as long as Ian bought a lottery ticket later today, he would talk to me.

9

I never liked hospital rooms.

Though I imagine not many people do. No one wants to sit in a tiny room watching someone you care about unconscious and with machines hooked up to them. Aside from the birth of a baby, there is no happy reason to be in a hospital.

Bert wanted to see me and Ian.

Now.

When we got to the infirmary, Bert was wide awake.

For a man who was zapped only an hour or so ago by a trap set in the mind of a dead body, Bert was looking pretty good. His color wasn't the best, but he was conscious and sitting up in bed. I was glad to see both.

Not only was he awake, he looked pissed. Really pissed.

It appeared that Bert was taking the attack personally. Since he was the only necromancer in SPI's New York office, I couldn't imagine who else the killer thought would go poking around in Sar Gedeon's head.

"Looks like you went one round too many with one of the boys downstairs," Ian told him.

My partner wasn't talking about the guys in SPI's motor pool.

Bert just nodded. "After what you two saw in that apartment, I was an idiot for getting in the ring." The big guy shrugged. "But taking punches is part of my job."

I nearly said, "It shouldn't be," but he was right. We knew the risks of the work when we'd signed on. It was just that some of us risked more than others. I merely pointed out warded supernatural criminals. Bert talked to dead people, and most of those people had gotten themselves dead by violent means. To me, that was the psychic equivalent of going around and sticking your bare hand in a hole in the ground. You never knew what you were going to find.

Or what was going to find you.

I had a good idea of what had found Bert.

The same thing that'd seen me from the other side of that portal.

"I need to talk fast before Doc Stephens comes in here and tries to give me a sedative."

I didn't miss Bert's emphasis on "tries." I could see the necromancer being a bad patient.

"What did you see?" Ian asked quietly.

"For starters, I can confirm that class-five demon."

"Too bad."

"Yeah."

I concentrated on taking air in and blowing air out.

Today was my first experience with demons. Like many Southerners from small towns, if someone asked you if you thought demons were real, you gave the Sunday school answer of "yes." But they weren't something you thought about on a day-to-day basis. Even working at SPI, you knew certain things were real, but you never really put religion together with anything you might run into on the job. At least I hadn't.

Until now.

By helping Bert break a hold a demon had on him, I could've put myself in its crosshairs. And if that same demon was what I had seen on the other side of that portal, he'd now met me twice.

Cold sweat prickled across my skin at the thought.

I knew without a doubt that I'd help Bert again in a heartbeat, but I really hoped I didn't have to.

Bert noticed.

"You look like you need this bed more than I do."

"It's just been a long day already." That wasn't a lie. I tried on a smile for size. "Trust me, I'm gonna do my best not to end up in an infirmary bed."

Or in a stainless steel drawer next to Sar Gedeon.

Bert grimaced as he pulled himself up further in the bed. Dr. Stephens might have the right idea of sedating Bert to make him get some rest.

"I saw them kill the elf," he told us. "I saw it because they wanted me—or whoever tried a PML—to see them work."

"PML?" I asked.

"Postmortem link."

All corporations had their acronyms, but SPI was a special snowflake.

"Your higher class demons are arrogant bastards," Ian said.

Bert snorted. "Or drama queens. You two talked to Marty yet?"

"Martin DiMatteo," Ian said in response to my confused expression. Then he grinned. "You don't want to get Marty and Bert started at company parties. They try to outdo each other with work war stories."

"I'll try to avoid doing that." Some stories are better left untold, especially if they involved demons and dead people.

"No, we haven't seen Marty," Ian said, "but the boss wants to bring him in on this one."

"A demon coming through a portal and ripping the insides out of an elf drug lord. Marty will love this one."

No, I definitely didn't want to be around when Bert and Marty started storytime.

"Our Class Five—or his cohort—left me that present on purpose," Bert told us. "The elf never had a chance."

"You saw this from Gedeon's point of view?" Ian asked.

Bert shook his head. "I saw through the eyes of whoever was working with that demon. They were the one in charge."

"So one was a demon and the other was . . . ?"

"Unknown."

"The accomplice planted the trap," I said.

Bert nodded. "The demon had its hand wrapped around the elf's entire neck. It was a big Class Five, and it was wearing a classic form: red skin, horns, tail, hooves."

I swallowed, or tried to.

"It picked Gedeon up off the floor and squeezed his neck until he stopped struggling but was still conscious. Then he tossed the elf on the floor and put one hoof on his chest to hold him still. Though I don't think it was necessary. The accomplice had already paralyzed the elf. There are spells or drugs that can do that but leave the victim fully aware."

God.

"So he felt it when they opened up his chest and cut out his heart." Now Bert did look sick. "In his last moments of awareness, Sar Gedeon was forced to watch as the demon ate his heart."

"There weren't any screams?" I asked quietly.

"His vocal cords were paralyzed, too."

And now so were mine.

"What about the soul?" Ian asked.

"Held immobile until the demon was ready for it."

"He ate it." Ian's voice was flat and without emotion, but I knew my partner. He was feeling plenty of emotion. He was just keeping himself from putting his fist through the nearest wall. Sar Gedeon may have been a merciless criminal who killed people and destroyed lives, but no one deserved to die like that.

"What kind of thing can do that?" I asked Bert.

"Unfortunately more than a few. Equally unfortunate is that the perp foresaw Sar Gedeon's murder leading to a necromantic investigation. This thing took great pride and enjoyment in its work, and wanted it to be seen and appreciated." His blue eyes went hard. "I hate to disappoint him, her, or it, but I didn't appreciate it one damned bit."

"Sar Gedeon was also a mage," Ian said. "Mid-level power, but it was enough that no one wanted to cross him."

"He got crossed all right," I muttered.

"I'm sure the killer knew that, which would only have increased his enjoyment." Bert said. "I sensed a sadistic satisfaction—glee, even—because of Gedeon's inability to defend himself. This thing likes it when his victims are helpless."

Bert's telling of Sar Gedeon's last minutes terrified me, but it also made me mad as hell.

"The thing fed Gedeon's heart and soul to his demon muscle while the elf had to watch and couldn't do anything about it. Is there a descriptor beyond sadistic? 'Cause this guy would qualify in spades."

Ian spoke one word. "Monster."

10

WE left Bert in his infirmary bed, gearing up for the inevitable argument with Dr. Stephens about how long—or not—he was going to stay there.

My money was on Bert.

Ian and I had been issued new phones and were headed out to take the next step to finding out who murdered Sar Gedeon; and more importantly, who tried to fry the mind of our coworker and friend.

Part of me didn't want to find the trail that would lead me to what I'd seen beyond that portal, but that part was soundly outvoted by the certainty that the only way to get rid of fear was to confront the thing that scared you.

Even if that thing was a class-five demon that ate hearts and souls.

After being reamed out for letting the NYPD get the jump on them in discovering a new supernatural drug on the streets, SPI's narcotics team was left scrambling to get information for our Dragon Lady and get themselves out of the doghouse.

Ian and I had sources of our own that were more well-rounded in their knowledge gathering. If they could make a living selling or trading information about one segment of New York's criminal society, they figured that they could bring in even more if they broadened their base. Snitches, like investments, were more profitable when they diversified.

Ord Larcwyde had a financial goal and a life goal. Make enough money to retire well. Live long enough to enjoy both.

He was an entrepreneur and a veritable information clearinghouse.

And out of all of SPI's agents, he would only talk to me.

While I'd like to be able to say it was due to my street savvy, I knew it was my accent.

Twenty years ago, Ord had transplanted from Atlanta. Business was too good in New York to ever consider going back home, but talking to me helped ease his homesickness for all things Southern.

Ian was a barbaric Yankee who he tolerated only on my account.

I'd be lying if I said I didn't feel a wee smidgen of pride at being able to be one up on Ian, even if it was only with a single snitch. My partner was nearly legendary in the agency, so I took what I could get.

Ord Larcwyde did business out of a small organic greengrocer one block south of the Meatpacking District on Horatio Street in the West Village. He had many information-related businesses, but only one interested me today. If you were on an extremely selective pre-approved list, you came in, bought a hundred dollar lottery ticket, and you got to talk to Ord. How long he'd chat with you depended on the questions you were asking—and how much he enjoyed your company.

Profits from sales of New York's lottery tickets went to the public schools.

Ord Larcwyde was very civic-minded.

Plus, you might actually win. So there was something for everyone.

Because I was Southern and he liked me, I got to talk to Ord for free. But today I laid a twenty on the counter to let Ord know I was thinking of the children, and that this wasn't just a social call. Plus, it was good manners.

While the elven store owner was letting Ord know we were there, I scratched off the numbers.

To win back the money I'd just spent wasn't my objective, though it would've been nice. My reward would be information on Brimstone, the murder motive, the identities of the killers, or I'd love the jackpot of getting all three.

Dang. The tickets were losers.

Hopefully Ord would be the source of my payout.

Ord Larcwyde kind of reminded me of Colonel Sanders. That is if the Colonel was a three-foot-tall gnome who wore a blue velour tracksuit and gold chains instead of a white suit and black string tie.

Ord stood, came around his desk, and treated my hand to a most-proficient kiss. Ian was on the receiving end of a terse nod.

"Makenna, you are a sight for sore eyes. Please, sit and make yourself comfortable."

Ord had two chairs in his office: one for him and one for a guest.

Ian the Barbaric Yankee leaned against the open door.

Ord would close it for truly private conversations, but he knew I didn't like being closed inside what was essentially a vault.

The back room was spacious as far as Manhattan grocery stores went, but Ord's reason for choosing this particular location for his office was an oversized fixture left behind by the previous grocer tenant.

An old walk-in freezer. It was the Fort Knox of offices.

The present store owner had a newer model that he used, and the old one was too big and expensive to move. Ord offered to make it worth his while to keep it. It was big for a freezer, but small for an office. Ord was a gnome; he didn't need space, just security. It didn't get more secure than what was essentially a big steel box. Ord got his office. The grocery store owner got rent to compensate for the storage space he lost by having the thing in his back room, as well as additional store and lottery customers from those, like us, who came in to meet with Ord.

Once again, everyone was a winner.

Ord had the freezer part disconnected, and had a handle and lock installed on the inside as well. He'd also had an opening installed for air to get in, though he'd never told anyone where it was. Since Ord was small, I imagined the air opening was, too. If someone ever wanted to kill Ord for running his mouth, they'd have better luck trying to off him after office hours. Either that, or bring the world's biggest can opener.

Ord had a step stool behind his desk that let him get in his office chair without any undignified hopping or climbing.

The gnome settled himself in the leather chair. "I'd ask what do I owe this pleasure, but I've already heard. A human who can't hold his powder sets fire to a restaurant, and an elf who's responsible for the deaths of at least hundreds finally meets Death for himself. You've had a busy day."

Sounded like Jesin Nadisu, the building manager at the Murwood, wasn't as discreet as he'd claimed. Then again, goblins were known for having a different take on promises and agreements. He'd seemed like such a nice kid.

It must have shown on my face.

"Three representatives of Sarkowski Plumbing went in the back entrance of the Murwood, and they were seen wheeling out a black bag that could never be mistaken for a defective toilet."

Of course. "Your pixies," I said.

The gnome smiled. "Their loyalty and work ethic are unquestioned."

Pixies were tiny, winged, and nosier than your worst neighbor. New York and Los Angeles were thick with the things. About the size and speed of hummingbirds, they were the eyes and ears of the city's supernatural paparazzi, and individuals like Ord who dealt in information. Like hummingbirds, pixies lived on a liquid diet. Pay them with Mountain Dew, Red Bull, or any other high-sugar, high-caffeine drink, and they were yours for life.

"My winged friends provide me with the information I need; I keep them well stocked with the beverages they want. It's a partnership made in heaven." Ord looked at Ian. "While SPI really should change their disguises more often, in all fairness, there really is no disguising a dead body. You could hardly have folded up Sar and carried him out in a duffel bag. It would potentially destroy evidence on the body." He leaned back and put his hands behind his head. "So who did the elf finally annoy badly enough to kill him?"

"I was hoping you could tell us," I said.

Ian gave me a look. I'd just told a source that the all-knowing, all-powerful SPI wasn't all-knowing all the time, and Ian didn't like telling Ord that he didn't have all the answers. I liked the gnome, so I didn't have that problem.

"There is no shame in admitting ignorance, Agent Byrne," Ord told my partner. "The only shame would lie in willfully remaining that way. Considering their success in keeping their operation 'under the radar,' as you humans say, my guess would make the new boys and girls in town either elf or goblin. Both races are ever so adept at keeping secrets. What I do know is that the hornets' nest has been soundly kicked."

"It couldn't be vampires?" I asked.

"Unlikely. There are three families that are not associated with any of the vampire governing covens. Two of them—the Frontino and Báthory families—deal in drugs."

"Báthory? I asked. "As in Hungarian countess Elizabeth Báthory? Bathing-in-the-blood-of-hundreds-of-virgins Báthory?"

Ord gave me a nod. "That's her. The family's right proud of their ancestor."

I made a face. "Nice people."

"You don't know the half of it."

I held up a hand. "And I'm fine staying that way."

"And the Frontino family proudly traces their ancestry back to Cesare Borgia, who was also reputed to be a vampire."

I nodded. "A Machiavellian bloodsucker. I can see that."

"You got it. And . . ."

"And as interesting as the history lesson is," Ian interrupted, "could we stick to the present for now?"

"You'll have to excuse him," I told Ord. "He's no fun."

"I've gotten that impression." The gnome turned to Ian. "Their descendants aren't heavily into drug dealing, but they don't believe in ignoring a potential revenue stream, even though it risks contaminating their food supply, namely humans. For that reason, the vampire covens had nothing to do with the drug trade. These two vampire families market the standard products."

"Not much into R&D?" Ian asked.

"None. Which is probably why they're interested what the newcomers are selling. Supposedly Brimstone lets the user see through glamours and read minds."

I snorted. "So much for why the guy in the restaurant did a line or two before his meeting."

Ian nodded. "Anything that would let you read the mind of a potential customer—or existing competition—would be worth its weight in gold in this city."

"Too bad he couldn't get past the change of scenery."

"Which is why the locals want a piece of the action," Ord said. "The local businessmen asked, the newcomers refused. It seems they don't share well with others, though I can hardly blame them. Unfortunately some of our locals are slow learners. They asked again, and the newcomers began saying no in most impolite ways."

"Such as?" I asked.

"Four days ago, the partially eviscerated body of a Báthory courier was hung on the front gate of the Báthory family compound on Long Island."

Ian stood straighter. "Define partial."

Ord looked from one of us to the other. "The heart had been cut out."

"Anything else?" I asked.

"A hoofprint had been branded into what was left of the chest. Some of their street dealers are missing."

"The Báthorys didn't report any of it." My partner didn't ask it as a question.

"To have a body deposited in such a manner . . ." The gnome swallowed queasily. "And in such a condition would raise questions about their business activities that the Báthory family would prefer not to answer. They cleared one racketeering charge last year by the skin of their pointy teeth."

"Was Sar Gedeon one of the locals who wanted a cut?" Ian asked.

"Oh yes."

"And?"

"*His* chief courier was found three days ago in the driver's seat of one of Gedeon's prized vintage Porsches inside his locked—and warded—twelve-car garage."

I exchanged a glance with Ian. Sounded like Gedeon didn't take no for an answer until it'd been his heart and soul being scooped out.

"And the Báthorys aren't the only ones missing some dealers," Ord continued. "The Gedeon organization and Frontino family also have fewer employees than they had two weeks ago."

A buzzer sounded in the front of the store. The owner came down the hallway to the back.

"Delivery, sorry for the interruption." He went to open the back door.

Ord made an impatient sound. "If this place wasn't so perfect for me, I'd have moved by now. The noise lately—"

The owner's body flew across the small storeroom and smashed into a wall lined with steel shelving. The shelving fell against a stack of boxes filled with garlic, which toppled onto the floor.

None of this affected the stance of the balaclava-wearing gunman who fired a spray of bullets through Ord's open door.

Ord hit the floor behind his desk. I plastered myself against the wall next to the door. Ian made a flying dive out the door and onto the floor of the storeroom, his gun drawn. This unfortunately coincided with the boxes falling over.

On top of my partner, burying him in garlic.

The gunman turned and ran.

Oh, hell no.

"You okay?" I yelled over the ringing in my ears from the gunfire.

Muffled curses coming from under the boxes indicated the affirmative.

This wasn't a robbery. The shooter had been posing as a delivery guy.

He'd been aiming at Ord.

"In pursuit," I yelled over my shoulder.

Ian's muffled curses were less muffled. I chose to ignore the "No!" that I really couldn't be all that certain I'd heard.

What wasn't muffled was Ord slamming and locking the door to his freezer/office.

Apparently there were limits to his Southern hospitality.

The one thing I hadn't needed any training on when I'd started working at SPI was running. I'd mostly used it to run away from something trying to kill and eat me, though not necessarily in that order. Running was both offensive and defensive. Running *from* took the same skill as running *after*. Either one could help keep you alive.

Today I was running to apprehend an assassin who just

tried to kill my best source, even though Ord had locked me and Ian out of his office. I tried not to think that said assassin had a gun and had just displayed a willingness to use it. I also had a gun, but was lacking in enthusiasm.

Ian would follow as soon as he could wrestle his way clear of those boxes. Yasha was circling the block waiting for our pick-up call.

Yasha Kazakov was our driver. Catching supernatural bad guys was easier than finding a parking place in New York. A driver who wasn't shy about throwing his weight around was a must. Yasha was also a nearly hundred-year-old werewolf, but he didn't look any older than Ian. With the Russian werewolf's preternatural hearing, I was sure he'd heard the shots.

"Yasha, pursuing suspect on foot," I said into my new phone's earpiece. I sucked in a double lungful of air. "Approaching Greenwich Street."

If there was one thing that Yasha loved, it was running down bad guys of any shape or substance with the Suburban that he considered his partner. I'd never asked if he loved her more than me or Ian. I didn't think I wanted to know the answer.

"Am half block away," came the Russian werewolf's voice in my ear.

I hoped Yasha wouldn't do a three-point turn or drive on the sidewalk to intercept the gunman, but I wouldn't put it past him. Heavy traffic or no traffic, if Yasha thought he could do it, he would. The Russian werewolf's mantra was, "I saw it in a cartoon once and I think I can do it." There were two werewolf packs in New York: one in Manhattan and another in the outer boroughs. Yasha wasn't a member of either one. He considered SPI his pack.

There were plenty of disadvantages of working for a secret agency, but the biggest pain in the ass was not being able to yell "NYPD! Freeze!" At least not legally.

When in pursuit of an armed suspect running down a busy sidewalk, the goal was to catch the suspect without anyone being shot. In theory, a suspect trying to get away didn't want to bring any more trouble down on their heads by opening fire on a crowded street. And the West Village was definitely crowded with traffic and people.

Even with all the foot traffic, I had no trouble spotting him.

He'd taken off his balaclava to try to blend in, but all that did was give him a serious case of hat hair.

He definitely wasn't a goblin. He wasn't using a glamour of any sort, and silver skin would've been a standout. As far as I could tell, the ears had rounded tips, which eliminated him being an elf. Besides, he couldn't run nearly fast enough to be an elf.

Until I could get a closer look at him, I'd say he was human. About six foot. Dark blond hair standing straight up, presently weaving through the pedestrians near the end of the next block at Hudson Street.

Bingo.

Beyond that was Seravalli Playground. If I had anything to say about it, he wasn't going to get that far. Even though he was running from me, I didn't delude myself into believing he was scared of me; he simply didn't want to get caught.

Or he could be leading you into a soul-ripping, heart-staking ambush, my little voice said. Did you ever consider that?

I hadn't, but I had an assassin on the run in broad daylight, and I would chase him until my lungs exploded if it meant bringing in a man who'd been told to permanently silence Ord Larcwyde—and who had no qualms about me and Ian as collateral damage. That was someone worth interrogating.

All that being said, like a little terrier chasing a big truck, I hadn't given much thought to how I'd subdue him when— or if—I caught him. Though also like certain small terriers, come hell or high water, I wasn't giving up.

I didn't slow down until I reached a clump of what had to be tourists, stopped in the middle of the sidewalk, looking at an honest-to-god paper map. Did they even make those things anymore?

"'Scuse me, pardon me, coming through," I said, weaving, dodging, and bumping my way through.

The gunman had vanished around the corner.

Dammit.

I stopped at the corner long enough to peek around and make sure he wasn't waiting to blow my head off. I got a gratifying glimpse of him darting into a parking garage across the street.

"Yasha, parking garage on Hudson."

I crossed the street and quickly darted inside to keep from being silhouetted against the sunlight from the entrance. I drew my gun and sprinted as quietly as I could down into the garage to the protection of the closest concrete column and stopped to let my eyes adjust to the shadows.

The garage was below street level. I'd been in these before. Going through the low entrance made you feel like you were driving into a cave. If you had to go to the bottom level to find a space, it felt like there was barely enough clearance to stand up in, and if you weren't a claustrophobic wreck before driving in, you were then.

I didn't know how far down this one went, but I wasn't going any farther than this level.

When a predator went to ground, you didn't jump in the hole after it—and if you had to, you didn't go far.

Since the garage was small by Manhattan standards and the gate was both an entrance and exit, this was probably the only way in or out. I could simply stay put and wait. The only way this guy was getting out was past me. Unless his car was here, then he'd be trying to go over me.

I tried to turn down the volume on my breathing enough to hear the gunman moving or starting a car.

I opened my mouth to get even more air in. What the hell? I could sprint farther than this without getting winded. Apparently running after—or from—a guy with a gun who'd just fired shots inches from where I'd been standing kicked my adrenaline into overdrive. More adrenaline flowing equaled more air needed.

Once I could hear over my own wheezing, there wasn't anything else to hear, other than passing traffic and dripping water from somewhere below.

It was too dark to tell how many columns were down here, but it was highly likely the gunman was behind one nearby waiting for me to make the first move.

I had news, I wasn't going anywhere.

Only minutes away was a Russian werewolf in an armored Suburban that could block the gunman's exit or pin him against a back wall. Ian and I had been shot at, and Yasha was the protective sort. Since there'd never been a day when a shelf and a pile of boxes had stopped my partner, he'd follow, if for no other reason than to yell at me for running off without backup.

None of that would keep the gunman from taking an elevator up into the building above, but I had one elevator in my line of sight, and chances were in a garage this small, there was only one. It was the only decently lit thing down here. Only half of the lights in the rest of the garage actually worked, the rest were either burned out or flickering on and off, like they were powered by anemic fireflies instead of electricity.

Looking out into the silent, too-poorly-lit-to-be-down-here-by-myself hole in the ground, I began to have second thoughts about my show of initiative, or as my Aunt Vicki, who was the police chief back home would have said, I'd "run off half-cocked."

As my adrenaline rush faded, realization started to set in, and it wasn't pretty. A trained and experienced agent could do something like this. I was neither trained, nor experienced.

I was a dumbass.

If I managed not to get myself killed, the next time I found myself in a similar situation, I'd think twice. I'd probably still do it, because the way I saw it I didn't have a choice, but at least I'd think about it more before it did it.

The garage was almost full, except for the far corner, which, considering the size of the garage wasn't all that far, was twenty spaces at the most.

No one had parked there.

I couldn't really blame them. There was no light for five spaces in either direction. I wouldn't have parked there. The corner didn't even have shadows, just a big chunk of dark.

I looked closer.

A chunk that was less dark than it'd been a couple of blinks ago.

The source of light wasn't a bulb, it was the wall itself. A wall that should have been a solid slab of concrete.

Underground garages smelled like gas, oil, and the left-overs of whatever fast food someone had most recently tossed out of their car.

Even then, chances were nil to none that those leftovers would smell like rotten eggs.

A smell nearly identical to sulfur.

I jumped as explosive pops and showers of sparks rained down from overhead as every light in the garage blew, leaving me in near total darkness.

Except for the far corner.

A thin, glowing line appeared, spreading, disintegrating the dark as it went.

An orange glow.

Oh shit.

The gunman didn't have a getaway car down here; he had a getaway portal.

— 11

TIME for me to leave.

I turned.

Less than ten feet away—standing between me and the only exit—was the gunman.

His hands were loose at his sides, there was no gun in sight, and his jacket was unzipped all the way, exposing a bare and seriously pasty chest.

He was smiling.

This was wrong on so many levels, I didn't know where to start.

He kept smiling and shrugged out of his jacket.

Add another level to the wrongness.

I raised my gun and took a step back.

"You need to stop." I backed up another step. "There's an easy way to avoid this whole confrontation—or whatever it is you have in mind. You step aside. I leave. Simple."

He stopped smiling. Not because he was any less happy, but because his mouth was changing, along with the rest of his body—at least above the waist. If there was anything going on below the belt, he was still wearing his pants, so thankfully, I didn't have to see it.

His arms lengthened and became serpentine as if his bones had melted. Other appendages sprouted from his shoulders and sides.

Tentacles.

The bottom half of his face writhed and snake-like tentacles emerged like a fleshy beard.

Oh yeah, this was definitely wrong.

And it sure as hell wasn't human.

The gunman was a shapeshifter.

A type of shapeshifter I'd never seen, heard of, or had a nightmare about. Though I'd be rectifying that last one tonight, if I lived through this.

The squid guy had forced me away from the column. The opening portal was still the length of the garage behind me, but it wasn't nearly far enough away.

I aimed for the spot right between his eyes. "Stop or I'll shoot."

He didn't stop.

I fired.

The bullet hit him right between the eyes—and made a dimple. Then the flesh beneath rippled and popped the bullet right out. It landed with a metallic plink on the concrete.

I didn't get a second shot.

A tentacle shot out like a whip around my legs and swept me off my feet.

I landed hard, hitting my head on the concrete. I saw stars and heard my gun clattering away from me.

Ian had been training me in hand-to-hand combat, not hand-to-tentacle combat. I couldn't win against two arms, let alone six tentacles. And if this guy got on top of me, I was toast.

The tentacle continued to constrict like a python around my legs until I couldn't feel them anymore.

I rolled sharply. At least that's what I tried to do.

My gun was out of reach.

I had a knife inside the top of my tentacle-wrapped right boot. My other knife was at the small of my back.

I twisted, scrambling wildly to get at it. Another tentacle shot out and wrapped around my waist, as he started dragging me toward the portal.

A portal that was now open to the width of a car.

I couldn't see through to the other side, but I could make out restless shadows shifting and passing across the opening just over the threshold.

One shadow stood still on the edge of the portal where it met and melted the dark.

I'd seen it before.

It was waiting.

I didn't need three guesses to know for whom.

I didn't believe in coincidences. I believed in traps. And I was being dragged toward one.

The squid had two tentacles wrapped around me and the other four were flailing around my squirming self, trying to get a hold. If he dragged me across that threshold, I was worse than dead and I knew it.

I panicked.

I got my knife in my hand, stabbing and sawing frantically at the tentacle wrapped around my knees, black blood soaking my hands. I gripped the knife harder. It was all I had and I couldn't lose it.

My whimpers turned to enraged screams. They could have been girly screams for all I knew. I didn't care. Screaming tapped my primal self, the terrified animal that kept me cutting and fighting with everything I had.

I cut through the tentacle's tough core and through the rubbery flesh on the other side, freeing my legs. I drove the heel of my boot into my attacker's knee, simultaneously hooking the toe of the other boot behind his ankle. One sharp pull and he went down. I stabbed the knife's blade into the tentacle at my waist and started sawing. The thing's high-pitched keening echoed through the garage.

It went well with my screaming.

If something was trying to mug you, rape you, kill you, or drag you through a fiery portal to your eternal doom— make noise. Help could be just one good shriek away.

The tentacle tightened around my waist, and I sawed faster. The squid thing was still keening. My screams had turned back to frantic whimpering.

I severed the tentacle, slicing into my numbed waist before I could stop. Black blood pumped from the tentacle's severed stump, the end of it still wrapped around my waist and constricting as if unaware that it was no longer attached.

With a keening squeal, the squid dropped me, staggering toward the portal, its remaining four tentacles cradling the stumps of the other two. I desperately pushed against the blood-slicked concrete with the heels of my boots as my hands scrambled and clawed for a hold to pull myself away.

At least I tried.

In my mind, I was making all kinds of progress getting away from that portal. In reality, I couldn't move. Not one muscle.

I didn't have to move to see the portal. The squid demon was gone, and the shadow standing silently beyond was still silent, but he had moved. The shadow had become a silhouette of a man. Tall and thin. Long fingers flared like a fan and my whimpers froze in my throat . . .

And my blood froze in my veins. Not from the paralyzing effects of what must have been a spell launched from the other side of the portal, but from the knowledge of who had done the launching.

Sar Gedeon's murderer. The thing that had held the elf still while a class-five demon had cut out and eaten his heart—then his soul.

A horned figure suddenly loomed behind the mage.

Oh God . . .

Tires screeched behind me.

In that instant, it wasn't my life that flashed before my eyes. It was gratitude. I was grateful that I was about to become the city's newest speed bump rather than a demon meal.

Just as the stink of burned rubber overrode my senses, the portal snapped shut, leaving no sign that it'd ever been there.

My body went limp in a fit of shaking.

I could move again.

Doors opened and arms were lifting me off the concrete. Ian's arms. Oh God, that hurt. The parts of me that weren't still numb had concrete burn.

I couldn't make sense of Ian's words over the sound of my ragged breathing. Since the ones I did hear were creative variations on the four-letter variety, my partner appeared to be going for emotional expression over sentence structure.

"Sq . . . squid." Great, my teeth were chattering, too.

I tried to point toward the portal.

It was gone. The Suburban's headlights lit the garage like high noon. The corner walls were just concrete. There was nothing left of the portal but the stink.

And the black blood on the floor—and on me.

Ian had one arm around me; the other hand held his gun. Yasha wasn't encumbered.

When in human form, Yasha's favorite weapons were his Suburban and his Desert Eagle. The Eagle was the only handgun large enough for his hands. He had it in his hand now. The other held a flashlight that could fry your retinas.

The Russian swept the entire garage with its beam.

"Is gone."

"It was a shapeshifter," I told them "I didn't do this . . . to myself."

Ian's expression was grim as his eyes scanned the cars. "I know you didn't. Yasha, get a—"

"Sample for lab," the Russian finished for him.

"Thanks, buddy." He looked down at me with an expression that said, unlike Yasha, I wasn't his buddy right now, or at the very least he was pissed at my show of initiative.

I pulled at my shirt. "I've got lab samples, too. He bled all over me when I cut off his tentacles."

Ian's expression changed from definitely pissed to possibly impressed.

"Just the two," I clarified. "He had six. It was kind of like cutting bait."

Really big bait.

For now, I left out the panicking and whimpering part. I wanted to keep my badass illusion going for as long as possible. Impressed while looking at me was a new expression for Ian, and I was enjoying it. Besides, he didn't look like he wanted to yell at me—at least not as much.

I thought I had enough breath now for the really bad news. My partner was going to have a lot of questions, and I needed the wind to answer.

"Ian, there was a portal . . . and a mage."

Within fifteen minutes, SPI had investigative and cleanup teams on site, complete with agency demonologist, Martin DiMatteo. The teams were disguised as elevator repairmen. Their job was to get in, get readings, get rid of the evidence, and get out. And they actually did do what the name on the van blocking the garage entrance indicated. They repaired the elevator—which was needed after they disabled it to keep anyone from descending into the garage.

Both teams had plenty of practice in being thorough and fast. The NYPD could have closed the garage as a crime scene for hours. Since SPI didn't officially exist, we couldn't officially do anything, and didn't have time on our side. The disguise was to keep the curious from asking too many questions; the speed was to prevent anyone from seeing squid demon blood splattered on both concrete and cars. Fortunately for evidence eradication, squid demon blood dried to the consistency of blackberry jelly and was easily powerwashed down the garage's storm drains. Unfortunately for the cars, it ate through the paint.

That was why I was wearing Yasha's spare sweats that he kept in the Suburban. My clothes had quickly developed holes. To keep those holes from being eaten into me, I got into the back of the Suburban with its conveniently tinted windows and stripped down. Going werewolf quickly was hell on a wardrobe. The Russian was tall enough in his human form; going wolf added another eight inches in height, and let's just say an impressive amount everywhere else. If he didn't have time to get naked before going wolf, his clothes didn't stand a chance.

Right now, I was glad he kept spares.

Yasha's sweatshirt hung nearly to my knees. If it hadn't been November, and cold, I'd have left it at that; but it was, so I couldn't. Keeping his sweatpants where they needed to be on me required sitting down and staying there. After running five blocks then wrestling for my life and soul with a determined squid demon to keep from being dragged through a portal to Hell, sitting down was exactly what I wanted to do. It ran a close second to drinking the massive hot chocolate Ian had gotten for me. I loved New York. There were coffee shops on every corner. My partner knew exactly what I needed. I was still shivering, and I didn't think it was from cold. At times like this, a girl needed chocolate—or a stiff drink. Despite what we did for a living, drinking on the job was still frowned upon, so a hot chocolate it was.

At the moment, Ian was talking to our lead investigator, but he kept the Suburban in sight at all times. I smiled around my cup. Yasha wasn't the only protective one.

I was sitting curled up in the Suburban's second row of seats in the exact middle. Just because the portal and Sar Gedeon's murderer were gone didn't mean I didn't want as many exit options open to me as possible—or the protection of armored glass on every side. It probably wouldn't stand up to demons, but it was what was available, so I gladly took it.

Except for the partially open driver's side window. I'd rolled that down myself. Just because I'd had the hell scared out of me didn't lessen my curiosity. The lab folks were having a field day with this one. It wasn't often they got to play with squid demon blood, and I didn't want to miss a word of it.

The rear passenger-side door opened. I had a visitor, an expected one.

SPI's director of demonology, Martin DiMatteo.

I saluted him with my gargantuan paper cup. "Hi, Marty."

We'd only met once before on my first day on the job, and he was many levels of agency bureaucracy above me, but after what'd just happened, I had no fracks left to give.

Not that he was intimidating or anything. I think the term "mild mannered" was coined with this guy in mind. Average height, average build, average looks. The only thing that wasn't average was the complete lack of hair above the neck. Below the neck, he was covered by a navy blue suit with a non-descript tie. Even the tie's pattern was muted.

Martin DiMatteo gave me a cool nod. "Agent Fraser." He got in and closed the door.

I took a big gulp of my hot chocolate. Interrogation, here we come.

"You can call me Mac, if you want to," I told him. "Or . . . Agent Fraser if you don't."

"I understand you've had quite the eventful day, Agent Fraser."

So much for friendly small talk.

Though one element of my eventful day wasn't going to be a topic of talk, small or otherwise. Ian had notified Vivienne Sagadraco about what had happened; and until after an official debriefing, she wanted us to keep the mage to ourselves. I had absolutely no problem with that. I didn't want to think about what'd nearly happened to me, let alone have a chat about it. As the director of demonology, Martin DiMatteo would probably be hearing about it soon enough, but I was fine with him being told by the boss and not me.

"I think we can safely call it the day from Hell," I said.

"Technically, no. A more accurate description would be

a day from an anteroom of Hell, but then that doesn't have nearly the dramatic flair."

"I don't want drama in my life." I nearly added "Marty," but decided against it. I could only claim shock-induced familiarity for so long. "What's the difference between a portal to Hell and an anteroom?"

"One's a direct flight; the other has a layover." He didn't crack a smile, or show any emotion whatsoever.

"So it's true what we say back home: to get to Heaven or Hell, you've gotta go through Atlanta."

Still no smile. I don't think the guy understood humor.

"In a manner of speaking, yes."

"But if I'd been dragged through, I could have been taken to Hell from there."

"Yes."

Gulp.

"There is no way directly into our dimension from Hell," he continued.

"That's good."

"It's the only reason any of us are still here."

Gulp again.

"The vast majority of demons cannot cross over," he said.

"Let me guess, squid demons can."

"Actually, that's what makes this incident so interesting. They shouldn't be able to, and definitely not so far from open water. Then there was what happened this morning, both in our morgue and with that elf's murder. Both highly unusual demonic behavior."

I'm glad only one of us considered all that merely interesting. I'd broken out in a cold sweat at the thought of what I was about to ask. "So demons don't like to torture humans— or elves—and eat their hearts?"

"They derive great enjoyment from that. However, they generally don't do it here. Contrary to what most major religions believe, demons really don't find us all that fascinating on an individual basis."

I probably didn't want to know, but couldn't help asking. "And as a group?"

DiMatteo shrugged. "I've heard that we're tasty and addictive, rather like buffalo wings. It's our dimension that they covet. They consider our dimension—or any dimension other than their own, for that matter—to be much more hospitable than theirs."

"Must be the beaches," said an unexpected voice.

I danged near choked on my chocolate. "Bert?"

"Mac." He nodded in greeting. "I escaped."

"I see. Should you be here?"

"You saw another portal—and the bastard who attacked me standing on the other side. Where else should I be?" He nodded to my visitor. "Marty."

"Bert."

"Where you should be is still in bed with Dr. Stephens fussing over you." I spotted a flash of white on the back of his big hand. My mouth fell open. "Is that tape from your IV needle?"

Bert looked down, grunted in acknowledgment, and ripped it off.

"You really did escape."

"I didn't have a choice," Bert said. "I'm fine, Stephens didn't believe me. That's his problem, not mine."

"I hate to disappoint you, but the portal's gone. You came here for nothing."

"There've been two portals today, and you've been there for both of them. You're batting a thousand, kid. If I stick with you, I'll be there for the next one."

I couldn't believe my ears. "Did you hit your head on the table in the morgue? It's more like I've got two strikes, and the next one means I'm out. I'd like nothing more than to take myself out of the game before that happens."

"What proof do you have that a class-five demon was with the elf's killer?" DiMatteo asked Bert.

The necromancer gave the demonologist a flat look.

"Seven foot tall *without* the horns. Tail as long as Mac here is tall. Turn-ons include chest branding, heart eating, and soul sucking. Yeah, it was a Class Five."

DiMatteo either ignored the sarcasm or he didn't get that, either. "Were there bony protrusions like a ridge down the length of its back?"

Bert shook his head. "Smooth back."

"Slender build or heavy?"

Bert looked confused.

"Swimmer or linebacker?" DiMatteo clarified.

"Somewhere in between, but more toward swimmer."

"The horns. Were they upward-, forward-, or backward-facing? Forward would be like a bull. Backward is like a goat. Upward is . . . up."

That question gave Bert pause. "I'm not sure."

"Think."

"It's important?"

"Critical."

"Upward, but curved and slightly tilted toward the back."

Martin DiMatteo would have raised his eyebrows in surprise if he'd had any. Two little crinkles appeared where his eyebrows would have been.

"Are you certain? Not like a goat or bull?"

Bert closed his eyes, mentally reviewing his "game tape." He opened them. "Upward. The base was about as thick as two of my fingers. They narrowed to a sharp point. They also had circular ridges like growth rings down the length."

The demonologist sat back on the seat next to me with a genuine smile. You'd have thought Bert had just handed him the best present he'd ever gotten. "Then it wasn't a Class Five."

"Well then, what class was it?"

"Demon lords are above the BCS."

"BCS?" I asked.

"Brinkman Classification System."

"Someone got close enough to demons to classify them?"

"Affirmative. But he's not around anymore."

No doubt.

I swallowed. Hard. "A demon lord sounds bad." My voice sounded tiny. I'd just had firsthand experience with seeing one, at least a silhouette, which was more than I ever wanted to see again.

"That would depend on your perspective, Agent Fraser. If what Bert says is accurate, and I don't have reason to doubt him, now that I've extracted more details, this is the opportunity of a lifetime."

"After Sar Gedeon got up close and personal with that thing, his lifetime was over. And if Gedeon's killer used a demon lord as their hired muscle, what does that say about what the killer is?"

"Precisely." The demonologist added a delighted eye twinkle to go with his smile.

He was getting happier than a pig in mud.

I was getting even more scared and creeped the hell out than I already was.

"Demon lords—and ladies—only leave Hell for special occasions," DiMatteo said. "This particular lord must consider it to be very much worth his while. They are proud, arrogant, and utterly self-absorbed, and would only consider subjecting themselves to Hell's aristocracy."

I felt the blood run out of my face. "So the killer is a—"

"Not necessarily the aristocracy, but a being that the demon lord could tolerate partnering with until he gets what he is in this to obtain."

"What would that be?"

"Unknown at this time. Whatever it is, 'catastrophic' would probably be the best description for how bad it would be if he got it."

12

DR. Stephens wasn't all that disappointed—or surprised—that Bert had flown the medical coop. It was obvious that the necromancer was a less than ideal patient.

Besides, now he had me.

The squid demon bouncing my head off the garage's concrete floor earned me a CAT scan and a stay for overnight observation in SPI's infirmary.

I was in the same bed—with fresh sheets—that Bert had occupied until he pulled a Houdini. Bert had said earlier that I had looked like I needed to be in that bed worse than he did. If I'd had a lick of sense, I'd have just crawled in then and saved myself the pain, possible concussion, and definite emotional trauma.

All of the tentacle constricting hadn't interrupted the blood flow to my legs long enough to do any permanent damage. My feet still felt a little tingly, which wasn't exactly conducive to standing, let alone running after or away from anything. The scrapes and cuts from being dragged across the concrete had been cleaned and spritzed with some kind of miracle spray that not only took the sting out, but dried to provide a bandage that wouldn't move or come off. It needed to be reapplied every twelve hours.

Because of all that, Alain Moreau—and more importantly, Vivienne Sagadraco—after they had come to talk to me about what had happened—and what had almost happened—had ordered mandatory bed rest and observation for at least the next twelve hours.

They'd both listened in grim silence as I'd recounted my experience. They'd asked few questions, all of them to clarify details, then the boss had told me to get some sleep, and they'd left.

If they knew who or what my attacker was—and I strongly suspected they had an inkling—they weren't telling me. Probably because I needed to sleep, and sleep would've been hard to come by if Dr. Stephens had to sedate me during the panic attack I would've had if they'd told me what they knew.

If ignorance was bliss, I was fine with being stupid and happy for as long as possible. I knew it wouldn't last, so I'd enjoy it while I had it.

It was nearly nine o'clock in the evening of one of the longest days I could ever remember; and to tell you the truth, I really didn't mind the thought of spending the night at headquarters. And since Dr. Stephens had come in and told me I didn't have a concussion, I wouldn't have either him or one of the nurses waking me up every hour, to make sure I *could* wake up, and shining that little penlight in my eyes.

My eyelids were getting heavy, and I thought with a little silent cheer that I might actually get some much needed sleep.

It'd been only two days ago that we'd been racing against entirely too little time to protect the supernaturals of the tristate area from death by cursed diamonds. Those who depended on glamours and other magic to hide what they really were from humans would have had that protection stripped from them; they would have been the lucky ones.

Needless to say, during the forty-eight hours leading up to that, no one had gotten any sleep. Halloween had been on a Saturday. Sunday, I'd still been too keyed up to sleep. Today was Monday and I was running on fumes.

Yes, I was in a hospital room, but I could mostly feel my legs, and there wasn't any permanent damage to them or to the insides of my skull. Whether I merely felt safe being in a secure complex with one of our commando teams on duty and the other on call, or I was simply exhausted, or a combination of both, I slept like a baby.

The nurse on duty, God bless her, didn't wake me up during the night or even the next morning. I got to wake up on my own. Aside from a brief bout of heart palpitations from waking up in a strange bed, it was a night well spent.

I really wanted to smell coffee, but instead, my nose twitched at the scent of flowers.

The nurse—or someone—had been in during the night and made a floral delivery. A cut crystal vase holding at least three dozen roses stood on the bedside table. Their petals went from a pink blush for the outer petals to a pale golden glow in the center. They looked like tiny sunrises. I made a soft sound. I loved roses, and these were the most beautiful I'd ever seen.

And there was a card.

I leaned over to get it and winced at stiff and seriously sore muscles. I saw a stretching session in my immediate future.

I opened the small envelope. Even the paper felt expensive. Rake.

I'd check with the nurse, and if she hadn't brought them in, I'd have Kenji check the security cameras for one stealthy and determined goblin.

I read the card.

Dearest Makenna,

Lunch (or dinner) awaits your pleasure, as do I.
    Be well and be careful.

                                                    Yours,
                                                    R

Very nice. Caring, polite, yet not pushy. Brownie points earned.

Sleeping in, floral delivery . . . the SPI infirmary was starting to feel more like a hotel. I was wondering if I could get room service and schedule a massage when there was a knock, and Ian came in with a familiar pink box and a cardboard tray with two cups of life-restoring coffee.

Ask and ye shall receive.

I wasn't going to push my luck with the massage request. A box of anything from Kitty's more than made up for it.

Katherine Poertner—or Kitty to her friends, and I was fortunate to count myself as one—was the owner and pastry chef extraordinaire of Kitty's Confections. She was a veritable wizard in the kitchen. Though to be perfectly accurate, Kitty Poertner was a witch. As far as those of us at SPI with a sweet tooth were concerned, Kitty's superpower was her baking skills. Everything that came out of Kitty's kitchen made people happy. She brought joy to the world—supernatural and mundane—one cookie at a time. Pink boxes turned up so often on SPI break room tables and in meetings that a lot of the folks here had started referring to her as the Goodie Goddess.

One thing Kitty didn't bake was gingerbread.

Between Thanksgiving and Christmas every bakery and coffee shop in the city was selling anything and everything gingerbread.

Kitty wouldn't touch the stuff.

In her defense, she had a good reason. Her entire family had a ton of bad karma to live down. Kitty's great-great-great-grandmother made Hannibal Lecter look like a cannibalism dilettante. She'd chow down on adults in a pinch, but she preferred children. She lured them in with sweets, most notably gingerbread.

Yep, she was *that* witch.

A cannibalistic child abductor was a heavy load on a family tree.

Ian saw the flowers on the bedside table. Everything else in the room was stark white. How could he miss them?

"Danescu?"

I tapped the tip of my nose twice in reply.

Ian held up the box, roses ignored, but, I was sure, not forgotten. "Lemon-blueberry scones fresh out of the oven."

My favorite.

I made a sound halfway between a moan and a . . . Okay, it was moan. Meg Ryan's deli experience had nothing on Kitty's scones. And from the size of that box, there were four warm wedges of pure heaven inside.

"Thank you, thank you, thank you," I said rapidly as I reached for the box with shamelessly greedy hands. "This is even better than Krispy Kreme when the 'HOT' light's on. I'm getting all kinds of presents this morning. If I didn't have to wrestle with a squid demon to get them, I'd do it more often." I opened the box and looked down. "One's missing."

Ian pulled the lid off his coffee to let it cool. "Pickup and delivery fee."

I remembered the previous pickup Ian had done—me off of a garage floor—and my appetite wavered, but didn't vanish. I was too hungry for even a near-death experience to ruin. "And a fee that was well earned and deserved," I told him. "Want another?"

If Ian had gotten my reference—and I was sure that he had—he wasn't going to bring it up, at least not now. That took considerate to a whole new level.

"I won't turn it down," he said. "We're both going to need to tank up today."

I stopped mid bite. "Aw, jeez. Can I at least eat one before you tell me who got slaughtered last night and how?"

"No one got slaughtered."

I took a bite and gave a thumbs-up. "Score one for the humanoids."

"At least not anyone that we've found. Ord sent me a message this morning via one of his pixies. Two more local dealers vanished last night. They had guards and they still got snatched."

A lump formed in my throat. "Portal?"

Ian shook his head. "No stink."

"But no bodies."

"Not yet, but the day's young."

"Heard anything from Fred and the NYPD?"

"Not a thing."

"Our people get any leads?"

"Still digging. Still nothing."

I grinned. "Even though Ord sent you a pixie-gram to make nice, you still gonna kick his tiny ass for locking you out of his office?"

Ian answered around a mouthful of scone. "Seriously thinking about it." He swallowed and drank some coffee. "I've also been thinking about a common denominator in all this, and I've found one."

"Good. What is it?"

"It's a who. A lawyer by the name of Alastor Malvolia."

"Sounds goblin."

"A lot of the best lawyers are. He's Sar Gedeon's lawyer—though now he's the executor of his estate. He handles all legal matters for the Frontino and Báthory families, and he's on retainer in one capacity or another with all of the other supernatural crime families."

"Elves using a goblin lawyer?"

"Not one of his clients has ever been convicted. In fact, Al Malvolia's been highly successful in countersuing any accusers—and winning most of the time."

"And the other times?"

"The suit was dropped due to the lack of a plaintiff."

"Lack as in gone?"

"Al's known for making problems—and sometimes the people who cause those problems for his clients—go away. He's a win-at-any-cost kind of guy." Ian glanced at his watch. "We have a meeting with him at eleven o'clock. That gives you three hours to get up, shower, get dressed, and get moving. You feeling up to that?"

"Sure. That is, if Dr. Stephens is willing to cut me loose. If not, I can just pull a Bert and leave. Thankfully I don't have any IVs to take out."

"You're sure?"

"I'm sure, but are you? You actually want me to go with you?"

"I need the benefit of your new skill set."

"How did you get a meeting with him?"

"I made an appointment."

"As yourself? He knows you work for SPI?"

"He does. I made the appointment not only as an agent of SPI, but as a personal representative of Vivienne Sagadraco. I told her my theory, and she's given me the green light to share any detail of the murder I need to in order to gain Malvolia's cooperation. It's in his best interests to help us in any way he can if he wants to keep representing living clients instead of handling dead clients' estates."

"I imagine he's gonna be popular. First us, next the NYPD will come calling."

"I'm sure they'd love to talk to him, but they can't."

"Why not?"

"They can't find him. That's the other reason why I need you to go. Let's just say he doesn't have a local address."

I'd heard about pocket dimensions, but I never expected to find a high-powered goblin lawyer's office in one. Though when I thought about it, what better place?

A pocket dimension is attached to a larger dimension, like a coat closet off of a ballroom. Though depending on the talent of the mage who did the construction, not all pockets are small. Like coat closets, pocket dimensions have a door—otherwise known as a portal. The big difference between the portal to Alastor Malvolia's office and the two portals to Hell's anteroom that I'd seen yesterday is an actual, physical connection. Malvolia's office is in our dimension. Our dimension and Hell's dimension, fortunately, aren't next to each other.

Malvolia's portal is permanent, like a door is permanent. However, it's still invisible to those not keyed to it.

Neither Ian nor I were keyed to Malvolia's office portal, but since we had an appointment, there would be someone there to escort us across. Ian wanted to know whether I could see it for myself. It'd be a test. If I could see the portal to this pocket dimension, I'd probably be able to see any and all kinds. That'd be great for SPI, but bad for me if people like Alastor Malvolia knew what I could do. If I could see the door to Al's hidey-hole, I wouldn't be making an announcement.

The goblin lawyer's office on Park Avenue occupied the same space as a prominent Manhattan law firm.

Ian and I went inside and he gave our names, and who we were there to see, at the front desk.

Without a word, the receptionist keyed in a code on his computer's keyboard, and a door clicked open that, until that moment, had looked like part of the wall.

Nifty. And more than a little concerning.

"Wait inside, please. Mr. Malvolia's assistant will be right with you."

Ian nodded. "Thank you."

My partner went through the door and I followed. The door/wall clicked shut behind us.

I'll admit it, I jumped a little. Ian glanced around, but otherwise didn't move. There was nothing to see.

That was my problem.

The room was no larger than ten by ten. No windows, no doors, all walls—and not a portal to be seen or sensed.

I casually went back to back with Ian. "I don't like this," I said, trying not to move my lips. I had an entirely unwanted image of the *Star Wars* trash compactor scene. Minus the trash and stink, that is. For a potential trap, it was actually a very nice room. Death by polished wood paneling.

"Easy, partner," Ian murmured. "It's a pocket dimension. They don't need doors."

Dimensions didn't need doors, but if an exit didn't show itself soon, I was going to either hyperventilate and pass out, or make my own door.

I continued with the whispering and not-moving-my-lips thing. "If I can see portals, why can't I see this one?"

"Because they haven't activated it yet."

Oh.

Before I had time to feel too embarrassed, a pale green glow appeared in a smooth seam down the same wall we'd come in through, though not in exactly the same place. It wasn't a friendly, springtime leaf green; this was a noxious acid green glow. Somehow it suited a guy who by all accounts could have single-handedly given lawyers of every species a bad name.

I'd never thought of myself as much of an actress, but I did my best to look past the portal as if I hadn't seen it, and moved to where Ian could see me checking my watch.

That was our pre-arranged I've-seen-a-portal signal.

Ian casually and quietly cleared his throat.

Message received.

I received a little message of my own. More like a confirmation. I could see portals, probably any and all of them.

I sighed. Oh goody.

The goblin lawyer took my partner's hand in an enthusiastic two-handed shake.

"Ian, my boy, how are you?"

With a name like Alastor Malvolia, I expected the goblin version of Mr. Burns on *The Simpsons*, not the bright-eyed, cheerful man who greeted us just inside the door to his office. Of course, someone would be less likely to expect a knife in the back from a happy guy.

Malvolia's assistant had walked us through an office that looked disturbingly similar to the human lawyer's office in our dimension—and that occupied almost the exact same space. That felt cosmically wrong on every level.

Goblins were known for being tall, but Alastor Malvolia was maybe an inch taller than me, if that. Goblins were also known for being sexy. I felt confident in saying that no creature—in our dimension or any other—would think Al Malvolia was hot.

"Mr. Malvolia, I'd—"

"Al. After all this time, please call me Al."

Ian smiled what I'd come to know as his fake work smile. "If you insist."

"I do."

"Al, this is my partner Agent Makenna Fraser."

Then I was on the receiving end of the two-handed shake as my hand completely vanished in both of his.

"A pleasure, Agent Fraser. Though I wish our meeting was under different circumstances. Mr. Gedeon was a long-time client of mine. The nature of his death has been a shock to all of us who knew him. Please, both of you, have a seat. May I offer you something to drink?"

Ian held up a hand.

I said, "No, thank you."

The goblin sat behind his surprisingly non-imposing desk. "Then we'll go directly to what brings you here. The killer who is preying on the citizens of our city."

At least he didn't say "innocent citizens." That would have been pushing it. How he described them was perfectly accurate. Drug lords and their underlings may be directly or indirectly responsible for hundreds—maybe thousands—of deaths, but they were citizens of New York.

"We believe Sar Gedeon's murder, as well as those of several of your other clients' employees, are linked to the arrival of the drug Brimstone and the individuals behind its manufacture and sale. We have reason to believe the source of the drug is extra-dimensional. However, we can't confirm this without access to the drug."

Malvolia laughed. "And you think that I would happen to have a sample lying around the office."

Again with the smile. "Of course I don't. Though it would make our job much easier if you did. If we can analyze the drug, we can determine its origin—and track down those who brought it here. We have reason to believe Mr. Gedeon was killed because of his desire to negotiate a business arrangement with Brimstone's manufacturers. His request was rebuffed with some finality in an incident involving one of his employees three days ago."

Malvolia laughed, a half-hiss, half-wheeze that didn't do a thing to make me feel more comfortable.

"Ian, you missed your calling," the goblin said. "You would have made a fine attorney."

My partner inclined his head in acknowledgment, though he'd been a cop long enough to take anything coming from a creature like Alastor Malvolia as a compliment.

"From what we saw of Mr. Gedeon this morning," Ian continued, "he either hadn't taken the hint, or his killers wanted to make an example of him to those who wanted to make a similar business arrangement—or perhaps both." He paused significantly. "SPI wants to stop all of this. I'm sure you want the same. Your clients may have information that could help, either a sample of the drug, or names of the people who they attempted to negotiate with. Either would help us locate these individuals and stop the killings. We would greatly appreciate their cooperation and assistance."

Alastor Malvolia had steepled his fingers and was regarding Ian with calm, calculating eyes. *Now*, we were seeing some Mr. Burns. "And what would be in it for my clients?"

"They might get to live longer," I said before I could stop myself.

"Such charming honesty." The goblin smiled, but it didn't make it to his eyes. "I have spoken with several of my clients who have been affected by recent events. They consider themselves qualified to protect themselves, their families, and their employees."

They've done a crappy job so far. I thought it, but this time I didn't say it.

"If I decide to relay SPI's offer to them, they would want to know what they would receive in return for their cooperation. Where is the value for my clients?"

"Have you heard how Sar Gedeon died?" Ian asked.

Any pretense of polite vanished. "Your agency has been unwilling to release that information—or the body of my client. I have sent a request for access to the body and the murder scene, and that request has been stalled. Mr. Gedeon's widow has been denied permission to claim her husband's body."

"Our investigation is not complete. Mr. Gedeon is more than a victim; he is our only source of clues to the identity of his killer. I would think Mrs. Gedeon would want us to find who murdered her husband and why. As to how he was killed, I have been authorized by Vivienne Sagadraco to share that with you."

Ian shared—and he included the details Bert had seen.

Al developed a twitch in his left eyelid.

Looked like Al now had a newfound appreciation for the severity of the situation.

Hearing that a demon lord—and someone unknown, but even worse—was hunting down and butchering your client base would do that.

"I will contact my clients, and then get back to you."

"When?"

Al's eyelid twitched again.

"Eight o'clock tonight. A few of my clients prefer to sleep during the day. Will that be acceptable to Ms. Sagadraco?"

Ian smiled, and now it was genuine. "Perfectly."

13

"I'LL be interested to hear what Al comes up with by tonight," Ian said as Yasha stopped in front of the Park Avenue office building to pick us up.

I settled in the middle of the second row of seats and buckled in. "You enjoyed that, didn't you?"

Ian got in the front passenger seat. He always rode shotgun. "Just because a person knows the law does not mean that they respect it. No one has less respect for the laws of our dimension than Alastor Malvolia. So yes, I enjoyed rattling his cage."

"I don't think we're going to get as friendly of a greeting next time."

"I would be surprised—and wary—if we did. However, the next time SPI needs to twist Malvolia's arm, it'll be Moreau's turn."

"You guys take turns?"

"Mostly. This meeting should have been Moreau's, but the boss thought that since I'd seen Sar Gedeon at the

murder scene, I was better qualified to describe it to Malvolia, if he needed persuading to cooperate with us."

"And the fun was just a nice fringe benefit."

Ian grinned. "I'm not opposed to enjoying my work." He
glanced at his watch. "Want to grab some lunch?"

"Sure. If you can find us a restaurant that's not likely to
get set on fire."

We hit the Full Moon.

It was close enough to headquarters if we needed to get
back quickly, but far enough for a little peace and quiet.

We were all greeted with hugs by the owners, Bill and
Nancy Garrison. Bill was the king of the barbeque pit, and
Nancy had the brains for the business, and the Southern charm
and hospitality to keep the place full of happy customers.

They were also werewolves.

Best of all, they were from my home state of North Carolina.

I came here to get a literal taste of home.

The barbeque was slow cooked, the burgers were rare,
the steaks were tartar, and the regulars were furry. There
was always a booth reserved for hungry SPI agents, and
Yasha's Suburban was always welcome in the alley/delivery
area behind the restaurant. Needless to say, it was Yasha's
all-time favorite place to eat.

Part of Nancy's business savvy involved billing the Full
Moon as "New York's Official Werewolf Bar." She even turned
a section of the front of the restaurant into a gift shop selling
T-shirts, mugs, shot glasses, and if you wanted to build your
Pomeranian's street cred at the dog park, there was werewolf
gear for the small, but fierce, canine in your life. The restaurant
and bar were decorated with dark wood, dim lights, and every
werewolf cliché that existed. Werewolf movie posters and
props were on display, and everything on the food and drink
menus had a werewolf- or movie-monster-inspired name.

Fun place, good people, great food.

As soon as Bill set that plate of pulled pork barbeque in front of me, I forgot all about finding Sar Gedeon nearly twenty-four hours ago, and nearly coming face-to-face with his killer soon after. Good food that was much needed would do that. I didn't think I was all that hungry until I started eating. I was glad I ordered the large platter. I was small, but I could put away some groceries.

"Do you think Al's going to have any luck getting his clients to talk?" I asked Ian.

"He might. If he does, he might even decide to tell us what they said. I'm not going to hold my breath on either one, but I hope their survival instinct overrides their greed."

"Greed? You've lost me."

"If the families have gotten their hands on some Brimstone or the formula, they're going to have a hell of a time getting the main ingredient."

I was still confused, and apparently I looked it.

"She was not in meeting last night," Yasha reminded Ian.

I blinked. "There was a meeting?"

"You were asleep."

"You didn't tell me this morning."

"I was preoccupied this morning, and I'm telling you now."

I sighed. "Go on."

"While we still need a sample of Brimstone for the lab, we've got enough information now to have a good guess as to where it came from."

"And?"

"The main ingredient was imported directly from Hell."

Whoa. "Real, biblical hellfire and brimstone?"

Ian nodded. "In our dimension, brimstone is another, non-scientific, name for sulfur. What I found out from Marty last night is that our sulfur got the alternative name of brimstone because there's an actual mineral, found only in Hell, that stinks like sulfur. He showed me several samples in his lab. It's bright orange."

I remembered yesterday at the coffee shop. "And Fred told us that Brimstone is orange." Just like the portal I'd seen in Gedeon's apartment and the parking garage.

"Exactly."

"Okay, I have to ask. How did Marty get samples?"

"He said he gathered them himself on a field trip."

"To Hell."

"Wasn't Hoboken."

"I wonder if that was when he lost his eyebrows."

"Nope. That's an even better story. You'll have to ask him. He tells it better."

"So what does brimstone from Hell do besides stink?"

"That's where it gets interesting. Marty said its chemical composition contains elements found in our dimension's LSD."

"So much for why man in restaurant saw monsters," Yasha said.

"Before I got some shut-eye myself last night," Ian continued, "I touched base with Fred. When the man was questioned about where and who he bought the drug from and for what purpose, he couldn't remember. The NYPD has a vampire on the force who has a knack for lie detecting. The guy was telling the truth. He doesn't remember a thing."

"That makes absolutely zero sense," I said. "What good is a drug that lets you see supernaturals and read minds, but then wipes your memory? I mean, it's good for us; no one would remember seeing goblins and elves, but it's bad for tracking down the source of this stuff. Well, besides Hell. Though that doesn't make any sense, either. Marty told me that demons aren't interested in humans on an individual basis. Why would demons provide brimstone as an ingredient to presumably a mortal drug kingpin—or queenpin?"

To say we were missing something here was the ultimate understatement.

Ian's phone rang.

He looked down at the display. "Fred."

"Speak of devil," Yasha said with a grin.

I grinned back.

Ian spat his favorite four-letter word into the phone, and waved for Nancy. "We've got to go. Now. Would you put this on my tab?"

"Of course, sugar. Want some of it to go?"

"Love to, but no time." He stood. "There's been another murder," he continued when Nancy began speaking to other customers three booths away. "Goblin by the name of Kela Dupari."

I scooched out of the booth. "Drug lord?"

"Lady, one of the 'queenpins.' Her territory is the Upper West Side. This one's worse."

I suddenly wished I hadn't scarffed down all that barbeque. "Worse than a heart cut—"

Ian shook his head. "No. The NYPD got there first."

Yasha snarled the Russian equivalent of my partner's favorite word. It sounded better in Russian.

"Then what do we have to do?" I asked.

"We'll get there and then we'll see."

"See what?"

Yasha pulled the Suburban keys out of his pocket. "If we need to steal a body."

14

I'VE had some strange things added to my job description since joining SPI, but I never imagined body snatcher would be one of them. Though technically it would be ambulance robber, or if we were going to get picky, ambulance hijacker.

Regardless of the semantics, I hadn't signed up for any of it. So I was more than relieved when we didn't have to do it.

This was the NYPD we were talking about. Getting arrested—at least for me—wouldn't be *if* it would happen, but how fast. I didn't want Alain Moreau having to come down to whatever precinct they dragged me to and bail me out. It'd happened once, and I didn't want it to happen again.

Ian had just gotten the call from one of our dispatchers that the medical examiner had taken care of extending the victim's glamour for another few hours.

Dr. Anika Van Daal was the medical examiner. She was also a vampire and mage who had arrived in the city soon after it'd been taken from the Dutch by the British and the name changed from New Amsterdam to New York. That'd been in 1625. At that time, two-thirds of the island was still wilderness.

She'd begun her medical career as a midwife, and had become the first licensed female doctor in the city. Every few decades, she "retired" from one position and took another. She'd been in her mid-twenties when she'd been turned, so she didn't stand out when she went back to school after a retirement to catch up on the latest medical advances. She'd learned to glamour and glamour well. As a result, she'd never had problems blending in or being found out.

Vivienne Sagadraco had a lot of pull in this town, and one of the ways she used it was getting supernaturals placed in strategic jobs. In addition to supernaturals in the NYPD, there were mages who, like Dr. Van Daal, could replace a glamour on a dead supernatural and hold it there until the body was turned over to the family. Or if no one claimed the body, until it was cremated or buried by the city. These mages were in the homicide divisions, medical examiner's office, and CSI teams.

The boss had covered all the bases she could, but occasionally a corpse tried to steal home. When that happened, there was a lot of scrambling and improvising by whichever agents were closest.

Thankfully today, no one needed to scramble.

We watched from a parking spot on the street that by some miracle of maneuvering, Yasha had managed to wedge the Suburban into, without turning either the car in front or the one behind us into an accordion. I'd turned to look at something totally fascinating out my window, so Yasha wouldn't see me cringing the entire time.

Our cozy spot was half a block from the murder scene. Ian wanted to stake it out for a while to see if any of the curious onlookers behind the police crime scene tape looked a little too curious—or pleased with themselves.

"Dr. Van Daal will get a copy of her report to Moreau, but the preliminary is the same MO as Gedeon's murder."

"Portal stink?" I asked.

"Including portal stink."

"Bert won't get a shot at this body," I noted with no small measure of relief. "And I'm perfectly fine being half a block away from where there was a portal." I spotted a familiar face trying to act casual as he exited the building. It was a ten-story building, and hundreds of people would have a reason to be there, but it was too much of coincidence that this individual would be one of them.

Jesin Nadisu. The apartment building manager of the Murwood, aka murder scene number one.

"Do you see—?"

Ian was out the door before I could finish.

Since Yasha was legally parked for once, he joined us.

The young goblin's day was about to take a turn for the worse.

My day was going to be just fine. Not only did Ian not tell me to wait in the SUV, but if Jesin Nadisu ran for the closest parking garage and getaway portal, I'd have plenty of qualified backup this time.

The goblin didn't run for the nearest parking garage. When he saw us, he just ran. Fast. If Yasha could have gone wolf, he could have been on our Olympic wannabe in three bounds and a leap. It was the middle of the day in Midtown, going furry wasn't an option, so we had to do it the old-fashioned way.

Ian had missed out on snagging the assassin yesterday, and he wasn't going to take second place today. Jesin Nadisu didn't want to be caught, so he was motivated. Ian was just pissed. People were being killed, a coworker was attacked, and his partner was damned near dragged to Hell—excuse me, an anteroom—by a squid demon. As a motivating factor, anger topped fear anytime.

Shots rang out that weren't ours, and the goblin went down.

People screamed.

We instantly went from pursuit to protect.

"Police!" Ian yelled. "Get inside."

It wasn't a lie; he was the police, just not the NYPD, at least not anymore.

Regardless, when Ian ordered, people obeyed.

Soon we had the section of street to ourselves—until the NYPD investigating the murder came out to join us. We needed to be gone before that happened.

With bullets flying around, I would have liked to have been one of the people obeying Ian's order and getting the heck off the street, but instead I ran with Yasha to where the young goblin had pulled himself to the protection of a building doorway before he collapsed.

Ian ran in pursuit of the shooter, with a sharp wave to Yasha to get the car.

"Go," I told him. "I've got this."

Yasha didn't like it, but he went. The quicker he got back, the less chance that we'd all get arrested, and it wouldn't be for stealing a dead body; it be for taking a wounded murder suspect.

When I got to Nadisu, he was still conscious. He saw me and tried to drag himself farther away.

"Hey, we're the good guys here. *You* were running from *us*."

Pain kept him from talking, but from the dread in his eyes, being caught was worse than being shot.

Despite his presence at two murder scenes, I didn't think Jesin Nadisu was a murderer, at least not the kind of murderer who'd eat souls and be partnered with a demon lord.

I'd been wrong before, but I knew I wasn't wrong about this.

For one, other than the small magics needed for a glamour, I didn't sense any power coming from him. The only thing a demon lord would want him for was a snack.

Blood was spreading under his suit coat on his white shirt. His hands weakly fought me as I pulled the coat back to see the damage.

A package fell out of the inner pocket. The bullet must have nicked it. An orange powder from inside dusted my hand. I highly doubted it was Tang.

I glanced at Nadisu's face to see his reaction, but he'd passed out.

Tires screeched as the Suburban arrived, and Yasha leapt out and picked up the goblin like he weighed next to nothing, laying him out on the middle seat. I jumped up beside him and started buckling him in, and Yasha shut the door behind us. The Suburban had a second set of seat belts mounted like on a stretcher.

The passenger door opened and Ian all but dove into his seat. His face was flushed and grim, and looked about as angry as I'd ever seen him.

"Get us home," was all he said.

15

JESIN Nadisu was going to be in surgery for at least two hours.

In addition to an infirmary, SPI had a fully staffed and equipped trauma center and ER, albeit on a much smaller scale than most New York hospitals. When you fought monsters and powerful mages and supernatural criminals, your people could get injuries that would do more than raise eyebrows at the neighborhood ER. Vivienne Sagadraco valued her employees, and made sure that we had only the best medical care available to us.

Jesin Nadisu was presently on the receiving end of that expertise.

We couldn't question him until he was out of recovery, and then it would be up to the trauma surgeon as to when and for how long. Not that we thought the young goblin was guilty of anything other than having a kilo of Brimstone on him. Heck, we were grateful that he had.

While the doctors were working on Jesin Nadisu, the lab down the hall was working on the Brimstone. The analysis would probably take longer than the surgery. But we wanted to be close to get word on both.

I was standing in the hall outside the main lab, looking through the glass wall.

I'd never asked the reason for a glass wall in a lab, but I guessed that privacy was less important than someone outside seeing if something went very wrong inside—and then getting help. Fast.

After hanging out in the ER waiting room for a while, I'd walked down the hall to the lab. Ian had gone to make a few phone calls. I hadn't asked him about what had happened in the chase to catch Jesin Nadisu's shooter. All that Ian had volunteered was that he'd gotten away. Something important was going on here, but I'd learned that when my partner needed me to know, he'd tell me. I was learning to tamp my curiosity down until that happened. I didn't say it was easy; I said I was learning.

The elevator door dinged.

Ian.

"Anything?" he asked, indicating the lab.

"If so, they're not acting like it." I glanced back into the lab to make sure none of the white-coats had gone all giddy in the past ten seconds. "Nope, no high fives or group hugs."

My partner sat in one of the chairs lining this section of wall and put his head in his hands.

I sat next to him. "Want to tell me about it yet?"

Ian didn't move for another handful of seconds, then he sat up, thunked the back of his head against the wall, and stared at the ceiling with an expression of "Why me?"

I didn't take any of that as an indictment on my curiosity, but rather frustration at the situation we were neck deep in, so I leaned my head back and helped my partner look at the ceiling.

"Nightshades," he finally said.

"I'm assuming you're not talking about the plant."

"I wish I was. You could get rid of those with weed killer. We rarely see these, let alone get a chance to eradicate them. They just come back. Then again, maybe they are like the plants."

"Then they're a who, not a what."

"Nightshades are basically elven black ops mercenaries. They'll do whatever they're paid enough to do. Today one of them was paid to get Jesin Nadisu."

"He didn't do a very good job."

"It's lucky we were here so he couldn't finish the job. If we hadn't been watching—"

"He wouldn't be here and alive getting stitched up."

"Yeah."

"But you saw the shooter, and I take it you recognized him."

"He's one of their best marksmen."

"And he only got Jesin in the side?"

Ian gave me a flat look.

"He didn't kill him on purpose?" I guessed.

Ian nodded once. "There was an ambulance parked around the corner."

I knew where this was going and it wasn't anywhere good. "A fake ambulance to fool anyone who saw them. They wanted him alive."

"And afraid and in pain. They hired Nightshades to make it happen. And if he had died . . . there are necromancers who sell their services to the highest bidder. The Nightshades keep two on retainer."

Cripes.

"Jesin doesn't look like the drug-runner type."

"The best runners arouse the least suspicion, and neither one of us would have suspected the manager of an exclusive, high-rent apartment building to be running drugs."

"He does dress well," I admitted. "Do you think he knew who was gunning for him?"

"Maybe, maybe not. We won't know until we can talk to him. In the meantime, I'm having Ord Larcwyde brought in for questioning, though the agents picking him up have been told to go with 'protective custody.'"

I grinned. "Ord does value his safety."

"I thought it'd go over better. Whoever was pulling that demon lord's strings was worried enough that Ord had damaging information to send a demon assassin after him. I want to know what that information is."

"When he gets here, you might want to let me do the chatting. He likes me more than he does you." I thought of something and chuckled. "I wonder if he's come out of his freezer yet."

"If not, the agents are taking a blowtorch with them, just in case. Either he comes out on his own, or the boys go to work on his cube."

A door opened down the hall in the hospital wing and Dr. Stephens gestured for us to come down there.

Our patient was awake.

"I'll let you do the talking," I told Ian.

He gave me a bemused glance. "Really. You're sure about that." Neither was a question, at least not real ones.

"Hey, I've never questioned a shooting victim fresh out of surgery. I take it you have."

"I have."

"Then this one's all yours."

"I'll believe it when I don't hear it."

We went into the recovery room.

Jesin Nadisu looked like hell.

Though he didn't look nearly as bad as Sar Gedeon had. Thanks to the skill of our surgical team, Jesin at least had all his pieces and parts. Most of them probably hurt right now, but at least he still had them. Considering all that he'd been through in the past few hours, I thought I should keep that comparison to myself. The young goblin had gotten off lucky. For the sake of his continued emotional well-being, I'd keep that to myself, too.

SPI's chief trauma surgeon had told us not to stay for longer than five minutes. The only reason she wasn't in the room with us was that she didn't need to be. There was a two-way mirror next to the door that would let her see and hear everything that went on. At the first sign of fatigue or distress from her patient, I was certain she'd be in here with us a split second later, telling us to leave. Nicely the first time, then not so nice. SPI agent, suspect, or caught-red-handed clawed criminal, her patients were her top priority. One of the things we learned in new-agent training was not to argue with Dr. Barbara Carey.

"Mr. Nadisu?" Ian said quietly, but loud enough to be heard. "Mr. Nadisu, I need to ask you just a few questions, and then you can continue to rest."

The goblin's eyes fluttered open. Large, dark, and long lashed, he looked even younger than he had when he'd met us in the lobby of the Murwood. If he'd been human, he wouldn't have looked old enough to buy a beer, let alone manage an exclusive apartment building.

"Agent Byrne." His voice was rough from the breathing tube we'd been told they'd had to use during surgery. Apparently the bullet had nicked the bottom of his lung and a not-so-minor blood vessel or two. He blinked a few times and focused on me. "And Agent Fraser." He tried a weak smile that didn't quite make it. "I can explain about the Brimstone."

At least we had confirmation that what the lab was analyzing was Brimstone. Though right now, a plastic-wrapped, brick-shaped block of glowing orange powder taken from a demonic murder scene couldn't be much else.

"Do you know who shot you?" Ian asked.

Nadisu didn't answer.

"If you're worried about them getting to you, don't," I told him. "You're safe here."

Ian cleared his throat.

Oops. So much for letting him do the talking.

"Do you know where you are?" Ian asked.

"No."

My partner was silent for a moment. "How long have you been in our dimension?"

I refrained from doing a double take. Ian's voice was actually gentle. He clearly knew something that I didn't.

"If you're here illegally, we won't send you back," he continued.

Oh, okay, now I got it.

Both goblins and elves were very selective over who they let come through the permanent dimensional portal between our world and theirs. Though like humans, if you wanted to get here badly enough, you'd find a way. For supernaturals, that meant paying a small fortune in bribes to mercenaries with access to an illegal portal.

Both races operated under a controlling monarchy supported by a powerful aristocracy. Unless you were related to an influential family or had a magical talent that the nobility were interested in, you might as well not exist. No rights, no hope of a better life, and if you pissed off the wrong noble or mage—no life at all.

Humans weren't the only species who came to New York looking for a better life.

Unless they could afford papers to let them pass as a legal citizen of the good ol' U S of A, and could afford to have a mage fit them with a glamour to let them pass as human, they were just like the thousands of undocumented human immigrants in the city, but with goblins and elves, the term "alien" was literal.

In such an environment, it wasn't a surprise to anyone that organizations emerged to "govern" their people, to resolve differences without human interference, to serve up justice when it was needed, and to execute whoever they decided should be.

Police, judge, jury, and executioner.

Any attempt by SPI to intervene was called interference in a "goblin matter" or "elven business."

We saw them as the criminal families they were.

And Jesin Nadisu was apparently scared to death of one of them.

"You're at SPI headquarters," Ian told him. "So whoever it is that you're afraid of can't get to you here."

The goblin sighed. "Would you like to bet on that?"

"We know about Nightshades," Ian said. "You're completely safe from them or anyone else you may have reason to fear."

Including demons opening portals. Then I had another thought.

"Your employer, maybe?" I asked.

The goblin turned even pastier, if that was possible.

The door immediately opened.

"That's all, Agents Byrne and Fraser." Dr. Barbara Carey wasn't going to accept any response other than us getting away from her patient.

Within seconds, we were in the hall with the door firmly closed behind us.

If I could've kicked myself in the ass, I would've. "Dammit, I'm sorry."

"Don't worry about it. Our time was almost up. Dr. Carey wouldn't have let us have a second more. Sounds like the kid's afraid of his boss."

"Do we know who owns the Murwood?"

"No, but Kenji has a database of buildings owned by supernaturals. Murwood is the name of a forest in the goblin and elf dimension, so chances are good that a supernatural owns the building."

"I have a couple of follow-ups I need to do, so I'll check in with Kenji on that."

Ian nodded. "I'll wait for Dr. Carey to come out and see when she might let us talk to Jesin Nadisu again, though I'm not holding my breath for it being anytime soon."

I tilted my head down the hall. "And if you could listen out for any celebrations erupting in the lab."

"Will do."

I headed down to the bull pen and to my desk.

Only to find Alain Moreau sitting in my chair.

Aw crap.

Being called into your manager's office was stress inducing enough. But to have your manager camp out in your chair to wait for you?

I'd stepped in something serious. Even worse, I'd stepped in so much lately, I had no clue which pile this could be about. At least he hadn't had to come down to one of the NYPD's precincts to bail me out. Regardless, I was sure I looked like a kid with their hand in the cookie jar, even though I didn't know what I'd done.

Alain Moreau looked like a man about to fire someone.

He'd hired me. He could fire me.

"I can explain," I told him. That is, as soon as I knew what he was here for. "Or . . . do I just need to pack a box?"

Moreau looked baffled—baffled and tired. "I beg your pardon?"

"A box. To clean out my desk."

More bafflement as he regarded the surface of my desk. "It appears to be acceptably tidy. Why would you need to clean—?"

"You're not firing me?"

"You're not going anywhere, Agent Fraser."

I took an involuntary step backward. Maybe SPI management considered firing to be wasteful. If I was a failure as an agent, maybe I'd be a rousing success as a meal in the employee cafeteria. After all, I wouldn't actually have to do anything. I couldn't screw that up.

"Unless you wish to leave," he continued, still sounding tired.

Now I was confused.

He had the same expression as Ian had upstairs—too

much bad news and no idea how to deal with it. But instead of thunking his head against a wall, Moreau ran his hand through his perfect hair. Hair that was still perfect. I wasn't sure if it'd even moved. Maybe it was a vampire thing.

"We have questioned both Agent Filarion and Mr. Sadler, and neither have experienced any effects—ill or otherwise—from being exposed to the ley line convergence."

"Dang it."

One of Moreau's silvery eyebrows shot up in surprise.

"Okay, that didn't come out right. Sorry, sir. It's just that that wasn't what I wanted to hear. I mean, I'm glad that Caera and Ben didn't get zapped with some kind of mutant power, but it'd be nice not to have the only explanation left being a bizarre mind-meld, power-transfer thing with Viktor Kain. I'm not exactly enthused about catching anything from a multi-millennia-old, psychotic criminal mastermind." I paused for breath and sighed. "At least I don't have an urge to take over the world," I muttered. "Yet."

"That is not the only explanation left."

I perched on the edge of my desk. "It's not? But Ms. Sagadraco said—"

"We need to reconsider your family background. The contact with either Viktor Kain or the diamonds or the nexus—or even a combination—could have awakened a previously dormant ability."

"No one in my family can see portals. If they can, I never heard about it. Not to mention, I'd kind of hoped to be able to avoid calling home and asking."

"Why?"

"They worry about me enough as is, moving up here and all. Calling home and going, 'Uh, Mom . . . yeah, I'm doing great. I've got a question. Has anyone in our family ever been able to see portals? No, no. No problems here. Just asking out of curiosity.'"

"I can see how that might be awkward."

"And impossible to hide why I want to know. Mom's

relentless. And don't even get me started on Grandma Fraser. Trust me; you don't want my family coming up here. Nobody wants that. Least of all, me. Has Kenji taken a shot at it yet?"

Kenji Hayashi was SPI's CTA—Chief Technology Agent. Each SPI office worldwide had their own CTA, but Kenji was the best, which was why he was here at agency headquarters. If it existed in cyberspace, the Japanese elf could find it, and decipher it six ways from Sunday.

"I give him *full* permission to dig into my family background," I said. "Just as long as he promises not to laugh at my more colorful relatives."

"I'll ask Agent Hayashi to look into it as soon as possible." Moreau paused. "I have been unable to contact Rake Danescu to ask of any effects he may have experienced. I've left two messages, but he has yet to return my calls. He may be more willing to answer the question if it came from you in person."

"What makes you think I'll be seeing him?"

"Your lunch date was interrupted."

"He wanted to reschedule for lunch today or dinner last night. But that got nixed by a squid demon and a possible concussion." I decided not to mention the flowers I found on my bedside table this morning. Moreau probably knew, but if he didn't, I really didn't want to bring it up. "Are you visiting my desk because of Rake? Because if—"

My manager held up an elegant hand. "It is not about Monsieur Danescu. I will admit to having concerns, but after speaking with Madame Sagadraco, she and I are in agreement."

I gave him a small smile. "That I'm a big girl and can take care of myself."

"That and while Rake Danescu may be many things, he has never been foolish." He narrowed his eyes very faintly. "Do I need to explain that statement?"

My smile broadened into a grin. "Oh no, sir. I got it loud and clear. And I think Rake probably has, too. He behaves or there'll be a line to kick his ass, and you and Ms. Sagadraco will be near the front. Though Agent Byrne might want to argue for the right of first in line."

"No doubt. I wanted to speak with you concerning your satisfaction with your employment here."

I tensed. "Are you or Ms. Sagadraco not satisfied with my employment here?"

"I assure you we are most satisfied with your job performance. The question is how you feel about your job. I imagine it has turned out differently than you envisioned."

"Yes, it has." I thought back to the events of the past week. "I try my best to stay out of trouble. Problem is trouble keeps finding me."

"That is part of our concern. I encourage those who report to me not to hesitate to tell me if parts of their job are distressing to them. You haven't requested a meeting."

"Anything that's happened has pretty much fallen under my job description. More or less."

"On New Year's Eve, you chased down a fully grown grendel in a crowd of nearly a million people."

"I was the only one who could see her."

"A human without defensive magical powers taking on a monster out of legend bare-handed."

"I was the only agent there. I couldn't just let her start eating people."

"But it was not your job. It was far beyond what anyone would have expected or demanded of you."

"I had to do it."

"And last week with Agent Byrne, Yasha Kazikov, and Rake Danescu. You didn't have to go to that island to take on Bastian du Beckett and prevent those diamonds from being activated."

"Ben Sadler was being held prisoner. I felt responsible for him. Then there was Yasha, you, Ms. Sagadraco, and every supernatural in SPI. None of you are just coworkers; you've become like family." I said it without one bit of embarrassment. "If there was some way I could help, I was going to do it."

"And you have not sought me out to lodge a complaint about your life being in danger beyond what you were hired to do."

"I don't mean any disrespect, sir, nor am I trying to be rude, but you're getting at something. What is it?"

"Have you at any point during your employment with us considered turning in your resignation?"

"Not seriously."

"And why is that? Through no fault of your own, you've nearly lost your life on numerous occasions. Other times you have purposefully placed yourself in harm's way."

"I don't think I'm a danger junkie, sir, if that's what you're getting at."

"I don't think that you are." His gaze searched my face. "Why do you do it, Makenna?"

I suddenly knew the answer without having to think about it. I pressed my lips together not only against a tiny smile, but against the sudden sting of tears in my eyes.

"I feel needed. Sometimes I screw up, but I know what I'm doing is worthwhile. I can't imagine not doing it. I love my job."

Moreau stood. "That's all I needed to know. If that ever changes, I trust you will inform me."

"Absolutely, sir."

"Then I'll let you get back to work."

"Thank you, sir."

Moreau headed for the elevators, and I realized my teeth were clenched in a smile that'd probably scare small children.

The silence of the agents in the bull pen behind me was absolute.

I turned slowly and was met with dozens of pairs of curious eyes: human, elf, goblin, troll, gnome . . .

"I'm still here," I said loudly. When that didn't make them stop staring, I gave a double thumbs-up for emphasis.

At that, everyone returned to what they'd been doing, and the noise levels returned to normal.

I sat down with a sigh. Nothing about this place was normal.

16

I'D barely gotten started digging for an answer to a question that'd been nagging me, when I heard the click of Kylie O'Hara's stiletto heels coming toward my desk. I'd never seen her in heels lower than four inches. She was pretty much five foot nothing, and while human women of her height would have worn heels for added height regardless of the excruciating pain, Kylie wore them because they were fun.

It had to be a dryad thing. They must have tiny arches of steel.

She nodded toward the elevators. "Well, how did *that* go?"

"Good. He just wanted to be sure I was happy in my work."

"Are you?"

"Sure. Until something kills me, but then it'd be too late to lodge a complaint. Well, unless y'all get Bert involved, but I'd really rather you didn't."

"Noted. So you're definitely staying?"

"I don't think I'd be allowed to leave if I wanted to. And I don't want to," I hurried to add.

"Good." She shot a withering look at the bull pen. "Because there's way too much testosterone around here."

"And eavesdropping."

Kylie shrugged. "Agents. They can't help it."

She perched on the edge of my desk. In her stiletto heels and short pencil skirt, she did a better job of it than I had. The boys in the bull pen agreed. They eavesdropped on me; they ogled Kylie.

"I found out from Baxter the Bastard about those *Sex in the City* segments," she said.

Both monikers were her creation. The first was the God's truth. Baxter Clayton, news anchor, was most definitely a bastard. The other was a cute and clever name for the series the aforementioned bastard was doing on New York's high-class sex industry.

"And?"

The dryad leaned in closer. "His producer shut down the project last month. The sex industry in this town must have a lot of pull."

"Pun intended?"

She thought a moment. "No, lucky coincidence. And it wasn't the station that pulled the plug. The *network* brass axed it."

"Oooh. Wanna bet some of those bad boys are clients?"

"I'd put money on it, though it sounds like they already have."

"So would anyone who was going to have their business featured have known that the series had been scuttled?" I asked.

"Definitely." Kylie gave me a fess-up look. "Why do you need to know?"

"Yesterday in the coffee shop, Rake needed to leave. Fast. He claimed it was because Baxter had been stalking him for his segment."

The dryad sighed. "Honey, think about the goblin mind for a minute."

"I'd rather not."

"Too bad. Besides, if you decide to make this thing work with Rake, you'll need the practice. Technically, he didn't lie. I have no doubt that Baxter would have been stalking him for that segment. The total truth was that Bax wasn't stalking him *anymore*. So, the question then becomes, why the sudden need to leave?"

I sat back and wished I had a wall behind me to thunk my head against. "It was obvious he didn't want to get away from me. So we can toss out fear of commitment. *Aversion* to commitment maybe, but not fear. I think he saw someone he either needed to get away from . . ."

"Or chase after," Kylie finished for me.

She hopped off of my desk. There were a couple of sighs from the bull pen. Kylie ignored them.

"Sorry hon, you're on your own to pry that out of Rake." She flashed a dazzling smile to a few more sighs from the boys. "But if you play your cards right, you could at least have fun doing it. And yes, *that* pun was intended."

"Thanks, Kylie."

"Anytime."

Damnation.

About an hour later, I didn't want a wall to thunk my head into, but I'd sure take one to use on Rake.

Kenji had gotten me into the databases I'd needed, but I'd done the digging myself.

I'd hit pay dirt all right. The operative word there being "dirt."

The Murwood *and* the office building where the second murder had taken place earlier this afternoon were both owned by none other than Rake Danescu, under the name of Northern Reach Holdings. That made Jesin Nadisu—with his kilo of Brimstone and Nightshade bullet—Rake's employee. An employee who had looked ready to faint at the mention of his boss. On a hunch, I ran a search on the office building where Alastor Malvolia's supersized pocket dimension contained his law firm.

Yep, Northern Reach Holdings, aka Rake Danescu's personal property.

Jesin Nadisu's reaction could have been his morphine getting low or any number of sudden pains after having a sniper's bullet blast through his insides, but eyes don't lie. That wasn't pain; that was fear. As a result, I had several urges bubbling to the surface, but the front-runner was an overwhelming need to kick Rake Danescu's ass.

The goblin was capable of a lot, maybe even murder. Who was I kidding? Definitely murder. But what had been done to Sar Gedeon and Kela Dupari wasn't Rake's style. If he wanted someone dead, he'd just kill them, not make a B horror-movie production out of it. And then there was all that blood and the brimstone stink. I couldn't see Rake getting within smelling distance of a demon, let alone partnering with one. No dry cleaner could get demon stink out of a silk suit. Plus, my gut told me that his hand would never go fishing around in a chest cavity for a heart treat to toss to his demon accomplice. "Innocent" was the last word I'd use to describe Rake Danescu, but he wasn't the murderer.

I knew in my gut the man whose silhouette I'd seen on the other side of that open portal had been the one to paralyze Sar Gedeon and the others while his demon used his claws to go grocery shopping. That silhouette didn't belong to Rake.

My desk phone rang.

It was the receptionist at Saga Partners Investments, our cover office on the surface. Rake Danescu was there to see me.

Speak of the devil. Pun and cliché intended.

"Shall I tell Mr. Danescu that you're in a meeting?" she asked.

I smiled, though to the guys in the bull pen it'd look more like a baring of teeth.

"No, no. Not necessary. I would love to see Rake Danescu," I said. "I'll be right up."

Rake stood in the reception area of Saga Partners Investments, impeccably dressed, and looking uncharacteristically grim.

Good. We were in the same mood. It'd save a lot of time getting past pleasantries if neither one of us had any.

When he saw me, grim turned to guarded. He knew I was mad. At him. Yes, the last time we'd seen each other was across a table in a coffee shop when he'd been kissing the palm of my hand. Now he knew that if he went for my hand, I'd give him my fist.

But he didn't know why, hence, the guardedness.

I was about to enlighten him.

But not here, not now.

What I'd just discovered wasn't personal; it was business. Rake was now a suspect, if not of murder, then of drug running, or at the very least, collusion—but most of all of being an asshole of a boss who terrified his employees. Until all of those had been thoroughly addressed, the one thing he was not was a potential boyfriend.

"Karen," I asked the receptionist, "is the conference room available?"

"Yes, it is."

"Would you put me down for half an hour?"

I closed the door. The main Saga conference room was essentially an interrogation room with fancy seating. I fully intended to bring Rake downstairs for Ian and possibly Ms. Sagadraco to question, but first I had to confirm that there was justification to take that next step.

"Before we get started, I wanted to thank you for the flowers. They're beautiful, and they were the first pleasant surprise I've had in days. Now your turn. You're here, asking for me, and you're not happy. Why?"

"You have my employee Jesin Nadisu here. Has he been arrested?"

Interesting. Rake didn't know he'd been shot.

"No, we're merely asking him a few questions."

"With an attorney present?"

"There's no need for—"

Rake reached for his phone. "I want him to have one. Anything he might have said to this point is inadmissible without an attorney present."

"I don't see why he would need one."

The goblin's dark eyes narrowed. "Oh, you don't, do you?"

I wasn't taking the bait. But with that attitude, I didn't feel guilty tossing him a curve.

"Because we don't think *he* is the one who's guilty—at least not of murder."

"Murder?"

"Murder. As to having a kilo of Brimstone on him . . ." I shrugged. "For all we know, he could have been holding it for a friend."

Rake paused, his long index finger poised above a key. Jeez, the guy had his lawyer on speed dial. I really hoped it wasn't Alastor Malvolia, though with Rake being his land-lord, I wouldn't have been surprised.

"Unless *you* think he's guilty," I continued, "in which case, you need to seriously reevaluate your hiring practices, hiring psychotic serial killers. I'd have thought you would've been more careful about things like that, being a savvy and successful big-city businessman and all."

"Not guilty?"

"That's what we think."

"Then why do you have Jesin Nadisu in custody?"

"We don't have Jesin Nadisu in custody. We had him in surgery."

The goblin went dangerously still. "What?"

"He was shot outside a building that was the scene of the second murder in as many days. He had a kilo of Brimstone on him. We're analyzing it in the lab now. But it would help greatly if you'd care to tell us why the demons peddling the stuff are thinning out the competition by killing drug lords in your buildings?"

"My buildings?"

"Your buildings. You own—and Jesin Nadisu manages—the Murwood, scene of the first murder. Two hours ago, he was shot outside an office building on West Seventy-Ninth Street, aka murder scene number two, also owned by you. And the lawyer who represented both victims—as well as probable future victims—has his cozy pocket-dimension office in yet another of your buildings."

"Alastor."

"That's him. A real sweetheart. Met him this morning. You know, if you'd give us a list of all of your real estate holdings, maybe we could get ahead of the killers and keep Al from losing any more clients."

"You've been busy."

"I'm not the one hosting a demonic murder convention—and terrorizing your employees."

"Terrorizing my . . . What the hell are you talking about?"

"We were telling Jesin that he didn't have anything to be afraid of, that he was safe here. We tried to determine who he was afraid of. When we mentioned 'your employer' the poor kid damned near fainted. Imagine my surprise when I found out just now that he works for you."

"I can't imagine why he would be afraid of me."

"Can't you?"

"No, I can't. Though at least I know why you're upset."

"I'm not upset, Rake. I'm about to become violent."

He exhaled heavily. "How is Jesin and who shot him?"

"He'll live. He's in recovery. Apparently the Nightshade sniper who shot him just wanted to clip him enough to justify using the fake ambulance waiting around the corner to come pick him up. Trust me, the poor kid will be a lot happier waking up here rather than wherever those elf ninjas would've taken him."

Rake swore and dropped into one of the chairs. Then he was silent, but there was a lot going on behind those dark eyes, mostly disbelief, confusion, and concern. "Thank you," he finally said.

Okay, that was unexpected.

Rake could have been pretending to care more about Jesin than defending himself, but I didn't think so. When I'd said "Nightshade," he'd gone a shade or two paler than usual. You can't fake that; at least I didn't think so. I wasn't going to back down, but for now I decided to back off.

"Could you tell me what happened without compromising your investigation?" he asked.

Pale *and* polite. There wasn't any part of what had happened that Rake wouldn't be able to find out himself with a few questions in the right places, so I wouldn't get in trouble for telling what we knew, which wasn't really all that much.

"The NYPD arrived at the second murder scene before we could," I said. "We got there and were staking out the location when we spotted Jesin leaving the building. He looked nervous."

Rake gave a halfhearted smile and shook his head. "Contrary to what you may believe, goblins aren't born knowing how to conceal their emotions."

"So it's an acquired annoyance?"

"Touché."

"Jesin saw us and ran, there was a shot and he went down. Ian ran after the shooter, I stayed with Jesin until Yasha got back with the Suburban. We got him back here and into our ER as fast as we could."

"Thank you, again."

"You're welcome, but we were just doing our jobs. We would have done that for anyone."

"Even me?"

"Including you. Though Ian might not have run so fast after the shooter. And Yasha wouldn't have been as gentle putting you into the Suburban. It probably would've been more like a quasi-aimed toss."

That got a slight smile out of Rake.

"Why would Jesin be afraid of you?"

"He's not. At least he wasn't as of yesterday when he told me about you and Agent Byrne coming to the Murwood and about Sar Gedeon's murder." He spread his hands in exasperation. "I have no idea why he would react like that. I'm his favorite uncle."

"Uncl . . . he's your *nephew*?"

"Yes. He's extraordinarily bright, a hard worker, with an uncanny knack for business. He's also one of the few in my family whom I actually like. When he came here, he wanted to work, so I put him in charge of the Murwood. The boy has a head for management."

I couldn't resist. "What? You didn't have him working at Bacchanalia?"

"His mother, my oldest sister, would skin me alive herself."

Oldest sister. That implied more than one. "Sounds like a nice lady."

"You have no idea. She was against him coming here from the beginning. I will have much explaining to do."

"If Jesin wasn't afraid of you yesterday and is today—"

Rake's eyes tightened in disapproval. "He wasn't carrying a kilo of Brimstone from the scene of a murder yesterday."

There was a soft knock. The door opened a crack and Karen stuck her head inside.

"Excuse me, Agent Fraser, Mr. Danescu, but Ms. Sagadraco would like to see you both."

I couldn't say I was surprised. Karen probably had a standing order to let the boss know whenever an agent asked to use a conference room for a chat with a perpetual suspect.

I wasn't in the least bit nervous. Alain Moreau had already told me that he and Ms. Sagadraco were very pleased with my job performance, so I wasn't having another what-the-hell-did-I-do moment.

Rake, on the other hand, had probably done, initiated, been directly or indirectly responsible for, or merely involved in so many nefarious activities that the concerned crease on his forehead was from trying to figure out which one all this was about. Was it about Jesin, Jesin's reaction to the mention of him, the murders, or Brimstone? Or something else entirely? I guess it was hard to cover your ass when you had so many irons in the fire.

We got into the elevator and the doors closed.

Both of us faced forward, neither saying a word.

"Makenna?"

I noticed he left off the "dearest," "lovely," or "beautiful" Makenna. Wise move.

"Yes?" I asked.

Out of the corner of my eye, I saw Rake's lips twitch upward at the corners.

"Well played."

17

ALAIN Moreau met us when the elevator opened on the executive level.

Okay, maybe I was in a little bit of trouble. Rake was a suspect, or at the very least a source of information we didn't have but needed, and I had shared elements of an ongoing investigation. I'd be finding out soon enough.

Vivienne Sagadraco's office door was open, a table had been brought in, and there was her formal silver tea service, china cups and saucers, and those little cakes and pastries from Kitty's that always looked too pretty to eat. Either the boss wanted to lull Rake into a false sense of complacency, or we were going to be here for a while and we'd need caffeine and sugary snacks to get through it—Ms. Sagadraco's version of a civilized interrogation. I knew Rake could never be lulled into anything, but the boss was civilized, so I was going to go with the latter.

"Rake." Not Lord Danescu. Ms. Sagadraco said it as

though the hand caught in the tea-cake jar had been his. But she still extended her hand for the requisite kiss. Rake didn't disappoint. "You could not have paid us a visit at a more convenient time." Her sapphire-colored eyes narrowed ever so slightly. "This chat is long overdue. Agent Byrne will be joining us momentarily. Alain, would you please close the door and ensure that we are not disturbed?"

Alain gave Rake a level stare. "It would be my pleasure, madam."

So much for who was in trouble, or at least more of it than I was.

If there was tea involved, Vivienne Sagadraco would make pleasant small talk until everyone had been served. But now as she poured the tea, she made no effort at conversation: small, pleasant, or otherwise. She was like a Southern lady in that regard: if you didn't have anything nice to say, don't say anything at all—at least until the individual in question wasn't around to hear you.

Yep, this was going to be a civilized interrogation.

"In the interests of complete disclosure," she began, "anytime an agent asks to use the Saga Investments conference room, video and audio recording is activated for the duration of the meeting."

So Karen had not only told the boss, she'd flipped the AV switch. I was kind of glad that she had. I wouldn't have wanted to summarize *that* exchange for Ms. Sagadraco.

The door opened and Ian came in.

"Have a seat, Agent Byrne. We were just getting started."

"The lab's completed the first part of their analysis," he told her. "Dr. Cheban sent the preliminary report to you. They're still isolating the individual ingredients, but they've determined enough to know what the drug is supposed to do. She'll forward the ingredient list as soon as it's complete. Though she did confirm that one of the ingredients is actual brimstone. And one of the murderers is a demon lord."

I glanced at Rake to get his reaction.

One perfect eyebrow, slightly raised. He may have been shaken, but he wasn't stirred.

Ms. Sagadraco reached over to her desk for her tablet. She scanned through her e-mails and opened the report. We were silent as she read.

Ian typed a few words on his phone, then tilted it so I could see: Saw the tape. ;)

Jeez, had they been playing it in the break room? I didn't know what the boss thought, but Ian approved—or at least he'd found it entertaining.

"Without the benefit of further testing, does Dr. Cheban believe the drug does what was intended by whoever made it?" she asked Ian.

"Yes, ma'am."

"How many doses are contained in the sample we obtained from Mr. Nadisu?"

"Hundreds."

Rake made a low sound in the back of his throat.

I didn't know if he'd intended it as a groan or a growl, but either way I think I understood why Jesin wouldn't want to see his uncle right now.

Ms. Sagadraco finished reading and put her tablet on the table next to her cup. "Lord Danescu, in our laboratory is an impressive quantity of a drug that our chemists believe would enable any elf or goblin who inhaled it to see through glamours and read minds."

"Damn," Rake muttered. "They did it. They actually did it."

"I take it you were aware of their efforts?"

"I'd heard rumors about their efforts, but nothing about their success."

Ian spoke. "According to Dr. Cheban, the drug works for elves, goblins, and humans. However, and fortunately for us, humans don't remember what they saw while under the influence." My partner gave Rake a less than friendly look. "Goblins and elves would recall everything, which leads Dr. Cheban to believe that it was developed for use by either goblins or elves. For humans who aren't aware of the supernatural world, seeing through glamours could easily be misinterpreted as hallucinating and thinking you were seeing monsters, which is what happened in the restaurant yesterday."

Ms. Sagadraco took a sip of tea, and then carefully set the cup and saucer on the table, leveling her gaze on Rake Danescu. "I believe it is time that you told us what you know."

The goblin had put his elbows on the arms of the chair and had carefully interlaced his fingers in front of him. Interrogation Posing 101.

"I had heard that the elves were attempting to develop a drug that could enable them to spot any undercover goblin agent by sight, and detect any goblin spies or elven traitors by thought. Conversely, it would also let goblins see and hear any elven agents."

It was said that elves and goblins originated from the same ancestors. Just never say that out loud to either one. Hate was a mild word for how most elves and goblins felt about each other. At least in our dimension they'd stopped trying to exterminate each other, settling instead for hostile corporate takeovers—with only minimal bloodshed.

"I imagine both goblin and elven intelligence would give or do anything to get their hands on the Brimstone formula," Ian noted coolly.

Rake didn't take the bait. "If it was a stable and viable formula, then yes, there would be considerable interest."

"And competition."

"What are you getting at, Agent Byrne?"

"Only that you appear to be in a unique position to hear of any interest or competition—and possibly even have a member of your family unwillingly pulled in."

Nice that Ian gave Jesin the benefit of a doubt. Might have even earned a point or two with Rake.

At that, Rake regarded Ms. Sagadraco, his expression unreadable. "Vivienne, I would be willing to share what I know in exchange for my nephew's safekeeping here."

What that implied about the situation in the city didn't bode well for any of us.

By all accounts, Rake was one of the most powerful dark mages in New York, perhaps *the* most powerful. For him to ask for help protecting his nephew by keeping him in here meant the situation out there was even more dangerous than we could have imagined.

"While we were upstairs, Makenna alluded to a connection between the murders and properties I own, and by association, myself. Her suspicions may not be unfounded. If so, at this time, Jesin would not be safe outside of this complex. I know that Sar Gedeon was the first victim. Who was the second?"

"Gedeon wasn't the first victim," Ian told him. "The killers started at the bottom of the ladder and have been working their way up. The most recent victim—at least that we know of—is a goblin by the name of Kela Dupari," Ian said.

Rake closed his eyes for a moment.

"I take it you knew her?"

"A foolish woman who routinely toyed with and taunted powers beyond her ability. The same actions can be ascribed to Sar Gedeon."

"What are their connections to you?"

"Both were actively involved in the drug industry, not only in New York but down the entire East Coast to Miami. Contrary to what you may believe about me, I am *not* involved—actively or otherwise—in any drug industry. Aside from Ms. Dupari and I both being goblins, we have no connection or association. That being said, an elf and a goblin, both prominent in locally based crime families, were brutally murdered in buildings that I own. This could be a coincidence, or an attempt to frame me, or at the very least cause me substantial inconvenience and embarrassment."

I stared at him in disbelief. "People get their hearts and souls ripped out and you're embarrassed because it happened in your buildings?"

"Yes," he said matter-of-factly. "You must admit neither death was unwarranted given their past professional activities, and their removal will no doubt make the city a safer place."

"So now you're playing Batman?"

"The costume would suit me, as would the nighttime activity, but no."

"Your nephew can stay here regardless of what information you share or do not share with us," Ms. Sagadraco said. "We will care for him as if he were one of our own. It's called decency. I know you're at least familiar with the concept. Your cloak-and-dagger dramatics are affecting and endangering others, and one of those others is Makenna. I assume you have heard what happened yesterday afternoon?"

His expression hardened. "I did."

"My agents are charged with protecting the supernaturals and humans of this city from any and all threats. Brimstone is a threat—both its manufacture and the battle among opposing forces for the right to sell it. My agents and the people of New York are caught in the middle. I arm my agents with what they need to do their jobs. A vital part of that armament is information. I believe you have this information, if not all of it, at least more than we have."

"Mac could have been killed yesterday in the same way as Gedeon and Dupari," Ian told Rake, his tone low and forceful. "Or even worse, dragged through that portal."

"I am more than aware of that," Rake shot back. "Which is precisely why we're having this conversation. Vivienne, from what I *do* know, neither you nor your people want to be involved in this. It is beyond their abilities."

"This, as you so obliquely put it, is precisely why I founded SPI. This is my world, Lord Danescu. I live here, *all* the time. I will defend it to my last breath. Can you say the same?"

Silence.

"As to my agents' abilities, I know their capabilities, you do not. You know what they would face, I do not. You tell me what is happening in this city, and I will be the one most qualified to make that assessment. Though from what I know of my agents, you have seriously underestimated them." She glanced at me. "All of them. You have yet to choose a side. It's understandable. One is the world of your birth, ours is merely a place of business."

Rake recoiled as if Ms. Sagadraco had slapped him, which I think was what she was going for.

"Or is it?" she continued. "If you have not made up your mind, it is time that you do so. You can help, or you can continue to hinder. You can no longer do both. Which will it be?"

"Very well." Rake leaned back in his chair. "Elves have been in your dimension far longer than goblins. Their established foothold forced us to play catch-up, strategically speaking."

Ian barked a humorless laugh. "Strategically speaking? You make it sound like you're planning to take over."

"Not take over, Agent Fraser. Merely ensure that the elves don't gain access to a resource—and thus an advantage—that we do not gain for ourselves. Much of what is called magic in the Seven Kingdoms can be replicated by science and technology here. Some cannot be replicated. Elven extremists have worked to gain power and influence here to obtain such technology for use against my people. It pains me to say it, but there are similar groups among my own race. Goblins and elves have been at war off and on for thousands of years."

I was dumbfounded. "You're saying elf-terrorists-trying-to-get-nukes kind of advantage?"

Rake actually smiled. "That would be extreme even for these people. They want to annihilate the goblin race, not render their kingdom uninhabitable. In their minds, that would be a waste."

"Thank God for small miracles."

"Both of our races use the excuse that we're merely trying to stay ahead of the other to protect our own people."

Ian sat back. "Brimstone's the source of the latest tug-of-war."

Rake nodded. "There are more than a few companies and laboratories run by both elves and goblins that develop drugs, weapons, and technologies to use against the other. Such organizations are routinely infiltrated to steal formulas, sabotage research, copy new technology. Much like human industrial espionage. Brimstone would allow select people to see through the glamours these corporate spies use to hide their identities, as well as detect spies by their thoughts." Rake poured himself another cup of tea. "Brimstone would be a valuable commodity for whoever has it. If it is effective, it would be worth killing for. From events of the past two days, apparently the drug is quite effective."

"Elves, goblins, and vampires have been killed by a demon lord and something worse than a demon lord," I said. "So who made the drug?"

"I suspect the individuals you need to pursue are not those who are physically manufacturing the drug. At least they wouldn't be your primary target. Brimstone—the ingredient itself—comes from the Hell dimension, making it particularly difficult to get."

"Not necessarily. Marty picked up a couple of rocks on a field trip," I noted.

Rake's teacup paused halfway to his lips. "I beg your pardon?"

Ian regarded the goblin with a knowing expression. "You know a lot about spies, espionage, and strategic advantages for a billionaire playboy, real estate mogul, and owner of an exclusive sex club."

Rake almost smiled. "Successful and undetectable espionage isn't cheap, Agent Byrne. Some of the buildings I own have been leased to elven companies and research facilities. I made the financial terms and incentives impossible to pass up—as would any developer vying to get a profitable client in a previously vacant building. Refitting the space to suit their needs presents all sorts of opportunities for installing undetectable surveillance equipment. The income from one building often pays for another; and the revenue from my other businesses funds the buying and bugging of those buildings. As you humans say, sex sells. It also makes an absurdly impressive amount of money. More than a few key elven power brokers spend time—and their money—in my club, little knowing that they're funding intelligence operations against themselves."

Rake Danescu. Sex broker and spymaster. I didn't know which was worse.

Or if either one was truly bad.

"And you have bugs planted in the tables at Bacchanalia," I said, recalling my first night on the job when Ian had felt the need to distract those listening in on us by seriously distracting me.

"One can hear all kinds of interesting and valuable tidbits," Rake noted smoothly, knowing exactly what I was remembering.

Bastard.

I glared at him. He smiled at me.

"Heard any interesting chatter concerning a new drug?" Ian asked.

"Not that my monitors have told me, but I will contact them when I leave here."

"And let us know?"

Rake just looked at him. "Yes, Agent Byrne. And let you know."

"I found a list of buildings that you own under Northern Reach Holdings fairly easily," I told him.

"Which is what makes me think the murders taking place in my buildings isn't a coincidence. I have allowed Northern Reach Holdings to trace back to me with relative ease. My other holdings are very well and deeply hidden. It's in a goblin's nature to hide your strategic advantages until they're needed—or until you need someone to find them."

Great. So much for me being clever.

"So Northern Reach is like the outer threads of a spiderweb," I said. "You're in the center, and if you sense movement, you know you've caught something."

"A nearly perfect comparison, Makenna. That is why I believe there is a very distinct possibility that someone is going to a lot of trouble to stage murders in my buildings."

"So I take it the elves know you're a spy?"

"I'm more of a freelance consultant for goblin intelligence. They use me, and I use them. It's a mutually beneficial relationship."

I remembered what Kylie had told me. I wanted to know the answer; not to mention, Rake had just gotten one up on me. I'm competitive, so sue me. "In the coffee shop yesterday, you needed to leave fast to keep Baxter Clayton from seeing you."

"That is correct."

"It also wasn't necessary, at least not anymore."

"I don't follow you."

Oh yes, he did.

"The series Baxter Clayton was planning had its plug pulled last month," I said for Ian and the boss's benefit; Rake already knew damn well that it'd been canceled. "You didn't really need to avoid him anymore. Though having heard more than a few Baxter stories from Kylie, I could understand why people wouldn't want to get cornered. But with the series canceled, you didn't *need* to avoid him." I eyed him. "Sitting at the center of the web like you do, I can't imagine you not knowing the series had been canceled. So that would mean that you were either avoiding someone else—or you saw someone who was desperate to avoid you. Which was it?"

"It had nothing to do with Brimstone." Rake's dark eyes were steady on mine. Eyes that said in no uncertain terms that he was not going to tell me or anyone else here what it was about.

If the boss had had a fireplace in her office, I'd have held his feet to it. Not only did I think she wouldn't have minded, but since she was a fire-breathing dragon, she could've done it herself. I glanced at her. From the hard glitter in her eyes, it looked like she wouldn't mind raising the temperature in the goblin's designer shoes.

"Rake, do I have your word that this incident isn't connected to this investigation?" she asked.

"You have my word."

"And if it does reveal itself to be connected, I trust you will inform me immediately."

Ms. Sagadraco knew how the goblin mind worked.

"Of course, Vivienne. I will contact you immediately." He looked to each of us in turn. "I have a question."

Ms. Sagadraco selected a pastry from the silver tray. "Please ask it."

"Makenna mentioned that the two of you met with Alastor Malvolia this morning," he said to Ian. "What were you attempting to learn from him, and were you successful? Though knowing Alastor, I would hazard to guess that you weren't, at least not after only one meeting."

"We're supposed to hear from Malvolia by eight o'clock tonight," Ian told him. "But we're not holding our breath."

"Nor should you," Rake said. "If his clients were able to give him any information he believed was useful to you, he would want to negotiate for additional benefits. What did you promise him?"

"Not a damn thing," Ian said bluntly. "I simply told him how Sar Gedeon was killed. In detail. He decided to cooperate."

"I would have enjoyed seeing that." Rake took a sip of tea, his dark eyes glittering with what I could only describe as delight over the rim of his cup. "Dearest Vivienne, you are quite right, I have underestimated your agents."

18

ONCE Ms. Sagadraco was finished with her tea-party inquisition, and extracted a promise of cooperation from Rake, she asked me to stay after Ian and Rake had been excused.

The tea and goodies were gone, but maybe the inquisition part wasn't over yet—at least not for me.

I decided to be proactive. "You want to talk about what happened up in the conference room with Rake, don't you?"

"I thought that would be a good idea, yes."

"From what you saw and heard, I didn't mess anything up, did I?"

"If you're speaking professionally, no, you did not. What I wanted to bring to your attention is on a more personal note. You may have created more of a problem than you solved."

"I don't understand."

"If your intention was to discourage Lord Danescu from pursuing you, then you may have made a tactical error."

My eyes widened. "What?"

"Goblin men of Rake's caliber aren't attracted to intellectually passive women. If I were to venture a guess, I would say that your performance just now and upstairs has probably rendered you absolutely irresistible. If you want him to cease his attentions now, you may have to kill him."

I recalled my violent urges toward Rake in the conference room, and thought it highly likely that before this was all over, I'd be feeling those same urges again.

"The day ain't over yet, ma'am."

The Dragon Lady smiled.

Ian met me by the elevators.

"Well, that was interesting," I said.

"That's one way to put it."

I waited a few moments before I spoke again. "You don't believe Rake's involved anymore, do you?"

The muscle in my partner's jaw flexed. "No, I don't."

"But you'd like him to be."

"If it'd keep more people from dying, then yeah, I would."

"Nice dodge. That's not the question I asked."

Ian grew some silence.

"I'm still worried about you, Mac."

"Rake or being snatched through a portal?"

"Yes. I can keep the second one from happening, but not the first."

My instinct was to tell him that I could take care of myself and that I didn't need his help or approval choosing the men in my life. But I didn't say any of that even though all of it was true. It wasn't Ian's fault for feeling the way he did about Rake, or any other man who kept his private life, business interests, and motives for nearly everything he did locked up tighter than Fort Knox.

Heck, I was still circling Rake like he was a rattlesnake coiled in front of the only way out of a cave, and I planned to do that for the foreseeable future. When I got to the future, and Rake still wasn't guilty of anything, then I'd reevaluate my reasons for continued caution.

Not blaming Ian one bit for his feelings left me with only one response to his statement. It was also the one I wanted to give him.

"Thank you," I said simply.

That earned me a surprised look.

"Really," I added with a slight smile. "There's no need to worry. I don't plan on diving into anything, but I know where your concern's coming from, and I know it's a good place. So thank you."

"It's not *your* plans I'm worried about."

I grinned. "You sure you aren't part Southern? Sounds like you don't think my gentleman caller has honorable intentions."

"Rake Danescu is no gentleman, and it's beginning to look like honor isn't a concept many goblins are familiar with."

In preparation for a meeting, Ian had rolled a big whiteboard into a conference room just off the bull pen that the Brimstone team had taken for our own. Photos of the victims were posted across the top of the board, with crime family affiliation listed beneath.

The NYPD had probably started a board like this, though theirs would only have three bodies, and there wouldn't be two additional bullet points under each victim's name noting their species and missing soul. And there certainly wouldn't be an asterisk next to Sar Gedeon's "missing soul" bullet indicating that "The agency necromancer attempted contact but was bitch slapped by a demonic booby trap for trying."

Fortunately there was only the one asterisk.

All of the victims had had their chests sliced open with a scalpel-type instrument. Or claw. Their hearts had been torn from their chests, all while alive with a demon lord holding them to the floor with one hoof, branding its imprint into their breastbones. None had died without a struggle.

The details of Kela Dupari's murder had already been leaked online, and the public and press were having a field day, especially when they found out that her murder hadn't been the first. The NYPD had been the first to arrive on the scene of two more murders: one late last night, the other about the same time as Dupari's killing. As the medical examiner—and a mage—Dr. Anika Van Daal had kept Dupari's goblin features hidden. Either the two most recent victims were human, or Van Daal—or one of her people—had concealed the pointy ears from curious eyes, because there'd been no mention of odd ears or silvery skin, only missing hearts and branded hoofprints.

When a murder was particularly gruesome, it didn't matter what security measures the city's medical examiner's office had in place, juicy details always found their way out. And they found their way onto home pages and front pages even faster when there'd been more than one murder with the same lurid MO—and a photo. Yep, the person who'd stumbled onto the most recent body had taken plenty of pictures before they'd called the cops. Nowadays you didn't have to commit a crime to get your fifteen minutes of fame, just be the first person to take a picture of it.

I was a big fan of the Internet, and it had it uses—like the glorious world of online shopping—but right now it sucked. As recently as a couple of decades ago, the three networks (yes, that was all there were) would have had it on their evening news, and the newspapers would have gotten hold of it, and it would spread only as far as their signal or circulation.

Not anymore.

All it took was one tweet to turn a secret into worldwide news. Send that tweet with a bloody photo of a gaping chest and hoofprint brand, and within five minutes it'd have its own trending hashtag.

Our not-so-secret-anymore secret had garnered itself three hashtags at last count: #devilmurder, #killerdemon, and—my personal favorite for sheer dramatic impact—#SatanInNY.

I sighed. This was going to be a very long day.

Crackpots, conspiracy theorists, religious nuts, and the tin-foil-hat crowd had started coming out of the woodwork, and Kylie and her department were busy as hounds in flea season.

So far, the focus was on the sensationalist details, which fortunately didn't out any supernatural creature the public didn't already know about. Nearly every major religion had more than its share of demons or devils, many of them even named. Hearing that one was making it his mission on Earth to slaughter people in the illegal drug trade was being met with cheers, not panic in the streets. Panic and terror were reserved for those in the illegal drug trade. The opinion of the average Jane and Joe on the street was "Good riddance!" and "Give that demon a medal."

Right now, Kylie O'Hara was doing the rounds of the local news programs as the founder of the internationally known website hoaxbusters.com. She'd made a name for herself online and beyond as a debunker of the supernatural. Heck, Syfy was still after her to host her own show. However, her "secret identity" job was SPI's director of media and public relations. The goal of both of her jobs was to have a mundane explanation for supernatural events and creatures. With the latest in CGI technology available to any kid with a computer, exposing anyone looking for their fifteen minutes of fame had never been easier. That being said, those photos of the latest victim hadn't been faked. Kylie had readily confirmed that. However, she'd added that they didn't need to be faked to be explained. There was a killer on the loose in New York. Unfortunately, that was nothing new. This one simply limited its work to a subset of criminals, and for some reason known only to it, carried a branding iron and liked to cut out hearts. That didn't indicate supernatural, just a deeply disturbed individual.

Kylie was doing a fine job of doing her job. It'd be nice if Ian and I could say the same. A board full of the names of dead drug dealers didn't equal success; it just meant we were organized. Success meant putting that demon lord and his mage partner permanently out of business.

Our friendly neighborhood source inside the NYPD's drug enforcement unit, Detective Fred Ash, stopped by to share what they knew with us. The NYPD didn't know about SPI, but with supernaturals on the force, we had eyes and ears where we needed them. What Fred's eyes and ears had seen and heard in the last few hours was a bombshell to us; like we hadn't had enough of those ourselves.

Ian was incredulous. "They want to do *what*?"

I was a mite stunned myself.

The NYPD was going to put the city's top drug lords and ladies under protective custody.

"Yeah, protecting the people who no one really minds seeing dead," Fred told us. "Makes all kinds of sense. They're all drug-dealing, murdering, lowlife scum. But apparently they're *our* drug-dealing, murdering, lowlife scum. Most importantly, drug kingpins are taxpayers, too. Taxpayers who haven't been convicted of a crime. In the eyes of the law that makes them innocent taxpayers. Gotta protect all of them." Fred took another bite of doughnut. "This case is just chock full of irony."

Before coming over for a fact-sharing session with us, Fred had made a Krispy Kreme run. And before coming to the bull pen, he'd taken two raspberry-filled doughnuts up to Bert in his office. Our necromancer didn't want to let on, but he still wasn't back in fighting shape from the trap the murderer had set in what had been left of Sar Gedeon's mind. The favorite doughnut of the guy who worked with dead people was filled with gooey red stuff. Go figure.

For a Southerner like myself, Krispy Kremes were the holy grail of doughnuts. And when the "HOT" light on the sign was lit, that meant the sugary-glazed goodness had just come out of the oven. The first couple of bites would melt in your mouth. In my family, we held to the rule that the fresher the doughnut, the fewer calories they had. Fluffy when passing the lips, no fat on the hips.

I knew it wasn't true, but I'd never let scientific facts get in the way of enjoying a good doughnut.

I snagged a chocolate-iced one before they got gone. "I'd ask if you were pulling our leg, but I know you're not."

"I think the big problem with the city hall people is the way the city's not-so-law-abiding citizens are getting killed," Fred noted. "Chest branded, heart cut out, stink of hellfire and brimstone."

"Technically, it's just brimstone," I said. "Hellfire doesn't stink." Jeez, I was starting to sound like Marty.

"Whatever. It's our job to make it stop. Now."

In addition to doughnuts, Fred had brought news of another murder. It had been committed on a yacht in the Hudson River. The NYPD had gotten to that one first, too. In our defense, the NYPD had an advantage—we didn't have patrol boats on the rivers and in the harbor. And screams coming from an obscenely expensive mega-yacht wasn't something a patrol boat full of cops was likely to ignore.

It'd been a vampire. A high-ranking member of the Báthory family. Celeste Báthory had gotten scared and taken refuge on her yacht. She obviously hadn't heard that portals can be opened anywhere.

That murder scene had a deviation from the others—the heart hadn't been stolen and/or eaten; the vampire's heart had been staked to the teak wood floor next to her body.

We could now add "dark sense of humor" to the murders' descriptions.

"Báthory's people had checked every square inch of that boat," Fred told us. "There was no one there but them. One swears Celeste Báthory had him check her cabin. Hell, I think she'd have had him looking under the bed if the thing had an underneath. Half an hour later, no sounds at all, the guard posted outside her door saw blood soaking the carpet under the door. Didn't hear a peep, no struggle, nothing."

"He smell sulfur?" Ian asked.

"Yeah, seemed to be coming from under the door. That's what made him look down. Wards had been set and locked. She even had battle mages on board, real heavyweights. Likewise, they didn't hear or sense a thing."

"Damn."

"Yeah, our gruesome twosome are good. They've got the local pharmaceutical distributors about to crap themselves at seeing their own shadows. Whatever they do to protect themselves, it's not enough. By the time Báthory's boys got through that door, it was all over except the cleanup—and according to our guys that was some cleanup." He dug a manila folder out of his messenger bag. "I brought you two eight by ten glossies of Celeste for your board—undead and permanently dead." Fred read the "bitch slapped" comment next to the asterisk and chuckled. "Who wrote that?"

I raised the hand not holding the doughnut.

"I like it," he said.

"My journalism degree at work."

"Your mom would be proud."

"I think so." I also thought I was getting the hang of using dark cop humor to relieve tension. Fred Ash was my spirit animal. Besides, Bert wouldn't mind; he'd laugh his ass off. In fact, I'd written it for him.

Ian added the photos to our board. "You're a sick man, Fred." He gave me a look. "And you're an enabler."

"Never claimed to be anything else," Fred said.

I popped the last bite of doughnut in my mouth. "Ditto."

"So what'd the first responders have to say about the heart staked to the floor?" Ian asked.

"With that and her fangs, their first thought was vampire," Fred said. "Their second thought was there's no such thing as vampires, and that Celeste must have had some kinky dental work done. My momma—and my first sergeant—always said that first impressions are important. Our boys and girls should've gone with what their gut was telling them they were seeing."

"They can't charge something with murder that doesn't exist," Ian noted. "And as far as the NYPD is concerned, demons don't exist."

Fred snorted. "Yeah, I'd like to see my precinct try to put one of those in the holding tank."

"They can try to protect those people all they want," Ian continued. "It's not going to do any good, even if they believed the reason why. I wish them luck. If they could stop the killings, more power to them. But they won't because they can't. They can't because their minds won't let them believe. Their lizard brains know what's happening, but then they'll look at the modern city they live in and the primitive truth they know in their gut gets pushed aside. They're looking for mundane explanations, and this is magic, black and as dirty as I've ever heard of."

Fred waved his second doughnut. "Yeah, yeah, I know. You're preachin' to the choir. The killer is a dark mage with a demon sidekick, who's using a portal to get in and out, so my brother and sister officers are gonna be seriously frustrated. The classic murder in a locked room. Damned media's already calling it the perfect crime."

The tabloids like the *Informer*, which I used to work for, had gotten it right. Well, partially. Demons were involved, and while it was ironic that all of the victims were involved in the illegal drug trade, there was nothing divine about the retribution. Though it would be nice if God would do a little judicious smiting every now and then. Clean out the troublemakers. The world would be a better place for the rest of us.

"You can count us among the frustrated," Ian was saying. "With your guys tailing our most likely future victims, we can't do the same ourselves. Though it's not like there's much else we've been able to do."

"Normally multiple vics killed in a freaky way means

serial killer," Fred noted. "Make those vics connected to some of the biggest names in the city's drug trade, and the folks downtown think we're seeing the beginnings of a drug turf war. New dealers come in, want a slice of the business for themselves, our existing drug lords and ladies say hell no, and the newcomers start making examples to get them to change their minds. Which is surprisingly close to the truth except it's the established lords and ladies who want a piece of the newcomers' action."

The NYPD had had Kela Dupari's home and office under tight surveillance due to an ongoing investigation that had nothing to do with Brimstone. When her body was discovered in her office with the heart missing and the chest branded, all of the doors and windows had been locked. The surveillance cameras from the building showed that no one other than Kela Dupari had entered or left the office.

The NYPD was stumped, embarrassed, and getting pissed.

We were just pissed.

The NYPD thought the killings were a new cartel moving in to make a name for themselves by simultaneously slaughtering the kingpins while scaring the bejeezus out of the survivors—or as we were beginning to think of them, "future heart donors."

Aside from the demon and actual Hell elements, Fred was right, they'd pretty much hit the nail on the head.

19

WHEN Dr. Cheban and her team released their final report two hours later, I seriously doubt there was any high-fiving in the lab.

It was bad enough that one of the ingredients in Brimstone was actual brimstone from Hell, but it was the form of the brimstone that turned just another evening at SPI into all hands on deck.

At least the hands experienced with portals and demons—finding the former and battling the latter.

The brimstone in the drug had been combined with the other ingredients while still in its molten state. Martin DiMatteo's samples were rocks, dried and old. We were dealing with brimstone fresh from Hell itself.

According to Marty, fresh, molten brimstone could be obtained from only one location.

We had a Hellpit open somewhere under New York.

Some people would say that New York was the modern equivalent of Sodom and Gomorrah, and more than deserved to have a Hellpit gaping open under it, and the sooner it fell in, the better for everyone else. Others would argue that dishonor went to Las Vegas. I'd have to disagree with both. The majority of New Yorkers were the best folks you'd ever want to meet. I'd never been to Vegas, but since the place had gone and gotten itself Disneyfied, I figured they were out of the running.

Regardless of how those who didn't live in New York felt about the Big Apple, it didn't need or deserve to be swallowed into the bowels of Hell.

Our job was still the same.

Find it and close it—without anyone finding out.

And ensure that what happens in a Hellpit, stays in a Hellpit.

We'd had food sent up from the cafeteria, with Martin DiMatteo hosting a Lunch 'n' Learn on Hell and demons. Though since it was eight o'clock at night, it was dinner, but the concept was the same. Most of us hadn't had time for dinner yet, and with the Hellpit news, we were going to sit down and eat while we could. Fred had had to leave, but we promised to fill him in on what was said and decided.

"I know you say there is a Hellpit," I was saying to Martin DiMatteo. "And it's *here*."

"Correct."

"The demon lord and his mage partner are launching their attacks here through a portal from a dimension *close* to Hell, because there's no direct access to our dimension from Hell."

"Also correct."

"Then why can't the Hellpit be physically located in the same neighboring dimension where they're launching their attacks from rather than here, and the brimstone brought in through a portal? I'm not doubting your expertise," I hurried to add. "I just want to understand what's going on and why."

"Never apologize for seeking knowledge, Agent Fraser."

Our director of demonology didn't seem to be offended. Quite the opposite, in fact. I'd just asked him to talk about his favorite topic; no one minded doing that. Though asking did give me a bit of an unpleasant flashback to asking Bert for an explanation of what he'd been about to do with Sar Gedeon's corpse. I didn't like what I'd heard and seen then, and I didn't think I was going to be too fond of Marty's explanation, either. But I needed to know; we all did.

"Dr. Cheban reported that her team's analysis of the drug showed the chemical composition to be too complex to have been manufactured in any dimension with direct access to Hell. Therefore, it was manufactured here. In order to be manufactured here, the molten brimstone has to be harvested here. The magic necessary for creating, stabilizing, and maintaining a portal would have an undesirable side effect on any molten brimstone being brought through a portal, thickening it enough to be rendered unusable for the drug manufacturers' purpose."

I think my mouth might have been standing open. "How do you *know* these things?"

DiMatteo actually looked a little embarrassed. "I have tried to bring molten brimstone back with me on more than one excursion."

"To Hell and back."

"Yes. Passing through the two portals I had to navigate to get home turned my sample into a substance that can only be described as warm goo. Even when I took every precaution and put the samples in a container that can withstand a nuclear blast."

"That's one heck of a thermos," I muttered.

"Yes, it was," DiMatteo readily agreed. "Since demons can't gain direct access to our dimension from Hell, they have to go through portals to get to a dimension closer to ours, and then from there to here. But even then, only certain sizes and classes of demons can get through. Dimensions that can be accessed directly from Hell aren't nice places to begin with. I've called the ones you experienced yesterday 'anterooms,' which is an accurate description. These dimensions are similar enough to Hell in terms of temperature, air composition, and pressure that a portal between the two can be opened with relative ease. The dimensions that can open directly into ours—the elf and goblin realm, for example—are near perfect matches for our own. All of that being said, there are times during the year when the barriers between all of the dimensions are at their thinnest. We just experienced one of those, namely All Hallows' Eve."

"How long do you think the Hellpit has been open?" Ian asked.

"The optimal time to open one is at a combination of a full moon and a time like All Hallows' Eve, when our enterprising drug manufacturers wouldn't have had to work quite so hard."

"I thought you'd said there's no direct access to Hell from here," I said. "Then again, when you told me, I'd just hit my head on concrete."

"You're correct, Agent Fraser. There is no direct access *from* Hell to here. From here *to* Hell is another matter."

"You're saying that some dumbass on *our* side dug a pit to Hell?" Roy Benoit was the commander of one of SPI's two commando teams. He was proud to be from the Louisiana swamps, from a long line of gator hunters, and a retired Army Ranger. Though according to Roy, Rangers not only didn't surrender, they never retired.

"Not dumb, Commander Benoit," DiMatteo replied. "Greedy. In all likelihood, our demon lord offered them access to fresh brimstone. They had the other ingredients. All they needed was the brimstone. They either didn't know—or didn't care—that if a Hellpit is ever fully opened, it's open permanently, and any demon that ever wanted to come to our dimension and belly up to the all-you-can-eat human buffet could do just that. Since New York has yet to be overrun by demons, we obviously haven't reached that point yet."

"So the last time there was a Hellpit here," Roy began, "how did they get rid of it?"

"First of all, it's not a simple matter to open a Hellpit. There have only been a few documented instances, none of which have ever reached a state of being fully open. The first Hellpit was opened in the Gobi Desert in Mongolia in the 1320s. A Mongolian sorcerer sought the advice of a demon to destroy a rival tribe. The demon instructed him on how to conjure a small Hellpit in return for the sorcerer's soul after death, as well as those of his tribesmen. The sorcerer opened the Hellpit, the promised 'help' emerged, and the sorcerer closed it again. What emerged from that pit killed the rival tribe within a matter of days—then did the same to the sorcerer and his tribe, netting the demon his promised souls a lot sooner than the sorcerer had anticipated." DiMatteo paused uncomfortably. "The creatures were tiny, microscopically so. They spread throughout Mongolia to the Silk Road, and from there onto the fleas infesting the rats on merchant ships bound for Europe."

Holy. Crap.

Roy was incredulous. "The Black Plague was caused by demons? I've heard a lot in my time, but—"

"Like all living creatures, demons come in all shapes and sizes," DiMatteo countered.

"In other words," I said, "It doesn't take a big pit to make big problems."

Roy took a deep breath. "Okay, saying I believe 'demonic bacteria'—and I might as well—I wouldn't think whoever opened the Hellpit here would be inclined to close it again. When we find it, how do *we* close it?"

"We don't," DiMatteo told him. "It would take a portal-keeper. Two of the officially documented Hellpits were closed by extremely powerful portalkeepers."

Roy swore. "Those are rare birds."

"They don't openly advertise their presence for good reason. People who have the gift of opening or closing dimensional portals or tears are in great demand—and most often by individuals or organizations who you would not want to have notice you. Wars, invasions, and criminal acts of every sort can be greatly simplified with a strategically placed portal.

Vivienne Sagadraco will hopefully know the name of a portalkeeper who is powerful enough to close our Hellpit."

"It can be yours," Roy said. "'Cause it sure as hell ain't mine."

"I'm not that great with math," I said, "so correct me if I'm wrong, but it's been four days since Halloween and two days since the full moon. Detective Fred Ash of the NYPD told Ian and me yesterday that they'd only found out about Brimstone a few days ago. That would coincide with Halloween, but wouldn't the manufacturing process take longer than that? Wouldn't that imply that the Hellpit was open before Halloween?"

All eyes went to Dr. Claire Cheban, the SPI lab director. She didn't look old enough to be out of college, let alone have a PhD and be in charge of a lab like SPI's.

"We're still analyzing the drug sample," she said, "but brimstone in its molten state is unstable, especially when combined with two of the other ingredients we found in the drug. As Director DiMatteo said, the composition of the drug itself is incredibly complex. From raw ingredients to finished product would take at least four days, and that's a conservative estimate."

"Sounds like whoever opened the Hellpit missed his window," Ian noted. "Or didn't need one. Is it possible to open a pit anytime?"

"It's not only possible," DiMatteo replied, "but in the case we're faced with, I believe it is probable. Contrary to what Commander Benoit said, we're not dealing with a dumbass. Greedy, yes. Dumbass, no. To open a Hellpit regardless of dimensional thinness and moon phase would take an individual with a frightening level of power and skill."

An assessment like that coming from a man who took rock-hunting excursions to Hell meant a lot of scary.

Ian and I exchanged a glance.

Halloween night had been the gala opening of the Mythos exhibit at the Metropolitan Museum of Art. One of the exhibits had been Viktor Kain's Dragon Eggs. Another had been a marble statue of three harpies. The real statue had been way-laid in London and had been replaced with three actual Grecian harpies that had been put into a state of stasis until the night of the gala when an unknown—and scary powerful—sorcerer or sorceress had reanimated the harpies to steal the Dragon Eggs. Before, during, and after the theft, they'd also killed a couple of security guards, terrorized the guests, and shattered a section of the window wall in the Met's Sackler Wing when they escaped into the night over Central Park.

We'd never found who was ultimately behind the diamond theft, but we strongly suspected it was the same individual who had enough magical mojo to put three harpies into suspended animation and disguise them as a marble statue.

It sounded like one of those mega-mages hadn't left town and was now working with a demon lord.

"Just because it's called a Hellpit," said Sandra Niles, our other commando unit commander, "does that mean it's an actual, physical hole in the ground, or could it be similar to a door, like a portal?"

"It'll be a hole in the ground," DiMatteo confirmed. "But it can be closed like a portal—unless it's completely open."

"When it's completely open, how can it be closed?" Sandra asked.

"There's never been one completely open before, so I don't know if it can be closed."

Silence.

"Uh, Marty, there's a lot of holes in the ground under Manhattan." Leave it to Sandra to be able to ignore the bomb Marty just dropped and move on. "Could you narrow it down for us?"

"Brimstone solidifies within an hour after being exposed to surface air. It wouldn't matter how quickly it could be gotten into a sealed container. That would put the pit less than an hour from the lab, probably much closer. At the same time, it would need to be a location that could be easily secured."

DiMatteo paused, his expression slightly disturbed.

Again, coming from a guy who studied demons for a living, this was alarming.

"There is a rather concerning possibility," he said. "I've compared it to black holes—"

Hellpits and black holes? This wasn't gonna be good.

"Humans have never been near a black hole, yet there are certain behaviors that scientists accept as fact. Once a Hellpit is open 'all the way,' there's no reason that it would be limited to a finite size. In theory, the size of the Hellpit opening would only dictate what size demons could gain access to our dimension. Smaller opening, smaller demons. Larger opening, larger demons. Unless the individual who opened the pit is remaining with it 24/7 to control its growth, theoretically there wouldn't be a size limit."

No one moved. Those who were still eating stopped chewing.

"On the upside—"

"There's an upside to Armageddon?" Roy muttered.

"Yes, there is. The presence at this time of any smaller-class demons could indicate probable proximity to the Hellpit's location."

"So, if people are being eaten in Midtown, chances are the Hellpit's in Midtown?"

"Correct."

That confirmed it. Marty didn't get humor or sarcasm. Bless his heart.

"Regarding Dr. DiMatteo's comments on the proximity of the lab to the Hellpit," Claire Cheban began, "understand that they would need to have enough distance between them to ensure that no heat or flame from the Hellpit would come in contact with two of the ingredients found in our dimension. Those two ingredients are highly unstable and flammable."

Note the location in the city of any large explosion. Check.

"And Hell does have a well-deserved reputation for being flammable," DiMatteo noted, with complete sincerity.

"The lab where it's being manufactured would need to

be state-of-the-art." Dr. Cheban proceeded to launch into a ten-minute, PhD-level lecture of the chemical properties of each ingredient she'd isolated, with an accompanying run-down of how contact with molten heat would make them go "boom."

When she'd finished, Roy spoke up. "And that, boys and girls, is why there aren't any meth labs in Hell."

"So what kind of equipment are we talking about?" Ian asked. "And where would they get it?"

I knew where he was going with this. Some of Rake's real estate holdings were elven-owned laboratories and research facilities. We'd asked him to check if any had been working on any new drugs. He'd said he'd check and get back to us. It'd been a little over two hours. Nothing from Rake. Maybe his "monitors" had to check their records. Maybe not. Either way, I knew who Ian would be calling when we got out of this meeting.

"I'll e-mail you a list of the equipment, and where each item can be bought." Cheban was typing insanely fast on her phone. "You can't get these things on eBay or off the shelf at Labs 'R' Us, and the companies that manufacture them don't let just anyone walk in off the street and buy them. And then there's the cost—"

"We suspect that our pharmaceutical entrepreneurs have a loaded angel investor," Ian told her.

"If money's no object, they could buy—or pay to have stolen—whatever they needed."

There were beeps and tunes around the room as Cheban's e-mail came through.

"Check for thefts of items one through five," she told us, referring to the numbered list she'd sent. "One and two are the most expensive and hardest to get."

When the meeting concluded, Ian made a beeline for the elevators down to the motor pool and motioned me to follow.

"We going to see Rake?" I asked.

"Not yet. Now that we've had dinner, how about dessert?"

20

BY the time Yasha stopped in front of Kitty's Confections on Bleeker Street in the Village, Ian had told me that we were here for more than a nighttime snack of red velvet cupcakes.

Apparently Kitty had a secret—a big one—and she'd kept it from everyone. Everyone except Vivienne Sagadraco, who, when the need proved great, had told Alain Moreau and Ian.

Kitty could close portals—big ones.

That implied that Kitty had the same level of power as the mega-mage who'd opened the Hellpit in the first place. I was having a tough time wrapping my head around that one. I was betting that the mega-mage, who'd essentially put out the welcome mat for the denizens of Hell, couldn't bake an angel food cake that was reported to have made actual angels weep.

Too bad this magical confrontation couldn't be settled with a bake-off.

"I take it from the personal visit, Kitty's going to be less than enthused about helping us," I said.

"Significantly less than enthused," Ian replied. "She had a bad experience. Her last name, Poertner, is German for Porter. Most people with that name had a distant ancestor who was stationed at a castle door. Kitty's people opened and closed a bigger kind of door."

"Dimensional portals," I said in realization.

Ian nodded. "The name's the same; the job couldn't be more different. For over a thousand years, Kitty's family have been the supernatural world's doorkeepers, or to be more exact, portalkeepers. Her specialty is stabilizing and closing dimensional rifts, which is essentially what we're dealing with here. We need to secure Kitty's help now, because it won't do us a damned bit of good to find the Hellpit if we don't have anyone who can close it."

"I wouldn't think that'd be a problem. Kitty's awesome. When she hears that the world will literally go to Hell in a handbasket if she doesn't help, I'm sure she'll be glad to slam a door in some demonic faces."

"It's a lot more complicated—and dangerous—than that."

Lately, it seemed like everything was.

Kitty was due to close the shop in another fifteen minutes. Yasha dropped us off out front.

When we came in, Kitty took one look at our faces and motioned us straight back to the kitchen while she locked the door and turned off the lights in the front of the shop.

I'd never seen Kitty with any expression other than happy and smiling.

She wasn't doing either one now.

Mind reading wasn't one of Kitty's talents, but she seemed to know why we were there. Then again, Ian had come by to get lemon-blueberry scones for me after the squid demon had tried to drag me through the portal in the parking garage. Ian had known about Kitty's ability, so I was sure he'd told her what had nearly happened to me. I realized that he'd known then that we'd be visiting Kitty for just this very reason, and he'd given her time to start thinking about her answer before he'd had to ask her the question—and before there was the pressure of a critical need.

A wise man, my partner.

Yep, Kitty knew exactly why we were here.

But it didn't change the fact that we were here to ask Kitty to do something that terrified her.

It sucked to be the bad guys.

Being the one who'd nearly been dragged through the garage portal, I suddenly felt like the visual aid for Kitty's impending guilt trip.

Kitty stuck her head in the kitchen and looked at me. "Are we going to need cupcakes for this?"

I sighed. "I could sure use one . . . or three."

When life turned to crap, some people drank. I mainlined sugar.

Kitty returned to the kitchen, set a tray of miniature red velvet cupcakes down in front of us, and went to the big stainless steel refrigerator and brought out a gallon of milk. I found cups and a roll of paper towels and was good to go.

"And the people rejoiced," I murmured, eying the cream-cheese-iced mouthfuls of culinary perfection. The cupcakes in the cupcake shops that'd sprung up to rival Starbucks in their numbers all had a Mount Everest tower of icing. I'd admit (though not to Kitty) that when I hadn't been near her bakery and was hit with a craving, I'd gone in those shops. More than once, I'd ended up with icing up my nose. Kitty's cupcakes had a perfect cake to icing ratio. My ultimate cupcake test came when I took the paper off. If the cake couldn't support the weight of its own icing and fell over . . . no, thank you. It was possible to have too much of a good thing, and that included icing. I drew the line at what I called bobblehead cupcakes.

"Where is it?" she asked us.

I frowned around a mouthful of cupcake.

"The portal," Kitty clarified. "Where is it?"

I glanced at Ian.

"It's not exactly a portal," he said. "As to where, we don't know. Yet."

She regarded him with steady suspicion. It was an expression I'd never seen on her before. "If it's not exactly a portal, what exactly is it?"

I glanced at Ian again. I was really grateful to have a mouthful of cupcake. It'd be rude to answer Kitty's questions while eating.

"It's a Hellpit," he told her. "Open somewhere under the city."

"Full apogee?"

"Getting close."

"Who opened it?"

"We're trying to find out."

Ian told Kitty everything we knew so far. Sad thing was it didn't take long.

"And when you find it, you want me to close it."

"We would like your advice, and if you're willing, your help."

Kitty glanced at me. "Your partner's becoming quite the diplomat."

I tried a smile. "I haven't noticed. He must like you more than he does me."

"He just wants something."

I nodded thoughtfully. "Hmm, I think that's a man thing."

Ian raised an eyebrow.

"Hey, I'm just trying to lighten things up. If any situation ever needed lightening, it'd be an impending demonic invasion."

"Why?" Kitty asked.

I puzzled over that one. "Marty says demons have always wanted our world. Bert thinks it's the beaches."

Now it was Kitty's turn to be baffled. "I meant why would someone open a Hellpit?"

"Other than access to molten brimstone," Ian said, "we don't know."

"You said it was likely open before Halloween."

"That's right."

"That means a lot of power was involved."

"We think that, too."

"Such beings of power would have a motive other than getting an ingredient for a drug."

"Even if they were being paid a lot of money?" I asked.

"It's been my experience—and that of my family—that those who can open a portal at will are rarely lacking money, nor can the things they want be bought with money. If you can find out what that motivation is, you'd be a couple steps closer to finding them or the Hellpit."

"If we do find it, will you help us?"

"If you don't find it soon, you'll be beyond my help or anyone else's. After a major portal has been open for a full cycle of the moon, nothing short of a team of archangels can close it."

"We're going to find it," I told her.

"A word of warning: it could very well be contained in a small pocket dimension to conceal it from anyone who might stumble onto it."

"I can see portals," I told her.

Kitty gave me a quick, startled look.

"You didn't tell her?" I asked Ian.

"That information is need to know. When I was here yesterday, Kitty didn't need to know."

"As far as I'm concerned, she does now." I looked at Kitty. She was regarding me with something that looked almost like pity. "What?"

"If that gets out, you're in more danger than I am."

I shrugged. "I'm a seer. I already have a bull's-eye from that. I can be the same amount of dead from two bull's-eyes than one. I don't know how I picked up this portal-seeing thing, but I have a sinking feeling that knowing how I got it isn't going to help me get rid of it. Besides, from what I understand, it's quite the resume enhancer."

Kitty smiled. Now that was the Kitty I knew.

I smiled back. "Sucks to be us right now, doesn't it?"

She glanced at Ian. "I don't really have a choice, do I?"

"You always have a choice."

"One option could save the world; the other definitely damns it. Not what I'd call much of a choice. I'll make you a deal—you do your job—*and* get me what I need—and I'll do mine."

We really couldn't have asked for more than that. If we found the Hellpit, Kitty would close it—or at least she'd try. It wasn't like anyone, including her, had on-the-job experience slamming the stairway to Hell.

Kitty had sent us on our way with a dozen cupcakes in her bakery's trademark pink box.

We'd walked out with cupcakes *and* a promise to help prevent demonic Armageddon. Now that was what I called a good night's work.

I refrained from diving into the box. I had a question for Ian, and I knew Yasha would appreciate me not getting cupcake crumbs all over the backseat of his partner.

"What did Kitty mean by 'get me what I need'?"

Ian blew out his breath and leaned his head back against the seat rest. "An anchor mage."

"Which is?"

"Pretty much what it sounds like. A mage who can anchor Kitty to this dimension while she works."

"From the 'sigh of eternal suffering' you just let out, I take it there's not a one eight hundred number for anchor mages."

"No, there's not."

"Difficult to get?"

"Impossible to get," Yasha chimed in. "There are none in this country—at least not anymore. Only in Europe and Asia."

"So Ms. Sagadraco can't just send over a company jet and pick one up?"

The Russian snorted. "All are worthless cowards."

"Some aren't worthless, buddy," Ian said. "And there's a few left who aren't cowards."

Yasha took a particularly sharp turn, and I clutched the cupcake box to keep it from flying into the window. "Uh, a few left? Is there some kind of high job burnout rate for anchors?"

"More like a high rate of getting sucked into dimensions they're helping to close along with the portal mage and not being able to get back."

"I can see why that'd make someone want to switch careers," I said. "So what about the ones who are left?"

"They have established partnerships with portal mages, and only work with them."

"So we fly a team over here. Kitty doesn't have to take the risk. A win-win."

"More like a lose-lose," Ian said. "They only do smaller portals."

"Then what good are they?"

"Not much. Plus, if the portal's on American soil, they believe it's an American problem, and that more than likely, we'd brought it on ourselves and can deal with it the same way."

"Bullshit. When those demons start pouring through, they may get us first, but I don't think they're gonna let a little thing like an ocean or two stop them. Not to mention, Europe and Asia have some amazing beaches."

"These people would say they'd deal with that problem when it came to them."

"And bit their faces off. I'm with Yasha. They're worthless cowards."

From the driver's seat, the Russian werewolf vigorously nodded in approval.

"Even if there was a team who would be willing to help," Ian continued, "Kitty's the last of her family line. She's the best, and some would say good enough to do it by herself, no anchor needed."

"What about anchor mages she's worked with in the past?"

That question earned me some uncomfortable silence.

"Okay . . . let me rephrase that: Are there any *surviving* anchor mages who she's worked with in the past?"

"No."

I let out a low whistle. "Was she in some way responsible for that?"

"From what I've heard, no. Just piss-poor luck on the part of her anchors, and the fact that they were working on big and nasty portals no one else would touch. Higher risk, higher mortality. Other portal mages and anchors call her the Black Widow."

"How did she survive when they didn't?"

"Kitty is brave," Yasha said. "They are cowards."

"I have to agree with you there," Ian told him.

"How do you know all this?" I asked Yasha. "I thought only the boss, Moreau, and Ian knew."

"Kitty is friend. She talks to me."

I could understand that. Yasha was big, but once you got to know him, you realized his heart was as big as the rest of him. Our big werewolf was also a big teddy bear. I'd also told Yasha things I hadn't told anyone else at SPI. Now I knew I wasn't the only one. I was glad Kitty had realized she could trust him. Everyone needed someone they could tell anything to and not worry about being judged for it.

"So what happened?" I asked them both.

"The last major portal Kitty closed was eight years ago," Ian said. "The portal was to a previously unknown dimension that really wasn't that much better than Hell. A monster, for lack of a more descriptive word, started coming through. Kitty held on and kept working. Her anchor mage panicked and released the protective spell on both of them. The spell Kitty was using to close the portal gave her some protection; her anchor was defenseless—"

"Because he was coward and dropped shields on him and Kitty," Yasha said vehemently. "Deserved to be eaten by blue monster." He glanced at me in the rearview mirror. "My opinion."

"If Kitty hadn't been strong enough to shield herself and continue working, she'd have been eaten, too," Ian added. "She doesn't trust anyone to have her back now."

I snorted. "With good reason. I take it this wasn't the first time it'd happened?"

"Unfortunately, no."

"Then I can't blame her for telling people to close their own damn doors."

"If this were a normal portal, Kitty could probably do it alone," Ian said. "But it's a Hellpit. There's no precedent on what could go wrong."

Just everything.

21

WE were halfway back to headquarters when everything caught up with me and I was suddenly bone tired. As a result, I made a decision.

I'd spent last night in SPI's infirmary. Tonight I was going to sleep in my own bed.

I informed Ian of my decision.

"Sure, no problem," Ian said from the front seat.

"Did you hear me?"

"Yes, you want to sleep in your own bed tonight. I completely understand."

"Uh . . . good. I appreciate—"

"Just as long as you understand that I'll be staying with you."

"Me, too," Yasha chimed in.

Me getting snuggly in my own bed had just turned into a pajama party, with two coworkers who didn't have pajamas.

"Nice try," I told them both. "Threaten to stay and get me to change my mind. It won't work. I'm not going to change my mind."

"I wasn't asking you to," my partner told me.

"Because I don't mind you guys staying."

"You have popcorn?" Yasha asked. "And other snacks? And movies? I like musicals. I will keep sound low; I have good hearing."

Why me?

On second thought, maybe I'd just grab some clean clothes and go back to headquarters.

When we got to my building, Yasha turned his anger at Kitty's cowardly former partners into a hunt for a parking spot, while I hurried up the stairs to pack a bag with Ian doing his bodyguard thing.

I lived in a fourth-floor walk-up in the East Village. The building was from the fifties, and a lot of the tenants were, too. The rest of us were young professional types. Thanks to rent control, the only way the seniors in the building were leaving was carried out on their flecked Formica kitchen tables.

My apartment was at the end of the hall, with two windows that gave me an occasionally entertaining view of Bainwick's Art Academy across the alley.

Ian looked out the window. "I haven't noticed that before."

"Art school."

His face was profiled toward me. He was grinning. "There's a platform in the middle of the room. They use any nude models?"

"Guys when it's warmer, girls when it's not." I met his grin and raised him a smirk. "Must be that whole shrinkage issue. With the cold snap, the only thing in the raw right now are bowls of fruit. The heat over there works as well as it does over here, which is when it wants to."

"Need me to help you pack?"

"I got it."

In my bedroom I kept the usual arsenal that helped single women sleep at night, but I'd added a few of my own.

In homage to my Southern mountain-girl roots, I kept a

seriously huge flashlight next to my bed. It had a trigger for a switch, a camo finish, and could blind a buck at fifty yards. While my intruder was having his retinas flash fried, I'd let him have it with a stream of Raid. Accurate for up to ten yards. Blind 'em with light and chemicals, then run like hell.

Incapacitate while maintaining distance. That's what I'm talkin' about.

The best defense was avoiding contact in the first place.

Since I'd joined SPI, I'd gotten plenty of training in defending myself. When it came to hand-to-hand combat, I knew I had to have been the most challenging trainee Ian had ever been saddled with. After the first few months, Ian had told me that my brain was probably going to end up being my best weapon, and that weapon told me not to go around writing checks I couldn't cash.

I was smart enough to know and accept that I could be trained by the best and still never qualify as a badass. My goal was simply to make it to work each day and home every night. Ian was the badass-ninja-monster-fighter, not me. I did the best I could during our training sessions, and never stopped trying to improve, but I also accepted that the mayor or police commissioner would never shine the Bat-Signal in the sky to get my attention.

I was good with that.

I went into my bedroom and closed the door. I figured my duffel bag would be the right size for what I needed. My closet was the size of a phone booth, so I kept my luggage— along with anything else that would fit—under my bed. I got down on my hands and knees, stuck my arm underneath the bed, and started sifting and searching for something shaped like luggage.

I found something squishy instead.

I yelped and yanked my arm back, scrambling to my feet, tripping over my own legs in the process.

The back of my hand was bleeding from a two-inch gash. Must have raked my hand on the bed frame yanking it . . .

My eyes were even with the comforter on my bed, and they locked on the clear slime pooling in little indentations in the blanket. And on my pillow, a pool of wet filled the indentation that my head had made the last time I'd slept in it two nights ago.

Since then, someone had been sleeping in my bed, and it wasn't Goldilocks.

A raspy hiss came from under the bed . . .

. . . and from the half-opened door to my closet.

A door I always closed.

I drew my gun and slowly backed toward the bedroom door, my eyes quickly flicking between bed and closet. I bumped into my dresser.

"Ian." It came out one notch above a whisper. I swallowed on a bone-dry throat and tried again.

"Ian."

A thing came out from beneath the pillow, squirming through the slime to free itself, dropping from the bed to land with a wet plop on the floor.

It was maybe eight inches tall, with red skin hanging loose on a thin frame, its bald head topped with two tiny horns. A forked tongue came out from between thin rubbery lips as it opened its mouth, showing me a double row of jagged teeth. Its feet were hooves the size of a cat's paw, its hands thin, spidery fingers, curling and uncurling to reveal claws curved to razor points.

It looked like . . .

It couldn't be.

A baby demon.

Class Five, Class Seven, classless, who the hell cared? It was in my bedroom.

And there wasn't a portal to be seen or smelled. If they hadn't come through a portal, then how the hell had they gotten in here?

I opened my mouth, to shout, to scream, but nothing came out, not even a whimper.

The demon's yellow eyes focused on me and it hissed, its whip-like tail lashing the air behind it.

I found my voice *and* the volume dial.

"Ian!"

I fired at those teeth. The demon was gone before the bullet got there. My pillow exploded in a blast of memory foam, and wood splinters flew from my demolished headboard.

Simultaneous attacks came from under the bed and out of the dark closet. Every kid's nightmare was now mine.

A clawed hand shot out from beneath my dresser, clutching my ankle.

I stomped on the hand, and fired at the demon skittering across the floor at me. It squealed as a spray of pink erupted from its side, but kept coming, its eyes brightly glowing.

Four demons. Two more dropped out of the heating vent and scuttled on spindly legs off my bed and across the floor.

Six.

Squealing, hissing, eyes gleaming with a yellow light. They were fast. Too fast for bullets—at least my bullets.

Bullets weren't working. Leaning against my dresser, behind my door, was my Louisville Slugger. I landed a solid midair hit on a demon that launched itself off my bed, and heard a gratifying crack of the wooden baseball bat on spindly bones for my effort. I didn't have time to confirm that I'd killed it or even knocked the wind out of the thing, as the remaining demons came at me.

I'd never been more grateful to have a small bedroom. The demons leapt at me, and I dove for my bedside table, hitting the floor hard, but rolling onto my back with my can of Raid. The demon that reached me first took a direct hit in the eyes. Its shrieks were deafening. Any higher pitched and only dogs would have been able to hear it.

A demon scrabbled out from beneath the bed and sank its jagged teeth into my shoulder. I screamed and beat it in the face with the can, frantic to get it off me. The can and my hand that death-gripped it were slick with blood, mine and demon.

A flick of movement was all the warning I got of a demon jumping off my bed directly above me.

It exploded in a bullet-induced spray of red, the bits raining down on me.

Ian.

The other demons kept coming at me, completely ignoring Ian and his gun as if he didn't exist.

Ian had his gun in one hand, but was laying into the squealing swarm with a freaking machete. Where'd he been hiding that?

In a few seconds, my carpet went from beige to beyond able to be cleaned, as Ian and I hacked and bludgeoned our way through the remaining demons. When there were no more of the little monsters left to come at me, I just stood there, gasping for what air I could find, bat still held ready in a double-fisted, white-knuckled grip. Ian stalked around the room, checking for any survivors, and fortunately finding none. In the other room, Yasha all but took my apartment door off its hinges to get in.

Ian flicked his blade to clear it of gore. "Maybe they knew I'd taste bad."

I sucked in enough air to make words. "Yeah." Gasp, wheeze. "Right."

The Russian charged into my bedroom, sawed-off shotgun clutched like a toy in his big hands, eyes shining with an amber glow. The only sound was my ragged breathing. On my carpet was the sliced, smushed, shot, and sprayed proof that someone—alive, undead, or demonic—didn't want me finding the portal to that Hellpit.

Demon eggs.

That's what Yasha found under my bed. Six leathery and slimy eggshells. And they hadn't been left there by the Easter Bunny.

Someone had left me an early Christmas present. Now all I needed to do was find out who my Secret Santa was.

That, and have a screaming fit.

The three of us were at my kitchen table.

"If that squid demon hadn't gotten hold of me last night, I'd have come home to sleep," I told Ian and Yasha. "So much for whether the murderer and his demon lord cohort know I can see portals." I gasped. "Oh, shit. What about Kitty?"

Ian held up his phone. "Taken care of. I called this in and dispatched a team to Kitty's apartment. She's safe."

My shoulders sagged. "We didn't try to hide that we were going to see her, and I don't think anyone would believe that we just had the late-night munchies."

"Which is why we have people staying with her." He frowned. "She refused protective custody at headquarters. She insists on opening the bakery tomorrow, so our folks will stick close."

"Why isn't that reassuring?"

Ian glanced back toward my bedroom. He didn't look full of confidence for Kitty's continued safety, either. He looked down at his phone's screen and scrolled down to a number then hesitated, his index finger poised over the screen.

"What?" I asked.

"I really hate it when a situation's so completely in the can that I have to call the boss on her direct line." He sighed, tapped the screen, and put the phone to his ear. "Ma'am, it's Agent Byrne. We have a Code Five. I wanted you to hear it from me." He listened, and glanced at me. "Yes, ma'am, that's exactly where I'm calling from."

I groaned and rolled my eyes.

He listened some more. "Some cuts that'll probably need stitches, but other than that, she's fine. We just need containment, cleanup, and minor medical." He listened. "Yes, ma'am, I'll hold."

"What?" I asked.

"They're checking to see if we're about to have company from the police."

I dropped my head into my non-bloody hand. I hadn't even thought of that. Though if the cops were on the way, they were taking their sweet time.

"Thank you, ma'am." Ian put his phone back in his coat.

"So . . .?" I asked. "Yes? No? Maybe?"

"None of your neighbors called nine one one," Ian said.

"You're kidding?"

"Nope."

Lately, SPI's biggest crime scene challenge was getting there before the cops. This time, no one had even called them. There'd been gunfire, screaming, and pounding coming from my apartment, and not one call went through to 911.

Considering the hour, half my neighbors were out drinking with friends, and the other half must have had their TVs turned up, or were in bed with their hearing aids turned off. All of the above kept the NYPD from being called. Luckier still, Mrs. Rosini, who shared a wall with me, was watching Fox News right now. We could hear it through the walls. There was no need to check on her; she was perfectly fine. Mrs. Rosini was one of those people who liked to argue with the TV. Fox News provided a constant stream of something to piss her off. But she made awesome cookies, though usually while talking back to the TV. We could hear her now, giving Bill O'Reilly hell. She'd never noticed when hell had broken loose over here.

I slowly shook my head. "Gunshots, screaming, and no one called the cops."

"Is good," Yasha said.

"*This* time. What if I'd been on the receiving end of those bullets? Or had my face eaten off by . . . ?" I waved my hand in the general direction of my bedroom. I wasn't going to say what they were out loud. I'd already visualized at least half a dozen alternate outcomes where I hadn't come out the winner.

Mac, when a murderer sends their newborn minions to kill you, can you in all honesty call yourself a winner in *any* scenario?

"Got a first aid kit?" Ian asked me. "I don't want to wait for the medics to get some antiseptic on those bites on your shoulder."

"Yeah . . . in the bathroom."

"Got it." Yasha picked up my Louisville Slugger and disappeared into the bedroom, now known as the room with the slimy pillows and squishy carpet.

I sighed. "Damn, I really liked this apartment."

"The boss will have everything taken care of," Ian assured me. "New carpet, paint, pillows, headboard, bed stuff. It'll be as good as new." He took a quick look around my less than Martha Stewartesque kitchen. "Better even. Though I hate to be the bearer of more bad news, but you're going to have to lose your shirt when the medic gets here."

"Excuse me?"

"Those bites on your shoulder look bad."

"You're just full of compliments today, aren't you?"

"One of my many gifts."

I peeled back the dish towel I'd been holding against my shoulder. While it was far from being soaked, it was a respectable amount of blood. But when I thought about what was attached to the jagged teeth that had made those marks, I wanted to strip and run naked through a rubbing-alcohol shower.

"Yasha," I called.

"Da?"

"There's a tank top hanging on the back of the bathroom door. Could you get that, too?"

Silence.

Uh-oh. "Finding everything okay?"

"Find more than expected."

I sighed and my shoulders sagged. "But wait, there's more," I muttered. I pressed the towel to my shoulder and stood.

"Stay here," Ian told me.

"*My* apartment, and an attempt on *my* life."

Ian put up his hands. "Okay. *Your* blood on *your* floor."

"Damn straight."

We carefully picked our way through the bedroom and into the bathroom where Yasha stood staring down into my bathtub.

Ian and I went to either side of him, looked down, and had a collective WTF moment.

There was a pile of raw chickens.

Or what was left of them.

They'd been torn apart, meat stripped off, and then bare bones flung into the deep end of the tub. It looked like the aftermath of a successful tailgating party or the grandstand after a NASCAR race.

"Baby food?" Yasha ventured. "Maybe they need chicken."

I just looked at him. "Great. So now I'm not nutritionally complete?"

"Maybe was appetizer for main course."

"That's not any better."

I saw a new bedroom, refrigerator, *and* tub in my future.

22

I was a lot less bothered by an entire SPI investigation team being in my apartment than I thought I would be. I had dead demon bits scattered around my bedroom, and before the hatchlings had eaten their first meal, there had been enough raw chickens in my bathtub to stock a KFC kitchen. That more than made up for dirty dishes in the sink.

The SPI team wore navy coveralls with patches that said "Green Heating and Air Conditioning."

Dr. Stephens was sitting at my kitchen table, a suture kit spread out on a sterile white cloth. Just my luck, he'd confirmed Ian's assessment that I was going to need stitches. I was more than willing to go back to headquarters, but there was no way I'd sleep in the infirmary again. No *Groundhog Day* time loop for me, thank you.

I was used to eating meals at my table. Now here I was getting stitched up because a pack of baby demons tried to make a meal out of me.

"I'm ready to start," Dr. Stephens told me. "I need for you to be still. Okay?"

I nodded tightly and found an absolutely fascinating mystery smudge on the wall to study while he worked. He'd given me a local, but I still had no desire to watch him take a curved needle and thread to my shoulder. However, I took a quick peek before I could stop myself. He was in the middle of his first stitch, and the bottom dropped out of my stomach.

Your life had officially gone to crap when you knew you'd never feel safe in your own apartment again, regardless of how many guns, baseball bats, and cans of Raid you had. For security, most New York apartments made do with half a dozen locks and one or more of the following by the door: mace, a baseball bat, a butcher knife that was past its prime in the kitchen but just fine for puncturing anything trying to get through your front door, or a gun of dubious legality.

I had all of the above, except my gun was legal.

When Ian had talked to Ms. Sagadraco, I'd been promised more than that.

Wards.

Fierce, fry-you-where-you-stood wards.

Three of our best security mages were on their way from headquarters to put the magical whammy on my abode. Creativity counted with wards, and Vivienne Sagadraco only hired the best. Nothing was getting inside my apartment. However, no mage's work was guaranteed against portals, but at least I'd know before I came in if one was or had been open in my apartment. It wasn't the ideal solution, but I'd take what I could get.

Ian quietly leaned against the frame of my open kitchen door, waiting for Dr. Stephens to pause in his work before speaking. I was sure the doc appreciated Ian's consideration. I appreciated it even more. He was just the stitcher; I was the stitchee.

"I went next door to Mrs. Rosini's," said Ian. "Lucky she

remembered me from the last time I was here and didn't shoot me."

I smiled. "By the way, Mrs. Rosini has a gun. Got it for her birthday."

"Thank you for telling me."

"If you'd told me you were going over there, I would have. Did she hear anything?"

"No, but she saw plenty yesterday. You came home with a tall, skinny guy carrying what looked like a cooler."

My mouth gaped open. "Another doppelganger?"

"I don't think so. They just needed to get into your apartment without causing suspicion. Probably just a quick glamour."

"God, I hope so."

Ian gave me a crooked grin. "And just so you know, Mrs. Rosini's money is on me. She said I'm way better looking than the guy you brought home yesterday—and more polite, too."

I felt a faint tug on my shoulder, and took another quick glance before I could stop myself. Dr. Stephens had finished and had just tied off the thread. My mouth went dry. The stitches were neat, but it looked like Frankenshoulder. "Nice work," I managed. "Thank you."

He quickly and efficiently bandaged my shoulder, gathered his things, and left the room.

When he'd left, Ian's smile vanished.

"I just got a call from the team protecting Kitty."

I froze.

"Don't worry, Kitty's fine. She couldn't sleep and wanted to get an early start on tomorrow's baking—and she found something."

"Baby demons?"

"Definitely not."

23

IT was nearly one o'clock in the morning when we got to Kitty's bakery.

Ian had told me and Yasha what had happened, and we all were silent from shock and rage the rest of the way there.

Baby demons had been sent to eat me.

Kitty had been protected by a SPI security team, so the bastards behind this went for the next best thing. Make her such an emotional wreck that even if we found the Hellpit, she'd be in no condition to close it.

A body had been baked in Kitty's big cake oven.

They had just brazenly and sadistically stepped over the line into painfully personal.

What was her love and solace? This bakery.

What was her torment? Her bat-shit crazy, evil three-greats-grandmother's legacy.

Were the killers afraid of Kitty helping us? Oh yes. How to combine all of those into one soul-crushing deterrent?

Bake a body in her cake oven. Just like dear three-greats-grandmama would've done.

This wasn't personal. It had gone way the hell past personal. Whoever was behind this had made a monumental mistake by coming after Kitty.

We all loved Kitty. Ian's jaw clenched tight, taking even breaths to keep himself calm, and a deep growl had been rumbling out of Yasha's chest since he came through the bakery door.

Our CSI team was there along with our cleanup crew, and Alain Moreau had dispatched another of our field units disguised as city workers to block off the area in front of the store, citing a sewer line break in the street outside. Kitty's customers didn't need to get a whiff of what our lab folks were taking out of that oven.

Kitty had two security cameras, one in front, the other in back. When the killer had opened that portal, both had been fried.

Between the sulfur stink of the portal and the leftover stench of burned flesh, there was no way the smell would ever come out of this place. Not that Kitty would want to keep her bakery here after what had happened; now I didn't see where she had a choice.

That is, if she stayed in business.

She'd always known she not only loved to bake, but she had a gift, and a good head for running a business. She'd started from almost nothing and grown a successful business for herself—and a happy life doing what she loved. By New York standards, her business was only moderately successful, but it was beyond what Kitty had ever hoped, and now that had been ripped away from her.

Whoever was behind this would pay, and pay dearly.

Kitty would never be able to go into that kitchen again without seeing what she'd found. Everything she'd worked for had been ruined.

Thinking from the killer's point of view, what they'd done in that kitchen had been a stroke of evil genius. They wanted to ensure Kitty wouldn't be emotionally able to close that Hellpit even if we found it.

Good fucking job, asshole, my inner voice snarled.

"You said it, sweetie," I muttered.

Ian gave me a quizzical look. "What?"

"Where do you send someone who probably crawled out of Hell to begin with?"

"Don't know."

"Let's find out and get this guy a one-way ticket."

The lab guys started removing the body. Ian and I stepped back and gave them plenty of room to work. I didn't want to be in the way. The baked body was curled in a fetal position, cooked until it looked more like a mummy from the Met than a man that'd been walking around mere hours before. A man Ian and I had talked to just yesterday.

We now knew why Alastor Malvolia hadn't called us back.

I backed up until my shoulder hit the doorjamb, and my vision went white with pain.

Ian was there immediately. "Dammit, are you all right?"

I nodded tightly and concentrated on hissing air out through my tightly clenched teeth.

I swallowed and focused on pushing the pain away. Dr. Stephens had given me some painkillers. Groggy wasn't conducive to fighting for your life, so I'd stuck them in my purse. When I got out of here and back to headquarters, I might have to take one.

"Any idea how long he'd been in there?" I asked. I knew time of death would be a bitch to determine when the only cooling the body had done was once the oven had timed out. It was a question Kitty's three-greats-grandma would've been able to answer off the top of her head.

"He's been baked at least five hours," said an emotionless

voice from behind us. "He was cooked elsewhere and brought here."

Kitty walked into her kitchen with calm, measured steps.

The lab techs froze.

They had the body on a gurney on an open body bag, but they made no move to zip it. They were frozen in place.

Kitty glanced at the body, and her throat seized.

I wanted to take the steps that separated us, give her the biggest hug I could, and tell her everything was going to be all right.

I didn't do that. I couldn't do that. Nothing I could say or do would make any of this right for Kitty.

She had to do it for herself.

That was why no one moved. At least it was why I didn't.

The next few seconds would determine how Kitty recovered from this. Just by setting foot in this kitchen, I knew she would recover, but the extent and speed of that recovery depended on what she did next.

Kitty sniffed and took a breath that I knew smelled like burned flesh. She didn't flinch.

"Who was he?" she asked any of us who might know, never taking her eyes from the dead man.

"Alastor Malvolia," Ian told her. "A goblin lawyer who was the attorney for most of the supernatural crime families in the city. He may have been brought here not only in an attempt to intimidate you, but because he was short enough to . . ."

He stopped. If he could've sucked those last couple of words back in, he would've. Even I cringed at that one.

"Fit into my cake oven?" Kitty finished.

"Yes. Sorry."

"It's okay." She took a shuddering breath, tears pooling in her eyes. She angrily wiped at them with the back of her hand. "Dammit."

"We'll get him," Ian promised.

"Not unless you find that Hellpit, you won't," Kitty said.

Silence.

She wiped her hand on her apron. "And not unless I help."
More silence.

"He thought this would scare me, break me."

The clock ticked on the wall.

Her eyes blazed with determination. "He was wrong."

"We'll be there with you," Ian said quietly.

Kitty nodded once, tightly. "I'll take that protective custody at headquarters now." She leveled those normally cheerful blue eyes on me. "When you find that Hellpit, I want to be there and ready to work. I'll get my gear."

24

ONE A Day wasn't just the name of a vitamin; it had also become the murder rate in the Brimstone case. We were guaranteed at least one, and for most of the days this week, there'd been more. Some we found first; the NYPD had been the first responders on others. In this case, I had no problem with sharing the wealth.

I'd actually gotten a few hours' sleep before we were called to the latest crime scene. I'd slept better than I thought I would. Maybe it was my body preparing itself for what was to come. Maybe it was exhaustion after taking the world's longest shower when we'd gotten back to headquarters at two this morning, and washing my hair five times until I was absolutely positively sure I'd gotten all the baby demon bits out. Alain Moreau had met us in the SPI garage and had taken charge of me and Kitty, setting us up in the small but plush apartment SPI kept for visitors who needed to stay onsite for security reasons.

We sure as hell met those qualifications.

Until our cleaning crew finished their work, I didn't have a home and Kitty didn't have a business. Both of us were looking for payback.

This morning's corpse du jour was another vampire by the name of Dante Frontino. The demonic dynamic murdering duo apparently believed in racial diversity, or maybe they just wanted to ensure they equally scared the crap out of everyone.

Fortunately, SPI got to the murder scene first. I was sure Dr. Van Daal down at the medical examiner's office appreciated not having to hide the fangs on this one.

Ian and I hadn't been the first responders. I was completely fine with our CSI team having that honor. We stopped by long enough to confirm for our investigation that the other elements were the same. Dead drug lord? Check. Hoofprint brand on the chest? Check. Heart cut out? Check. Soul missing? Unknown.

Some would claim that since the victim was a vampire he didn't have a soul to take. I couldn't have disagreed more. Anyone who believed that had never met Alain Moreau. Last week, when the seven diamonds that comprised the Dragon Eggs had been on the verge of activation, my vampire manager had steadfastly stayed by Vivienne Sagadraco's side and refused to leave, facing what would've been certain death, the permanent kind. He would have remained a faithful friend to the end and beyond.

Try doing *that* with no soul.

One other thing was the same as the other murders, and another was a notable difference. What was the same? The building was owned by Northern Reach Holdings. Who called in the crime and the ID of the victim? None other than the CEO of Northern Reach, Rake Danescu.

The goblin called Ian to tell him that he was at the hotel across the street having breakfast, and would be delighted if we joined him.

I wouldn't describe Ian's reaction when he'd hung up as delighted, but I sure knew where we were gonna be having breakfast.

* * *

The hotel manager was waiting just inside the front door to escort us to where Rake was seated, alone, in a small palm court with a lavish breakfast buffet laid out seemingly just for him. Two uniformed waiters hovered by the door, entirely too attentive for just one customer, regardless of how rich. They'd look human to anyone else, but I saw the waiters and the manager for the glamoured goblins they were.

"Danescu," Ian said.

That one word was weighed down with all of the other, unsuitable-for-public words that Ian really wanted to say.

My mood was even worse.

Rake stood and, with a flourish, indicated the two empty chairs at the table with him. It seemed that someone had been expecting us. "Agents Byrne and Fraser. I hope you don't mind that I didn't wait. I wasn't sure how long you would be detained across the street." He gave me a quick, wicked grin. "Makenna, you look positively effervescent this morning."

The only meaning for "effervescent" that I knew of involved Alka-Seltzer. I tried unsuccessfully to find the compliment in that. I gave up in favor of the question I had.

"Do you own this hotel, too?" I asked.

Rake sat and began buttering a piece of toast. "As a matter of fact, I do." He glanced at the nearest waiter. "Carl, would you bring plates for my guests?"

Ian started to object and Rake held up a hand. It only held a butter knife, but I had no doubt he could commit murder most elegant with it. Heck, Rake could probably kill in thirty ways with a plastic spork.

"I won't hear of it," Rake told us. "You need to keep your strength up. Fighting the forces of evil and minions of darkness requires being at the top of your game. I promised Vivienne that I would do all in my power to assist you. A sumptuous breakfast is within my power."

Ian's phone rang, and he went back into the lobby to take it.

"This isn't the intimate breakfast for two I proposed the other day," Rake murmured, "but it will suffice. For now."

"What the hell are you doing here?" I wasn't going to tell Rake what had happened last night until—or unless—I had to.

"Other than enjoying a delicious and most satisfying repast?"

"Yeah, other than that."

"Considering that, again, I own the building the murder was committed in, and knowing that you and your partner would want to speak with me regarding that increasingly tedious coincidence, I thought I would save time, and provide a nutritious breakfast while you asked the questions I knew you'd have." He gestured at the palms and orchids that filled the space. "Isn't this a much more convivial setting for an interrogation?"

With that, Rake took a quick bite of toast. The goblin's fangs were out and fully extended. He wasn't experiencing tedium, he was furious. It was gratifying to see a genuine emotion from him for once, even if he was still trying to hide it.

I leaned closer and lowered my voice, though the goblin waiters would still be able to hear me perfectly well. As with Rake, it was all for show. "Nice act. If the murderer walked through that door right now, you'd rip his throat out like that toast, wouldn't you?"

"I am being toyed with." His voice was clipped with barely restrained anger. "We're all being toyed with. I will see all of this—and the person behind it—permanently stopped."

I poured myself an orange juice, and tried to calm the rage bubbling up inside. The juice had lots of pulp. Fresh squeezed. Nice. My gut told me that whoever Rake had seen outside that coffee shop was someone we needed to have a chat with. Now. "You didn't say 'unknown' person. Does this mean you've decided to tell me who you saw outside that coffee shop?"

"This doesn't have anything—"

"Save it!" I snapped.

Rake's eyes widened in surprise.

I kept going. Venting felt good, and right now Rake was

a target who deserved it. *He* had been toying with *me* since the day we'd met, and I'd had it.

"You wouldn't be this pissed unless you knew who was behind this and you just haven't been able to get your hands around his throat yet," I snarled. "I'm sure you have your reasons for not telling us—like thinking we're in over our heads—but as Ms. Sagadraco said, why don't you let us decide that? If you've been trying to catch this guy on your own, the body across the street tells us you obviously haven't had any luck. So does your nephew in our infirmary." And me and Kitty homeless and workless. "You're not the only one being toyed with, and I've got news, *none* of us like it!"

Rake hesitated for the first time that I'd ever seen. He knew I was in a frothing rage, and had rationally determined that while some of it was his fault, all of it wasn't. He opted for caution.

"I thought I saw someone."

"You *thought* you saw *someone*? You've got eyes that make us humans look like moles staggering around at high noon." I continued before Rake could throw up a wall of denial. "You saw who was behind the Brimstone and the Hellpit, and you chased him. I'm guessing from all the portals, demons, and murders that have followed, you didn't catch him."

"No, I didn't."

"Care to give us a description for our wanted poster?"

"I have no proof of his guilt."

"And we have no idea *who he is*. You've got more than we do, so start talking. I want answers, and I want him."

Ian's shadow fell over us both. "Sounds like progress," he said cheerfully. No doubt my partner loved seeing me tear into Rake.

I glared at the goblin. "I'm hopeful."

Rake regarded both of us, his eyes still inscrutable. "Yes, Agent Byrne. I believe we're about to discuss progress. Please be seated."

"Gladly, Lord Danescu." Ian sat and put a napkin in his

lap as Carl poured him a cup of coffee. My partner smiled. "I love the smell of cooperation in the morning."

I had to admit that Rake was right. Asking questions was ever so much nicer when you had a pair of waiters serving you the best breakfast you'd ever had in your life. But most of all, I was finally getting straight answers from Rake, which made it downright enjoyable.

Once again, Rake had been using goblin logic and evasion tactics. He hadn't seen a man outside the coffee shop, so he hadn't lied. He'd seen an elf. An elf and mage by the name of Isidor Silvanus.

"Isidor is of an older generation and prefers our home dimension," Rake was saying. "To the best of my knowledge he does not maintain a permanent residence here."

"You might want to check any recent apartment leases with Northern Reach or your other holding companies," Ian suggested. "You might have yourself a new tenant."

"It's being done as we speak."

"How old is he?" I asked.

"One generation older than myself."

I didn't repeat my question. Some things I was happier not knowing, and considering that the life spans of goblins and elves were longer than humans, Rake's age might very well be one of them.

"Why do you think Silvanus may be connected with the murders?" Ian asked.

"Because of family relation and past associations," Rake replied. "And my firsthand knowledge of his level of power."

"You've tangled with him before?" I asked.

"Our paths have crossed."

He didn't want to elaborate, and once again, it wasn't a question I needed an answer to, at least not now.

"Isidor's brother is the president and CEO of Hart Pharmaceuticals," Rake told us.

"Let me guess," Ian said, "they lease a building from you."

"Correct. They insisted on handling the retrofitting of their space themselves, as well as hiring their own contractors to do the work. I have been unable to get surveillance equipment inside to monitor their activities."

That had to have annoyed the heck out of him.

"However, I had glamoured agents inside that reported to me from time to time. For the past year, a small team of their best chemists had been working on a secret project. It was so secret and well protected that my people hadn't been able to get any intelligence concerning it for me. Projects of that level require funding, so I followed the money. I also have agents at the bank Hart uses. They investigated for me and reported an influx of money from an organization that's known for being a front for elven intelligence. From other sources, I know that there's only one drug that interests elven intelligence at this time."

"Brimstone," I said.

"Correct." His expression darkened. "My suspicions were confirmed last week when I lost all contact with my people inside Hart Pharmaceuticals. I had nine agents. One day they were there, the next they weren't."

Ian scowled. "Around the time we think they perfected the Brimstone formula."

"That was my conclusion as well. I believe that one of their test subjects was given the drug with the instructions to find any goblin agents. I haven't heard from my people since."

No wonder Rake was furious. First his agents, then his nephew.

Speaking of which . . .

"I know Dr. Carey is keeping Jesin's visitors to a minimum," I said. "Including us. We haven't been able to talk to him again. Have you—"

"Vivienne persuaded the good doctor to let me speak to him for a few minutes. We spent a little quality FaceTime." Rake smiled slightly. "I do love humans' modern technology.

When attempting to get an explanation for a young goblin's actions, it helps considerably to see their face. It's not a guarantee of getting an honest answer, but it helps."

"And?"

"I maintain an office in the building where Kela Dupari was murdered. Jesin has recently begun managing it for me as well. And before you ask, yes he's in charge of only the two buildings. His hours in my office there are from eight until noon. A package was delivered that morning addressed to me. Jesin is naturally suspicious, recently even more so. The package was not delivered by a courier service our receptionist was familiar with. When the murder was reported in Kela Dupari's office five stories below, Jesin opened the package. Unfortunately, my nephew isn't qualified to check parcels for spells, but when he opened it, he knew he'd set something off. This one triggered a call to the closest precinct reporting a suspicious package. When he saw what was inside, Jesin took the Brimstone out of the box and quickly left the building with the intent of concealing it. He was trying to protect me."

"That's a very creative story," Ian noted. "Do you believe him?"

"Jesin has a head for business, but not a nature for lying."

"Not going to make it far in this town," I muttered.

Rake sighed, but there was genuine affection in it. "No, he's not."

"Why would Isidor Silvanus want to involve you in three murders and frame you for drug possession?" I stopped and thought. "Let me rephrase that. Can you give us a *short* list, in order of likelihood, of why Silvanus would want you to rot in prison?"

Rake laughed. "You are learning, my dear Makenna. Isidor and I have been adversaries for years. To be blunt, he hates me." The goblin smiled. "I believe that any job worth doing is worth doing well, and I have more than earned his animosity. As to his motivation now, it could be any number of reasons ranging from damaging or destroying the operations goblin intelligence has in place in this dimension, to the demons offered Isidor a 'get out of death free' card for helping them gain access to this dimension, to he's simply bored and all of this amuses him. I assure you I am trying to ascertain his reasoning. No doubt you would find his thought processes nearly as convoluted as my own. I promise, if one option seems more likely than the others, I will tell you."

"You were telling us about Hart Pharmaceuticals," Ian said.

"Yes. In the city's supernatural criminal underworld, Hart is known for developing new recreational drugs that are then sold by the Balmorlans, an elven crime family in this dimension, a known name in elven intelligence in mine. Both they and the Silvanus family have been known to use Nightshades as enforcers. Hart Pharmaceutical's share of all profits is laundered through two offshore sources before it comes back to their bank accounts. From all reports, it's a lucrative partnership."

I tried to follow the tangled trail. "Okay, so Isidor's brother runs Hart. Hart has dealings with the Balmorlans, and both Hart and the Balmorlans have a connection to elven intelligence. So how do you know that Isidor opened the Hellpit?"

"Because, lovely Makenna, Isidor Silvanus has contacts in Hell, and is so obscenely powerful that he could open a Hellpit in his sleep."

I put my fork down. Appetite gone.

"How did you know about Dante Frontino being this morning's victim?" Ian asked.

"I began an analysis of the properties I owned under Northern Reach Holdings, noting the location of each murder in relation to the Hart Pharmaceuticals laboratory. Then I put that analysis on hold when a more immediate clue presented itself. While on my way here for breakfast, I saw Isidor Silvanus exiting my building across the street."

Holy crap. "Did he see you?"

"Oh, yes. I received quite the jaunty salute." Rake smiled grimly. "The bastard positively reeked of brimstone."

I glanced at Ian. I wondered if Isidor Silvanus had delivered half a dozen eggs to my apartment—and had been the figure I saw on the other side of that parking garage portal.

"What's this Isidor Silvanus look like? Tall? Skinny?"

Rake gave me a quizzical look. He didn't quite know where I was going with this. "Tall, yes. Skinny, no. Slender would be a better description."

Rake's "slender" might be Mrs. Rosini's "skinny." She'd told me more than once that I needed to put some meat on my bones.

"Good-looking?" I continued. "Average? Ugly?"

"The Silvanus family pride themselves on keeping their bloodline pure. They are high elves." Rake gave me a slight smile. "He is nearly as handsome as I am."

Mrs. Rosini had said that Ian was better looking than the delivery guy. In my opinion, and probably most women's, Rake was better looking than Ian. Not by much, but there was no denying it.

"Silvanus wasn't the delivery guy," I told Ian.

"Thanks, partner. You know how to make a man feel good."

So much for Ian not following my train of thought.

"Besides, a high elf wouldn't be hauling a cooler," I quickly added.

Ian gave me an arch look. "I can at least see that being true."

Rake's eyes were going back and forth between us as if he was watching a tennis match. "If you continue, will this eventually make sense?"

"No," we said together.

"That being said, any type of glamour is well within Isidor's abilities." Rake took a positively vicious bite of bacon. "He could be anywhere now, and posing as anyone."

_**25**_

"**THAT** could have been how he got close to Alastor Malvolia," Ian said.

"It appears I'm not the only party guilty of withholding information," Rake murmured.

"You had more to share," I told him. "Ours is just icing on the cake." I felt suddenly queasy. "So to speak." I looked at Ian. "You wanna tell him? I'd rather not even think about it."

Ian told about the baby demons in my apartment and Al in Kitty's cake oven. Rake listened and didn't say a word. His expression was calm—too calm. I didn't know if anyone could truly know Rake Danescu, but I'd learned enough to know that calm was the last thing he was feeling.

"Where are you staying?" Rake asked me as soon as Ian had finished.

"At headquarters for now."

"I have apartments. *Secure* apartments."

"Is that like your offer of an intimate breakfast?" I asked. Ian was right there, but I was beyond caring.

His dark eyes were steady. "No. It is an offer of a safe place to live. Full wards, and a full-time battle mage security staff on duty twenty-four seven."

"Wouldn't happen to be your building, would it?"

"As a matter of fact, it's in Vivienne Sagadraco's building."

"You own the boss's apartment building?"

"I do."

"Does she know?"

"She does. The building where I live is equally secure, but I know you'd never accept my offer of an apartment there."

And I knew I'd never be able to afford an apartment in either one.

"Last night, Ms. Sagadraco sent a security team to beef up the wards on my place."

I said it, but I couldn't say I was thrilled about it. I could see it being a short-term solution, but the thought of living in a place where, despite the best wards, a portal to Hell's anteroom could still be ripped inside my bedroom closet . . . I knew I'd never be able to sleep there again. Not to mention, I refused to endanger my neighbors. Those demons had run out of chickens. If I hadn't come home there'd have been nothing to stop them from taking the air ducts over to Mrs. Rosini's. I felt the prickling of impending tears stinging my eyes. I would *not* endanger her or anyone else.

"I'll think about it," I told Rake. And I meant it. "For now, I'm going to stay at headquarters with Kitty." I tried a smile. "It's like a pajama party. Tonight we could do mani-pedis."

"Tell her that I have several retail spaces in the Village and SoHo, should she want to relocate. Free of charge."

"No rent and no burned body stink? I don't see how she could turn that down. I'll tell her."

"And the apartment for you would likewise be rent free—"

I was about to make a comment about that, but his uncharacteristically somber expression stopped me.

"And no obligation—of any kind," he finished.

Wow. I wasn't entirely sure I trusted it, but wow.

"Thank you," I said simply. "When I have time to think, I'll give it some thought and let you know. It's a very generous offer."

"Agent Byrne has been working tirelessly to protect you since day one," Rake continued. "You're now in the worst kind of danger, and I am at least partially responsible." His brow creased in confusion. "Though I don't yet know why or even how. But I do know that I will do whatever's in my power to help him keep you safe."

"Thank you. Again." It was all I could think to say. Rake had complimented Ian, apologized to me, admitted he didn't know everything, and promised protection—all in a few, short sentences. For Rake Danescu, that was a staggering achievement.

Ian and Rake exchanged solemn man nods.

Looked like Ian was speechless, too.

"Is there a chance they're manufacturing the Brimstone at Hart Pharmaceuticals?" I asked Rake.

"They would certainly have the equipment they needed, but I wouldn't think so."

"According to Dr. Cheban," Ian said, "working with molten brimstone wouldn't be something you'd want to do in a multi-million-dollar facility filled with valuable, highly educated employees."

"Oh yeah." I spread my hands. "Boom. No meth labs in Hell, and all that. Though if Hart is bringing in beaucoup bucks on illegal drugs, what would stop them from buying some property of their own? They've probably got some labs hidden away around town. Should we let Fred know that Hart's the likely manufacturer?"

Ian nodded, took out his phone, and started texting. "I don't expect they'll find anything, but since Hart operates as a human company, the NYPD and the feds would be the best qualified to at least make life difficult for them. Maybe they can dig up enough probable cause for a search warrant."

I got my phone out, too. "I'll text Kenji and have him start digging for property Hart and any of its C-levels might own around town." I glanced at Rake. "Unless you have a list floating around in that goblin James Bond head of yours."

"Until now I haven't had a need to know."

"That's okay. Kenji probably already does. He's a collector: comics, movie memorabilia, dirt on supernatural-owned, multinational corporations. Like noticing that a drug company owns a run-down warehouse with state-of-the-art security. Things that jump out and wave red flags." My finger froze above my phone. Speaking of red flags . . .

"Just how badly does Isidor Silvanus hate you?" I asked Rake.

"The level appears to be approaching obsession. Why?"

"He's been going out of his way to murder people inside of buildings that you own. Why not open a Hellpit under one? What better way to humiliate a dark mage adversary than to open a Hellpit under a property they own without them knowing about it?"

There was silence around the table. So much for whether I might be onto something.

"Is that possible?" Ian asked.

"I own many properties, most of which I have no contact with on a day-to-day basis. This is why I have management companies."

"Then it is possible."

The goblin's dark eyes narrowed to angry slits. "Isidor is exceedingly gifted in the magic arts. Unfortunately, yes. It is possible."

"Marty said brimstone loses its molten state after an hour of being exposed to our air," I said. "That'd put the lab an hour—probably much less—from the Hellpit."

"We need a list of all of your real estate holdings in Manhattan," Ian told Rake. "And not just Northern Reach."

When a response wasn't forthcoming, Ian continued. "The list will be kept in a secure database."

Rake's lips tightened into a thin line. "A SPI database."

"If I'm right, then Isidor Silvanus already has that list," I said. "So you can slam the barn door if you want, but that horse is long gone."

The goblin sighed, though I detected a hint of a growl. "Very well. You shall have it within the hour."

"One more question," Ian asked him.

The goblin raised a brow. "You mean one more question—for now."

Ian ignored that. "Do you know if Alastor Malvolia represented Hart Pharmaceuticals?"

"He did."

"Did he represent you?" I asked.

"He did not. Believe it or not, but I do have standards, and Alastor Malvolia was far beneath them. It was nothing personal; I merely didn't approve of his methods."

I grimaced. "So somebody at Hart stuffed their own lawyer in an oven?"

Rake laughed, a genuinely happy sound. "Believe me, it could not have happened to a nicer guy."

26

FRED was thrilled to hear about Hart Pharmaceuticals being the cause of all of his late nights and early mornings. Fred was thrilled because Hart was already under investigation by local, state, and federal authorities. Kitty and I weren't the only ones who wanted payback. There was a line.

The latest incident in Fred's busy schedule was that he'd just come from the scene of yet another murder that could be connected to Brimstone. This victim was displayed in just about the most public way possible. A human drug lord with a small but profitable Wall Street client base had been found impaled on the horns of the Charging Bull statue in the Financial District. His heart was gone, replaced by the statue's right horn. Fred was of the opinion that this was the guy who had been selling Brimstone to humans like the man in Café Mina. Sounded logical enough to me. Who would want to read minds more than brokers, financiers, and other businesspeople? Fred said that this particular drug lord had been clued in to the supernatural world, which could connect him to what was really going on at Hart Pharmaceuticals. And it sounded like he'd either neglected to give his customers full disclosure on Brimstone's side effects, or simply told them that they might see things, but to ignore them until the mind-reading benefits kicked in.

That solved the mystery of how humans were getting their hands on Brimstone, but we still had the problem of no prosecutable evidence against Hart and its officers. Any that had been found had been refuted, and all potential witnesses had disappeared and had not been found—all thanks in one way or another to the late, evilly great Alastor Malvolia.

As the brains behind Hart Pharmaceutical's continued legal maneuverings and evasion, Al was now out of the picture and in a stainless-steel drawer at SPI headquarters. The feds' prosecutors would be happy about that.

If Hart's CEO, Phaon Silvanus—brother of Isidor—had been in any way responsible for Al's demise, he'd just gotten the ball rolling on his own downfall. If it hadn't been done at his orders . . . well, for the murderer's sake, I hope they got a running head start for killing the person who'd single-handedly kept the cops and feds from hanging Hart Pharmaceuticals out to dry.

I just loved it when the bad guys shot themselves in the foot, but it remained to be seen if it'd be too little too late.

Alastor Malvolia had been baked, but the finished product was in one piece—including heart and soul. Though with this particular goblin lawyer, one really had to wonder if there'd been a soul there to begin with.

Bert was determined to find out.

And Rake wanted to be there when he did. He'd given us a list of his Manhattan real estate holdings. It was in the hundreds. Money had never impressed me, and it still didn't. But, damn. We didn't have enough agents to check out even a fraction of them. Rake was hopeful that Alastor Malvolia might be persuaded to point us in the right direction—especially since his murderer was probably also located in that direction.

I'd said I never wanted to be in SPI's morgue for another of Bert's corpse Q&A sessions, but if the goblin lawyer was going to say anything, I wanted to hear it. I was betting that being betrayed by one of his corporate clients was going to make for one seriously vindictive ghost. No retainer was worth that.

I'd damned near been baby food for demons either directly or indirectly because of the Silvanus brothers. I was overdue for some fun.

The autopsy room's recording system had been double checked and was ready to go. Human courts didn't consider the testimony of a ghost to be admissible in court, but as far as supernatural law was concerned, alive, dead, or undead, it was all good.

The autopsy room had two tables and not much room for anything else. Bert had to be in there as did Al Malvolia. Bert took up enough space for two people, and in his present condition, Al was literally half the man he once was. Now he really did look like Mr. Burns from *The Simpsons*, if Mr. Burns had been baked into a mummy.

Dr. Carey and Bert had done an external examination of the goblin's body and determined that he had been knocked unconscious with a blow to the back of the head. I'd only met him once, and by all accounts Alastor Malvolia was as far from being a nice person as it was possible to get. I was still glad to hear that he'd been unconscious or already dead before he'd been shoved into Kitty's oven. After the questioning, Bert would guide the spirit to the other side, and there would be an official autopsy to determine the exact cause and time of death, as well as to look for any residue or fibers on the body that might provide clues to place of death and the murderer's identity—something a human court would accept.

Martin DiMatteo had been there to back Bert up in the past, and he was in there now. The rest of us were on the other side of the double-thick glass wall. Normal morgues didn't need that kind of reinforcement, but in the world of the supernatural, there were many kinds and levels of dead, and on occasion, they didn't need a necromancer to raise a fuss.

In addition to me, Ian, and Rake was Ms. Sagadraco, Alain Moreau, and—not so surprisingly—Kitty. After all, it was her oven the goblin lawyer had been found in; she wanted to know what had happened to him before he'd been brought there. I'd think it would help her considerably to know that Alastor Malvolia hadn't died in her oven.

Fred was busy with the Hart Pharmaceutical end of the investigation, but had made Ian promise to get a recording to him ASAP.

Bert was presently making a brief initial contact to ensure Malvolia's soul was still inside his corpse when the body's mouth dropped open and an enraged shriek damned near shorted out the sound system.

Holy Mother of God.

Normally spirits communicated through Bert. Not this time. Malvolia the dead lawyer wanted to do his own talking.

The lights might not have been on anymore, but the dead goblin was definitely home, and he was not happy.

Bert had shielded himself and wore a necroamulet to give himself even more protection. He wasn't taking any chances and I didn't blame him one bit. Contacting a newly dead angry ghost was like startling a big dog out of a sound sleep. Unpleasantness was likely to occur.

The necromancer glanced at Ms. Sagadraco and nodded. Showtime.

"Alastor Malvolia."

Once again the boom of Bert's deep voice filled the morgue's four tiled walls. There was an intercom on our side, but we really didn't need it. The glass was also warded, so the force of Bert's necromantic magic didn't affect me and

Ian as it had when we'd been in the room with Sar Gedeon's corpse.

The elf drug lord's soul had already been taken, so there'd been no response to Bert's command. Al Malvolia had been a lawyer in life; and in death, he couldn't wait to talk.

Almost immediately a silvery mist rose from the curled-up corpse.

And it solidified, complete with a face, an angry face.

Okay, that wasn't normal, either.

Even Bert looked a little taken aback, though for Bert that meant briefly raising one eyebrow.

There were soul contacts that had been memorable enough to enter into Bert's office party story repertoire. I bet this was going to be one of them—and I was getting to witness it firsthand.

Lucky me.

It was probably a good thing that Fred wasn't here, and that none of us were elves. The spirit that had once lived in the body of the goblin lawyer Alastor Malvolia hissed and spun, two glowing red orbs where his eyes had been, probably looking for the elves who'd killed him.

I wondered if Bert was in charge in there anymore.

However, Bert looked cool as a cucumber.

Those glowing eyes didn't find any elves, but he saw his own burned body curled on the autopsy table.

The shriek he'd let out before paled in comparison to the roar that came out of that pissed-off poof of mist.

Alain Moreau reached over and flipped the switch on the speaker. Either that or our ears were gonna bleed.

"Thank you," I said. At least I think I did.

The roar came down to a gurgling hiss. It took me a minute to realize that the goblin was laughing.

He was looking directly at Rake Danescu.

And laughing.

I didn't think any of us—especially Rake—were going to find what was about to happen amusing.

Alain Moreau flipped the switch again, turning the speakers back up.

"Danessscu," Malvolia hissed.

"Alastor. You're looking well."

More gurgling laughter. At least he'd kept his sense of humor.

"He isss coming for you."

"Isidor?"

"Yessss."

"I was beginning to get that impression." Rake nodded toward Malvolia's body on the table. "Did he do that?"

The glow in the red eyes faded a little, and his expression grew distant and puzzled. Both were impressive achievements for a mist you could see through.

Apparently he hadn't seen who'd killed him. Looked like Malvolia had been hit from behind like Dr. Carey said.

Bert stood next to the table, his hand resting lightly on the corpse's head, his eyes calm and steady on Malvolia's manifestation. Bert was still in control; at least I hoped so.

"Isssidor made a deal with the devil."

Rake's fangs flashed in a brief grin of delighted realization. "And you drew up the contract."

More gurgling laughter. *"Yessss."*

Now it was Rake's turn to chuckle. "You screwed them both over."

"Filthy, arrogant elvesss. Deservesss to burn."

"Alastor, if you weren't so crispy right now, I'd actually kiss you. Where's the contract?"

"Sssafe."

"Where?"

"You will sssee."

The mist that was Alastor Malvolia was beginning to fade.

"Hurry," Bert mouthed to Rake.

"Where did Isidor open the Hellpit?" Rake asked.

I could clearly see Bert standing behind the goblin. What was left of Malvolia was confused, looking around as if he'd suddenly become aware of where he was and didn't recognize it.

We were losing him.

Rake leaned closer to the glass. "Alastor. Listen to me. Where is the Hellpit?"

"Where the demonsss are coming from."

"Yes, demons will be coming from the Hellpit. Where. Is. The. Hellpit?"

The mist was drawn back into the burned shell of Alastor Malvolia's body.

Bert bowed his head, and took a couple of deep breaths.

"Can you get him back?" Rake asked urgently.

The necromancer shook his head. "There's a chance, but he'd be even more confused than he was now. Even if he could manifest, he would only be able to hold form for a few seconds. We need to let him go, Lord Danescu."

27

ALASTOR Malvolia hadn't been able to tell us where the Hellpit was. We were running out of time. While we hadn't been able to pinpoint exactly when Isidor Silvanus had first cracked open the Hellpit, it'd been long enough since the Brimstone drug started showing up on the street that the pit had to be nearing a fully open state. Once it reached that, it couldn't be closed.

So far, all of the murders had been committed in properties owned by Rake through Northern Reach Holdings. Even the yacht that Celeste Báthory was killed on had been leased through a yacht brokerage owned by, you guessed it, Northern Reach.

Kenji was working on pinpointing property that Hart Pharmaceuticals or Phaon Silvanus owned and those properties' proximity to buildings owned by Rake Danescu.

Rake had identified Isidor Silvanus as one of the previously unknown, obscenely powerful sorcerers who had been at the Mythos gala opening. Just our luck, he'd decided to hang around after the party to make more trouble.

In the meantime, Roy Benoit and Sandra Niles had their commando teams on standby, and Martin DiMatteo had four people in his department ready to deploy with the commandos to search each potential Hellpit site.

The first hits on both Rake's property and Phaon Silvanus were two buildings one and six blocks from Times Square. Even in legendary New York traffic, getting from one to the other would still take less than an hour, making them viable Hellpit locations. Sandra's team with two of Martin's demonologists were checking the tunnels nearby and beneath Times Square. After last New Year's Eve, we were more than familiar with them. A Hellpit was different from a portal. It'd be standing wide open, glowing orange like molten lava, and probably guarded by demons.

Considering the attempts on my life, the Hellpit was probably concealed in a pocket dimension, the entrance to which was a small portal visible only to the mage who made it—who would be Isidor Silvanus—and yours truly.

Kitty had confirmed that it was possible, that the Hellpit could be concealed in a small pocket dimension. If that was the case, I would be able to detect the doorway to the dimension, like I had done with Alastor Malvolia's office.

Worse still, if the Hellpit was being concealed inside a pocket dimension, it'd be highly likely that the Brimstone lab would be hidden the same way.

I could see portals, but I couldn't open them.

Fortunately for us, Kitty could open an existing portal as well as slam one shut.

At least that problem was solved. Unfortunately we had plenty more to take its place, and a line forming behind those.

We were stretched thin enough as is. Ms. Sagadraco had told me that under no circumstances was either I or Kitty to leave headquarters until a viable location had been found. The risk was too great. If the Hellpit or Brimstone lab was concealed by a pocket dimension, I'd be the only one who'd be able to see it, and I couldn't go chasing after every possibility. The demonologists would be able to detect signs of demonic activity that even a pocket dimension couldn't hide.

If I had to stay at headquarters, there was one thing I could do and still possibly help.

It was time that Ord Larcwyde and I had a talk.

Kitty and I had one of SPI's VIP apartments; Ord had the other one. Alain Moreau was in charge of assigning guests to accommodations. He liked me and Kitty more than he did Ord, so we got the larger apartment.

It didn't help Ord's cause that he was being an obnoxious asshat.

In the gnome's defense, he'd been brought here for protective custody and questioning, and while there was plenty of protection going on, there hadn't been time for any questioning.

The agent assigned to Ord told me that the gnome was in a foul mood, had been testing the patience of the SPI cafeteria's room service, and was presently binge watching *Game of Thrones*. Other than that, things had been relatively quiet.

I couldn't leave headquarters, so I had plenty of time on my hands for finding out what Ord knew that was worth killing him for—besides the number to room service.

The stacks of dishes were piled on a cart outside Ord's door. The SPI cafeteria's job was to keep agents fueled up so they could protect and serve. With the clock ticking on the Hellpit, our people had been working and eating overtime. Cleaning up after guests must be falling through the cracks. Though from the looks of the nearly pristine dishes on that cart, Ord had done everything but lick the plates. Our chefs were the best, and Ord was taking full advantage.

I knocked. I'd called Ord as soon as I'd left the morgue, so he was expecting me.

The gnome opened the door and I was treated to a vision in a green velour bathrobe.

His feet were bare, his chest was exposed, and I think the only thing he had on underneath was his ever-present gold chains.

Yikes.

Maybe I would have been better off spending more time with Al the Crispy Lawyer.

Ord's little face lit up. "Makenna, darling! I had begun to despair of ever seeing your lovely face again."

Okay, Ord might be naked as a jaybird under that robe, but he had Al beat on the charm scale.

"Come in, come in!"

I did, and Ord closed the door.

The gnome grabbed the TV remote and muted the slaughter on *Game of Thrones*. "To what do I owe this pleasure?"

"First, my apologies if you've felt neglected. We've had several emergencies that had to be dealt with."

"More murders?"

I nodded toward the now silent slaughter. It looked like the "Red Wedding" episode. "Not quite at that quantity, but it's getting there."

Ord considered that comparison for a moment, and that he'd narrowly escaped being one of the slaughterees. "I haven't had the opportunity to express my appreciation for allowing me to stay here until all this unpleasantness blows over. Thank you. And should you see Miz Sagadraco, please extend my heartfelt appreciation to her as well."

Yep, when properly motivated, Ord could definitely tip the top on the charm scale.

"You're most welcome. We're glad we can do it."

Actually, we weren't, and Ord knew it, but we were Southerners trading pleasantries before getting down to business. We both knew the game and the rules. It was older than the family pound cake recipe and just as revered.

Ord hurried to clear a tumble of newspapers out of a chair. "Please, make yourself comfortable. Could I order something for you?"

I waved a hand. "No, no, I'm fine."

Ord took his seat and arranged his robe modestly over his lap.

Thank God for the decency of a Southern gentleman.

"Do you really think I know something worth being killed for?"

"I sure hope so." I cringed. "Wait, that didn't come out right."

The gnome reached out and patted my arm. "I'm here, safe and sound, so don't you worry yourself about it."

The job of the agent assigned to Ord had been to basically keep him out of trouble until either Ian or I had time to question him further. The guest rooms had occasionally functioned as fancy jail cells, so the TVs had Netflix, HBO, Showtime, etc., but that was it. There was no contact with the outside world, and even if a guest had managed to smuggle in a phone, it wouldn't work unless we wanted it to. Kitty and I had full outside communication; Ord Larcwyde did not. Until we knew who he knew that might want to kill him, cutting the gnome off from the rest of the world was a prudent security measure.

The long and short of it was that Ord didn't know diddly squat about what had been going on since our people had picked him up and brought him here.

I brought Ord up to speed on the case, namely who had been killed, and who we suspected of doing the deeds. However, I left out the part about his unsuccessful assassin being a squid demon. I didn't think it had any connection to the information I needed to know, but most of all, I'd heard enough shrieking from Alastor Malvolia; I didn't want to have to listen to Ord's screams, too. My ears had had enough for one day.

"Do you know any of those people?" I asked when I'd finished. "Living or dead, victims or suspected killers?"

"I've heard of most of them, but am glad to say I don't know any of them personally."

"So your pixies haven't brought you information on any of them worth killing you for?"

"None."

"You're sure? This is really important. Like fate-of-the-world important."

"I sincerely wish I could help you, Makenna, but I've got nothing other than what I told you at my office. Between that gunman trying to kill me, and my pixies raising their prices, I'm considering an early retirement."

Huh? "Your pixies want a raise?"

"Two weeks ago, they come to me and say that they're no longer comfortable in the neighborhood; and that if I insist on remaining there, they'll continue to work for me, but they'll be forced to increase their rates."

"Are they getting mugged by fairies for their lunch money or something?"

The gnome drew himself up in righteous indignation. "They said my office stinks, if you can imagine such a thing."

I remembered the boxes of garlic falling on top of Ian. "That garlic was a bit much. He must do a heck of a restaurant business."

"Some. But mostly it just sits there."

That was more than odd. "So he stocks it, but doesn't sell it?"

"I don't mind. I like garlic."

"When did he start stockpiling garlic?"

"About a month ago. Pixies have extremely sensitive noses, though I've never heard of garlic bothering them—or even bothering vampires for that matter. That only happens in the movies. It is such an annoyance when Hollywood doesn't even bother to get the details right. The industry is positively rife with supernaturals, so there's simply no excuse. All the vampires I know love Italian food. Well, at least smelling it. And many of my pixie employees are Italian-American. You wouldn't think they'd mind garlic in the least." The gnome finished with a dramatic sigh. "I still may be forced to take the building's owner up on his offers of alternative accommodations. The noise the past few weeks has become tiresome."

Odd just turned into a waving red flag—two of them. "The building's owner wants you to move, *and* there's been noise?"

"He offered last month, and again last week. As to the noise, it's mostly vibrations coming up through the floor." He waved a hand. "There's a subway line running somewhere below. They must be using that track more often now."

Nervous pixies, stinking office, the owner wanted him out, plus noises—all starting within the last month. And I'd be willing to bet the farm that the squid-demon gunman sent to kill Ord had been a last, desperate measure to get him out of there. As to the stockpiled garlic, was it meant to cover the stench of occasional wafts of brimstone coming from a brand-spanking-new drug lab below?

I got my phone out and called Ian. "Ord, honey, when this is over, I need to talk you out of retiring. You're a treasure."

28

SO much for our theory of Hart Pharmaceuticals owning the building housing the Brimstone lab. Hart didn't own the building the grocery store was in; the Balmorlan family did.

The store owner was a veritable gold mine of information once Ian and I walked through his front door—and a SPI commando team silently came through the back and appeared directly behind him like supernatural ninjas.

The grocer hadn't been a willing accomplice. A Balmorlan family representative came to him a month ago and said that they required a few favors. In exchange, he would no longer need to make monthly protection payments. The grocer said the favors were simple, they weren't illegal, and weren't hurting anyone—at least not until two days ago when the gunman paid the store a visit.

Keep fresh garlic in stock at all times, and report who came to see Ord Larcwyde.

Two seemingly innocent favors, plus no more protection payments.

The grocer jumped at the chance.

If I'd been in his place, I would've done the same thing.

If he hadn't cooperated, another of Kitty's ovens might have had an occupant.

Vivienne Sagadraco had approved me leaving headquarters in case the lab was concealed in a pocket dimension. The reality turned out to be not nearly that fancy. In addition to the old walk-in freezer that served as Ord's office, the store had a trapdoor in the floor. The grocer knew about it. It'd been used in the past to store illegal liquor for a local speakeasy during Prohibition.

It had been expanded considerably since then.

The original storage room had been converted to house air treatment equipment. Brimstone stank, and regardless of how careful the lab folks in the even older chamber below had been with their main ingredient, stink had a way of getting out. That was where the garlic had come into play. One strong smell to hide the occasional whiff of another. And if Ord had ever gotten suspicious, rotten garlic didn't smell too good, either.

There could only be one reason why the drug lab had been under the store Ord Larcwyde used as an office.

It was close to the Hellpit.

"It's all clear below." Commander Sandra Niles was in full body armor. Yes, our target was a lab, but it was a drug lab, and one of the ingredients was being brought in fresh daily from your friendly neighborhood Hellpit—neighborhood as in nearby. All that considered, I thought body armor was a simply wonderful idea.

Ian and I were in dark street clothes. We'd needed to come in through the front of the store, and body armor or fatigues would have attracted attention to say the least. Sandra had brought everything we'd need if all this panned out and we'd be going underground.

She showed us the surprisingly clear image on her tablet. Considering the combustibility of Brimstone's ingredients, she'd taken the prudent precaution of snaking a camera in through an air duct.

I swore. "There's no one down there."

"The store has security cameras, but there aren't any monitors up here," Sandra said. "I have a feeling we'll find monitors when we go below."

"They knew when we got here," Ian said.

The commander smiled. "And they ran like rats when you turn the lights on. Don't worry, it's an active lab." She swiped a finger across the screen, and it went from full color to infrared. Heat signatures flared on two of the chairs, four of the lab stools, and all of the equipment.

Ian's grin joined hers. "Bingo."

"Where did they go?" I asked. "I don't see a door."

"We're hoping it's flush against a wall and just not visible on screen," Sandra said. "As with the monitor, we'll find out when we get down there."

Dr. Claire Cheban and four of her team had suited up in biohazard suits in preparation for going into the lab, complete with gas masks and air tanks, and they were bristling with enough shielding spells to make my teeth hurt.

Chances were good that the air was breathable and there weren't any booby traps of the fatal kind waiting for them when they got there. The Brimstone techs had fled when we'd arrived in case we found the lab. That didn't mean they hadn't expected us to find it. They'd probably done this drill before. You wouldn't want to contaminate a lab you fully planned to return to.

But, just in case, Sandra's team would go in first with sealed body armor and full helmets with small oxygen tanks built into the back. The lab crew was probably waiting nearby, and you'd think at least a few of them would be armed, but regardless of what they were packing, they were nowhere near armed enough. If Lady Luck had finally decided to start talking to us again, the lab crew would have enough sense to not come back.

The trapdoor entrance wasn't the main way in or out. It

functioned as an emergency exit only. They'd just had an emergency, and it hadn't done them a bit of good. As I'd found out the not-fun way on New Year's Eve, the underside of Manhattan was filled with tunnels and chambers. Most were for subway, sewer, water, and power—both used now and abandoned. However, some of those tunnels and chambers hadn't been dug out by human hands.

Somewhere down there was the way to the Hellpit. Martin DiMatteo had told us that the Hellpit would need to be no more than an hour away from the site of the lab, closer would be even better. Molten brimstone was unstable, so the quicker you could get it to where it needed to be, the fewer accidents of the "boom" variety you'd be likely to have. Since you couldn't exactly walk down the street in New York casually swinging a bucket of molten brimstone from Hellpit A to Drug Lab B, the tunnel leading to the Hellpit began somewhere beneath our feet.

The thought made my skin crawl and gave me a nearly overwhelming urge to find a chair and stand on it.

What I wanted even more was about two weeks of sleep. Then to go on a vacation somewhere exotic and sleep there for two more weeks.

Minutes later, Sandra found the door from the lab out into the tunnel. It hadn't been hidden, simply set into the wall and out of sight of the camera. The other side of the door was camouflaged so well that you could have been standing in the tunnel right in front of it and you'd have never found it. Though the Brimstone lab techs must have had a way to get to work every day.

The tunnel beyond had been used at one time for sewer and rain drainage overflow. Fortunately for us and the AWOL Brimstone lab techs, it wasn't used for either anymore. Once the lab—and its contents—had been secured, it was my turn.

Dr. Cheban and her staff had taken over the lab and were

working on documenting everything as well as downloading computer hard drives and securing ingredients. Because of the possibility of accidents, even when being handled by professionals, Ian and I had to suit up in hazmat suits, at least until we were through the lab and into the tunnel.

As we went single file down the narrow stairs that led from the air treatment room under the store and into the lab itself, the sound of my respirator was ridiculously loud in my ears.

"'Luke, I am your father,'" I rasped.

No response from Ian.

"Really?" I asked through the communicator. "Nothing?"

"It was only funny the first fifty times I ever heard it."

"It's my first time in a getup like this. It's new—and funny—to me."

Once down in the lab, there were glass-front storage cabinets with cylindrical stainless steel containers. Considering that the largest container said "brimstone" I half expected the others to be labeled like something out of a Grimm's fairy tale. I was disappointed.

"What? No eye-of-newt?"

That earned me a snicker from one of Dr. Cheban's techs.

"That gets a laugh, but Darth doesn't."

"Eye-of-newt's funny," Ian said.

"But Darth's a classic."

We passed through the lab and into the tunnel beyond. For the first time, I was glad to be in one of New York's old drainage tunnels. It meant I could ditch the biohazard suit. If we stumbled onto the Hellpit, the suit wasn't intended for prolonged exposure to high temperature, and "stumbled" would be the first perfect description for what I'd do if I needed to run away from anything while wearing it; the second would be "fall." So in the interest of self-preservation, Ian and I left the suits just outside the lab. Hopefully they wouldn't be needed by the time we came back.

Hopefully we'd be coming back.

A few of Sandra's commandos would stay behind to guard the techs while they worked. Sandra and the rest of her team would be coming with us.

I had a Hellpit to find.

The tunnel stank, though not of brimstone.

That was both good and bad. Okay, mostly just bad. We needed to find the Hellpit yesterday. It wasn't something we could pretend didn't exist just because we couldn't smell it.

The tunnel's natural aroma wasn't strong enough to mask something as pungent as brimstone. The tunnel smelled like what it was coated in: damp and mold. I was allergic to mold and glad I'd taken my meds and done my spray this morning. A sneeze down here would echo forever. If we were going to be ambushed by demons, I'd rather it not be my fault.

No brimstone smell didn't mean there wasn't a Hellpit.

It simply meant there could be a portal between us and it.

If there was a portal, it could empty out next to the Hellpit, or into one of Hell's anterooms filled with demons just waiting for the dumb mortals (that would be us) to come bumbling through.

"Let's go to night vision, people." Sandra gestured and we silently moved out.

Just because there hadn't been any booby traps in the lab didn't mean the tunnel presumably leading to the Hellpit wasn't going to be thick with them.

I could see through glamours and now portals. Half of the people on our commando teams could see wards, illusions, and magical traps of every known kind—and a few that'd never been known before they'd seen them. They were the best. If Isidor Silvanus had left any surprises on the path to the pit, they'd find them before we tripped them. I had the utmost confidence in their skills.

I had nearly none in the job I was being expected to do. Find the portal hiding the Hellpit.

Isidor Silvanus may or may not have wanted me to see those two portals. But I couldn't imagine any scenario where he'd want me to find the Hellpit.

But you're not the one who has to close it, said the little voice inside my head. Normally it was the voice of reason; right now it was the voice of shame—as in "Shame on you, Makenna Fraser."

My job was over when I found the Hellpit.

Kitty Poertner's job was to close it.

Alain Moreau was working to find an anchor mage who would help her. Last I heard, there'd been nothing to hear.

Kitty would be alone, facing not only closing the largest portal there was, but one that had been opened by a mage who Rake described as so powerful he could open a Hellpit in his sleep.

Kitty had to close that.

In addition to any traps Silvanus may have built into the magical mechanisms holding the pit open, Kitty would have to contend with demons determined not to lose access to our world. They wouldn't like a human *and* a mortal slamming the door on their eternal beach vacation.

Sandra's team was with us now. When we found the Hellpit, Roy's team would join us. While Kitty worked, SPI's commandos would keep the demons under control.

At least that was the plan.

I'd seen our guys and gals in action. They were beyond impressive. But these were demons we were talking about. Demons who had wanted our world for literal ages. They were closer than they'd ever been to having it all. If that didn't say motivated, I didn't know what did.

Mortals and former mortals going up against the combined might of Hell.

As good as they were, I really didn't want to bet on us.

But everyone else was.

* * *

The tunnel curved and turned, but there weren't any branches off of it that the Brimstone lab techs could have used for escape.

At four places there were ladders leading to the street above. At each, Sandra's team "navigator" would note the position on a GPS device strapped to his forearm armor for later investigation. We wanted the Brimstone lab folks in custody for questioning at the very least, but we needed to know where the Hellpit was. Locating lab rats could wait. Finding an open Hellpit wouldn't.

We were just out of sight of the fourth ladder when the air began to thicken. The two commandos who had taken the lead slowed and then stopped. Sandra went up to where they were. I didn't have to leave my spot in the center of the main group to know what was going on.

We were getting close.

I took calming breaths and told myself that what I sensed, what I thought I saw, none of them were there. None of them were real.

The ceiling wasn't closing in on us.

This was a major-league repelling spell.

Repelling spells were flexible; not only in composition, but in how they affected each individual who encountered it. When you got to the outer rim of the spell's area of influence, you felt uneasy. If you went farther, you began to breathe faster and sweat, experiencing fear you couldn't explain. A sense of "Get out!" would start ringing through your head. If you managed to go farther, the visuals would start. We were in a tunnel, so the hallucinations would contain scary things that you'd find in tunnels: rats, snakes, spiders, and, in New York, the ever-popular alligator. Whichever one you were the most afraid of would be the one that you'd see. A buffet of nightmares, so to speak. Though in this case you'd be picking what you didn't want.

Even though all of us knew this, what we imagined wasn't any less terrifying.

Being a country girl, I'd seen plenty of rats, spiders, and snakes in barns or under rocks. I'd never seen an alligator before, so my imagination wasn't up to reconstructing one of those for me to terrify myself with.

Having the walls and ceiling closing in on me? Now that I could imagine with no problem, and was doing a fine job of it right now.

One of the commandos quickly moved to the front, removed her gloves, and raised her hands as if she were putting them up against a wall. She pushed against it and a rush of words in a language I didn't understand filled our earpieces. Our commando teams dealt with the worst that the supernatural world could throw at them. They knew how to fight, but each and every member of both teams had unique skills specific to what they encountered on the job.

As the commando's words faded, the hallucinations stilled, and then began to fade. It took a few minutes to banish them completely, and the commando was breathing raggedly by the time she'd managed to completely disarm the repelling spell. The spell might be gone, but I was experiencing a whole new wave of uneasiness. I glanced at Ian. I wasn't the only one. We were getting close.

About twenty yards later, we came to an old brick wall. The corners were rounded, and the finish was smoother than modern bricks. The tunnel continued to the left and right.

On the wall in front of me, about chest high, was what looked to be a spigot for a water hose that you'd see on the outside of any house in the suburbs—except it was missing its handle. What it did have was protection. The air rippled in front of it from the effects of a shielding spell.

The spigot looked harmless enough, but I wasn't about to get any closer. And considering all the protection it had, I felt safe in saying that what would come out of it wouldn't be water. The drug lab techs had to get their supply somehow, and Martin DiMatteo did say that brimstone couldn't be taken through portals without going from molten to useless goop.

"Sandra, we're here." I pointed at the spigot. "Brimstone source, right there. Well, behind a shielding spell."

Sandra turned to the commando who'd taken out the repelling spell. "Deborah?"

"On it, ma'am."

It must have been a tough nut to crack because it took her nearly ten minutes to get rid of those ripples concealing the brimstone spigot.

By that time, Sandra had dispatched scouts down both side tunnels, and both had returned to report that there was no sign of anyone—human or demon. We dispensed with our night vision and had flashlights trained on that wall where one of Sandra's people was now scanning the pipe with some kind of device, while another scrapped a sample of the blackened and pitted concrete floor directly below the spigot. For me, what would come out of that spigot was a foregone conclusion. The water in the Hudson River was known to be nasty, but even that water wouldn't burn and eat holes in concrete.

The commando with the scanner glanced up from his display. "Ma'am, some of these elements I recognize, but the rest . . . Your guess would be as good as mine as to where they came from. And the handle that fits this thing would be just as exotic. It'd function as much like a key as anything else."

"Would the metal stand up to high temperatures?"

He nodded. "Judging from the elements that came from our world, that's exactly what it was made to do."

We had no intention of confirming that by finding a way to turn on that spigot. None of us wanted to go down in what'd be left of history as the modern-day Pandora if we released the next plague or an even worse disaster.

"What's on the other side?" Ian asked.

Sandra studied her wrist-mounted GPS. "We're below Ninth Avenue. Nearest cross street is West Thirteenth. We're about mid-block, directly below number thirteen."

"Why does that sound familiar?" I asked Ian.

"Because it's Bacchanalia."

29

WHETHER building a successful business or opening a Hellpit, it was all about location, location, location.

This situation was more like setup, setup, setup—and I could smell the stink of it from here.

Rake had wanted to open a business; Isidor wanted to open a Hellpit.

Isidor Silvanus had opened a Hellpit directly beneath Bacchanalia. When the pit was fully open, the center of the goblin intelligence spy network would be the first to fall in.

We hauled ass back to the Brimstone lab and got back on the surface in record time.

Sandra got her team to the two trucks that'd brought them there. They looked like the thousands of other slightly dinged-up delivery, transport, or construction trucks that filled New York's streets every day. SPI had signage for both of them that would be appropriate for any situation or destination. Inside of the trucks was essentially a SWAT command center.

Ian and I had come with Sandra and her team. Yasha had

stayed at SPI, ready to bring Kitty to the location of the Hellpit once we found it.

Ian called Vivienne Sagadraco and told her where we were, and what we'd found.

The boss then talked for at least a minute, and Ian listened.

"Yes, ma'am," he finally said. "I understand." Then he hung up.

"Well?" I asked, my patience long gone.

"Kitty's on her way here now with Alain Moreau."

"Not Yasha?" Though the way Yasha drove, and how emotional he was bound to be right now because of danger to Kitty, having a cool vampire behind the wheel might be the best thing.

"She didn't say, just that Kitty had left with Moreau."

Mid-afternoon traffic would put her here in around twenty minutes.

"Is she going to call Rake?"

Ian nodded once.

That was going to be a fun phone call. Ms. Sagadraco spoke goblin, so she'd know every word Rake blistered the phone lines with. An elf dark mage had opened a door from Hell directly into Rake's pride and joy.

One of the trucks carrying Sandra's team had gone around behind Bacchanalia to the loading dock area to wait. The other had by all miracles of nature found a parking place across the street and slightly down the block. They'd let us out two blocks before Bacchanalia so I could scout around.

Ian and I walked down the street, holding hands, just a couple on an afternoon stroll on a sunny but unseasonably cold day.

He lowered his head to my ear. "See anything?"

We were both wearing sunglasses to scan the people around us and up ahead without being too obvious about it. I was looking for glamoured lookouts. A villain wouldn't go to the trouble to open a Hellpit that would be unclosable in the very near future and not have people—or not-people—keeping an eye on his special project.

I saw a lot of people, real people and a smattering of supernaturals, hurrying to get where they were going and out of the cold, but I didn't see any loitering evil minions.

"Nothing yet."

Bacchanalia occupied what looked like just any other four-story, brick-fronted building in the Meatpacking District. Unless you were a member, or the guest of a member, you didn't know what was beyond its doors.

On each side, flush up against Bacchanalia's walls was a six-story building filled with high-end condominiums, and a four-story, mixed-use office/restaurant/retail space. Across the street were two more restaurants and a coffee shop, with what appeared to be lofts on the three floors above.

It was three o'clock on a Wednesday afternoon.

"People are gonna die."

"That's why we're here," Ian said, "to keep that from happening."

I gave my partner a double take.

"You said, 'People are gonna die.'"

"I thought I just thought it."

"Unless I can suddenly read minds . . . ? No, you said it."

Crap. I really needed a vacation.

"What about the people inside those buildings?" I asked. "If that Hellpit gets bigger than Bacchanalia's walls—"

"Those buildings are still standing, so it's obviously not that large yet. And Kenji's working on getting those buildings cleared now."

That made me stop in my tracks. "Okay, Kenji's good, but—"

"It's a procedure we have in place." One corner of Ian's mouth curved into a brief smile. "One of his superpowers is tapping into the monitoring system of any commercial or residential building and setting off his choice of alarms: fire, smoke, or gas. He's also good at calling in suspicious packages. I'm thinking in this situation, he'll go with gas. If he tripped a fire alarm, the people would evacuate, but after ten minutes of not seeing any fire or smoke, they'd start grumbling and want to go back inside. Especially when it's this cold."

"What about when the Con Edison guys show up?" I asked.

"Kenji would make sure the call went in to one of Con Ed's clued-in or supernatural shift managers. The boss ensures that there are plenty of those in positions qualified to smooth over anything that needs to be covered up."

I nodded at the simple brilliance of it. "With gas, you can't see it or smell it unless you're in the room with it, so people could whine all they wanted to."

"Right. And not one of them would want to set foot back in those three buildings until the police and Con Ed gave the all clear to go back in. We'll be getting some NYPD crowd control, too. An open Hellpit couldn't be a more perfect fit for a fake gas leak. Natural gas is scented so that if there is a leak, people would know by the rotten egg smell."

"And brimstone smells like rotten eggs."

Ian flashed a smile. "Like I said, perfect." His phone beeped with an incoming text. Ian took it out of his pocket. "Fred says he's on his way to the party."

I knew the elf detective wouldn't be working crowd control. I had to admit I liked the thought of him going in with us.

A cab pulled up to the curb a few feet in front of us and Martin DiMatteo got out dressed like he was going on another rock-finding field trip to Hell, either that or a safari, complete with an old-fashioned camera hanging around his neck.

Humor and sarcasm weren't all that he didn't get, apparently so was the need to blend in.

On the other hand, his priorities were in perfect order. If Isidor Silvanus didn't already know we were here, he would as soon as we crossed Bacchanalia's threshold. And if that Hellpit got out of control, no one was going to care how anyone was dressed.

Thanks to Kenji, those buildings would be evacuated and stay evacuated until the job was done.

If we didn't get that Hellpit closed, an explosion would be the nicest thing that would come out of those buildings.

All we could do now was wait for the rest of the team to arrive.

I wasn't worried about Kitty and Moreau getting in. The delay was probably due to the combination zoo and circus happening in a five block radius around Bacchanalia. Once Moreau got to the police barricade, he'd just do his vampire Jedi-mind-trick thing, and the two of them would be able to walk right through.

Meanwhile, Kenji's gas leak story had taken on a life of its own. As people hurriedly left the buildings, I'd heard the word "terrorists" more than once, though since 9/11 that probably happened every time something moderately big went wrong.

Rake arrived in a justifiably foul mood, and he quickly led me, Ian, and Martin to one of Bacchanalia's fire exits, conveniently hidden by a Dumpster, which I suspect was illegal in ten different ways.

Ian's phone rang and he stuck a finger in his ear and tried in vain to find a quiet place to take the call. I recognized the ring. It was Vivienne Sagadraco. After a few moments, he spat a word I didn't need to hear to recognize, and he sharply gestured Rake over. After Ian's first few words, Rake looked even more pissed than my partner.

Even Martin picked up on the fact that something was very wrong.

I sprinted over to where they were.

"Isidor Silvanus has Kitty," Ian snapped.

"But she left with Moreau—"

"Not Moreau," Rake said. "Silvanus, glamoured."

I forgot how to breathe. "How the hell did he get into headquarters?"

"He didn't," Ian said. "He was just outside the complex. He called in and Kitty came right out to him."

My heart leapt into my throat. "Yasha?"

"Is fine. If damned near shredding the motor pool when he found out is fine. Silvanus called him using Moreau's voice and told him to stand down, he'd bring Kitty here."

My shoulders sagged. "And Moreau's the voice of the boss."

"Exactly."

Isidor Silvanus couldn't scare Kitty out of helping us, so instead he . . .

"I'm not getting this," I said. "He kidnapped her. He couldn't scare her out of helping us, so he glamoured as Moreau so she'd go with him. Wouldn't he want to kill her? Why would—"

"It's me," Rake said.

Ian grabbed the front of Rake's leather jacket in his fist and slammed him up against the Dumpster, dark mage power be damned.

"What are you not telling us *now*, goblin?" he snarled. "Another spy secret to play with? Kitty's life is not yours to—"

A slender packet of papers fell out of the inner pocket of Rake's coat.

"That," Rake told him, eyes blazing, but making no other move against Ian. "Was just delivered to me. It's the contract Alastor Malvolia wrote between Isidor and Hell."

Ian's breaths came in ragged gasps. He let Rake go, but he didn't step back.

"Isidor will want to use Kitty to bargain with," Rake continued. "He wants the contract; we need Kitty."

"How did you get it?" Ian asked.

"Remember when Alastor told me in the morgue that the contract was safe? When I asked him where, he told me that I would see. Well, it took him being dead to keep a promise. He knew either Isidor or Phaon Silvanus would try to kill him. If that happened, he'd left several documents in a safe deposit box. They were to go immediately to me. I got them an hour ago."

I bent to pick up the papers, but I didn't hand them back to Rake. "You said he hates you, and it's mutual."

"I said I strongly disagreed with his methods. For goblins, hate is a personal emotion. I didn't care to get to know Alastor well enough to hate him." Rake glanced down at the packet of papers in my hand. "We both feel the same about Isidor Silvanus. *That* we agreed on. Alastor may not have liked me, but he trusts me to see to it that his last wish is carried out."

Ian took one step back, which in manspeak said he wasn't going to kill Rake now, but he reserved the right to do it later. "And what would that be?"

Rake bared his teeth in a sleek, vulpine smile. "Use the contents of that contract to ensure Isidor Silvanus burns in Hell. Today."

I handed him the papers.

30

WITHIN five minutes, our people had managed to get through the police perimeter.

The last time I'd been in Bacchanalia had been my first night at SPI. Ian and I had been undercover as a couple on a date. I'd really been there as a seer to locate a leprechaun prince and his four aristocrat buddies out for a night on the town before the prince's wedding the next day. The boys were drunk, they were danger junkies, and they'd intentionally gone to an upscale and highly exclusive sex club owned by a known, dangerous, and evil dark mage.

That would be Rake.

Back then we'd thought that Rake would capture the leprechaun prince and torture him to force him to grant three wishes, and use those wishes to bring destruction on the city and the entire supernatural world.

That same dark mage was now fumbling with an absurdly large bunch of keys trying to find the right one to get us into Bacchanalia. To his credit, he'd only dropped them once.

"Fuck it!" he snarled, slamming his hand flat against the center of the massive steel fire door.

It vanished.

The entire door. Gone.

No smoke around the edges, no tingle of magic, no boom.

Just gone.

As if it'd never been there.

"I didn't know those two words were an incantation," Martin said.

I think Rake was finished fumbling, and if Isidor Silvanus was somewhere inside with Kitty, he might want to consider leaving her and then leaving Rake's property. Now.

I'd only ever been in Bacchanalia through the front door during business hours.

The décor had been black. Completely, totally black. The floor was marble, the walls were black glass, and the ceiling appeared as a star-covered sky far from any city lights. There'd been constellations, stars, and even the Milky Way.

On the other side of the door that Rake had made go bye-bye, I heard the rapid click, click, click of three wall light switches.

Nothing.

Even the emergency lights weren't working.

Now the décor was *really* black.

Dammit.

The power was out, and I knew Con Ed didn't have a thing to do with it.

Ian and I reached into our coat pockets and pulled out our night-vision goggles. Sandra's team already had theirs ready to go.

Fred had a flashlight big enough to double as a battering ram. "We waiting on an engraved invitation?"

"Wait," Rake told us all.

How did he see—

Oh yeah, goblins could see in the dark.

Rake's low whispered incantation was like a warm breath against my ear, even though he was standing at least five feet away.

The words weren't for me.

They were for the soft glow that began around the edges of the floor and ceiling, a glow that grew brighter until even us humans could see.

"I never trust mortal lighting in an emergen—"

We all stared at what the lights revealed.

Bacchanalia's interior had gone from *Arabian Nights* to Dante's *Inferno*.

It looked like my baby demon-infested bedroom times ten thousand.

Clear slime ran down the walls, and dripped from the ceiling, pooling on tables and the floor. The bar area was covered in slickly glistening webs, punctuated by what looked like cocoons. A few were pulsing with movement from inside.

I couldn't see any demons, but I knew they were here, watching and waiting.

Sandra got word that Roy's team had gotten inside the police perimeter just before it'd been closed off. We weren't going to wait for them. They knew where we were going. Bacchanalia didn't have a basement, but Rake had what I'd heard was considered one of the finest wine cellars of any club in the city. From the dimensions Rake had provided, there'd be only so much room to maneuver down there, and when dealing with a pit of demons, backup would be needed. I wanted to know that Roy's commandos were at our back, not more demons.

I wasn't much for wine. Actually, I wasn't much for alcohol, aside from an occasional dark ale. And forget any kind of liquor. It didn't matter how long it'd been fermented in whatever fancy distillery, it all tasted like cough syrup to me. I could safely say I had an unsophisticated palette. Back home when I was growing up, we didn't bother with store-bought cough syrup. Moonshine, honey, and lemon juice worked just fine.

I prepared myself to make impressed noises if it was still intact; sympathetic sounds if it was all over the floor—or if the demons had drunk it all. What I knew about wine would fit on the top of a cork, but I'd heard that Rake had a small—or maybe not so small—fortune invested in the room and its contents. Now Isidor Silvanus had opened a Hellpit in the middle of it.

And Isidor Silvanus had Kitty.

We had no way of knowing which way Alastor Malvolia's soul had gone when Bert had guided him to the other side. But wherever he was, I knew he'd approve of there being a long line of people who wanted to help make his last wish in life come true.

There were two ways down to Bacchanalia's wine cellar: an elevator and stairs.

We took the stairs.

Elevators were death traps on steel cables.

Rake took the lead, with two of Sandra's commandos far enough behind to give him space. They'd wanted to go first, but one scowl from the goblin who'd made a steel fire door vanish into thin air, and the boys backed off. Rake could take care of himself. Ian and I followed.

There wasn't that much information available on Hellpits, but Martin DiMatteo knew all of it. I was the lucky one who could see portals.

If Rake opened the wine cellar door and the floor had been turned into a bubbling hellfire-and-brimstone pit, Martin was officially in charge. If it looked to everyone else like a perfectly normal and intact wine cellar stocked with obscenely overpriced bottles of fermented grape juice, and only I saw the bubbling pit, it'd be my turn for Show & Tell.

Rake opened the door.

Ian and I were still on the stairs, so I couldn't see inside.

Martin stepped up and looked in, then both he and Rake turned and looked at me.

Crap.

Ian stepped in front of me to go down the last few steps first. While my partner turning himself into an immovable object between me and a Hellpit was chivalrous, it wasn't going to do anyone any good, or change what lay beyond that door.

As far as anyone else was concerned, everything beyond that threshold looked perfectly normal. I didn't want to see a Hellpit, but I hoped I did. Because if I didn't, we had no idea where else Isidor could have opened the thing. He would be there—with Kitty—and we had to find her.

Rake stepped aside and I looked into the room.

I could see what Rake and Martin saw, and it was unexpected, at least to me. Rake had originally come from a Renaissance type of society, and I expected a wine cellar built to look like it came out of a European castle. Bacchanalia's wine cellar was a circular room, with pale woods and sleek brushed steel. The shelves and niches that held the bottles were glass, though it probably just looked like glass, and in reality was something more durable. Lighting radiated out like muted sunbeams from a circular central orb mounted in the ceiling. From the looks of the panel set into the wall with the gauges and flickering lights, it appeared Rake's cellar had the latest in wine storage technology. The room looked more like the bridge of a spaceship than a place to store wine. Rake was a techie. Who knew?

The room also had a portal slicing like an open wound down a narrow section of wall.

It wasn't like the portals at the scene of Sar Gedeon's murder and in the parking garage. For one, this thing stretched from floor to ceiling. The other two had been roughly man height. But the big difference was that this portal was red and it looked angry—or at least like anyone stupid enough to get close to it would get themselves chewed up and spit out on the other side. Knowing what was on the other side, that was a chow line I wasn't about to get in.

Though I didn't think I'd be risking life, limb, and soul just by crossing the threshold of the wine cellar.

I stepped into the room and Ian, Rake, Fred, and Martin followed. Sandra stayed by the door.

Time to break the bad news, but first I had a question. "Director DiMatteo, you said that the Hellpit would be a hole in the ground, not a portal."

"That is correct."

I nodded in the direction of the bloody and raw-looking gash in the wall. "Then at two o'clock we have a portal that will presumably take us to the Hellpit."

"What's on the other side of that wall?" Ian asked Rake.

"I had assumed it to be solid rock," the goblin replied. "This room was already here when I bought the property. Since it naturally maintained a steady temperature of fifty-eight degrees, I assumed it to be enclosed on all sides by more or less solid rock, like a cave. My wines have been quite comfortable here." He glared at the wall with the portal that only I could see. "At least they were."

"Apparently it's less solid than you thought," my partner noted.

Rake made a sound that under better circumstances would have been a chuckle. "My insurance will never cover this."

"What, no Hellpit portal policy?"

"It's one of those things you're sure will never happen to you. Like living in the desert and not getting flood insurance."

"At least this portal doesn't go into another dimension," I told them both. "It's just a way to disguise the entrance to a Hellpit."

"And its exit," Martin told us.

Like we needed reminding. Kitty wasn't here to close it, and as every minute passed, the Hellpit was opening wider, and the things inside were closer to being able to get out—as in out here with us and the rest of the world.

"So . . . how do we get inside?" I asked anyone who might have the answer. "Not that I'm eager to do it, but—"

"Isidor wants the contract," Rake said. "Since he has taken Kitty Poertner, apparently he knows that I have the only copy of the contract not in his possession."

"If he's as powerful as he would have to be to open a Hell-pit," Martin began, "couldn't he simply kill you and take it?"

Rake smiled slowly. "I welcome and eagerly anticipate his efforts. I would be most disappointed should he not try."

Even Martin didn't know what to say to that. Rake was homicidal and suicidal at the same time. Must be a goblin thing.

"There has to be another entrance." Fred was standing off to the side, studying the rest of the room.

"Detective Ash raises a logical point," Rake said. "Isidor Silvanus could hardly stroll into my establishment unno-ticed. Not to mention access to the elevator and stairs down to this cellar is controlled by a coded keypad."

"Then why put a 'back door' here?" Ian asked.

"For the same reason he has been staging most of his murders in buildings that I own," Rake said. "Embarrass the goblin intelligence agency—and me in particular. And for the coup de grace, should we fail to secure the Hellpit, the demons will emerge from here. It seems that Isidor now knows that the center of my web—as Makenna so astutely described it—is here at Bacchanalia. He wants it destroyed."

"You must have really pissed him off to get all this spe-cial attention," I said.

One side of Rake's lips curled upward. "Many times and on numerous occasions."

"Has it ever occurred to you to stop pissing people off? Or at least be more discreet about it?"

His crooked grin grew. "I am the very soul of discretion, lovely Makenna. I was merely doing my job. It is no fault of mine that my job is a source of great annoyance for Isidor. Besides, to obtain a source of brimstone, he simply would have opened his Hellpit somewhere else in the city. The danger would be the same, and we would not have had the trail of bread crumbs that led us here. When you look at it that way, it was a good thing I did piss him off. It made him predictable."

Ian snorted. "We haven't found him yet."

I stood perfectly still as the sides of the portal slowly peeled apart.

Ian tensed. "What is it?"

"The portal's opening." Then I saw what lay beyond. "And I think Isidor Silvanus just sent someone to let us in."

A red-skinned and horned demon, no more than two feet tall, leisurely strolled toward the opening from the other side, swinging what looked like an old-fashioned key that was nearly as big as he was.

That was surreal. Like *Alice in Wonderland* surreal.

"Any of you see the demon lord mini-me walking toward us from the other side?" I asked.

"No," Ian and Rake said.

With a smile revealing a mouth entirely too full of jagged teeth, the little demon embedded the key like a spear into the right side of the portal wall—or whatever it was that a portal had—and stepped right through into the wine cellar with us.

Ian and Fred reached for their guns.

Rake reached for his magic.

Martin reached for his camera.

Still smiling, the little demon stopped in front of Rake and held out a folded piece of parchment complete with a red wax seal.

Rake took the parchment and instead of breaking the seal, he put his thumb in the middle and the wax vanished in a poof of rotten egg stink—disarming whatever nastiness Silvanus had intended when the seal was broken.

He read it, then passed it to me and Ian.

The words began burning the paper as soon as it left Rake's hand.

We read fast then dropped the smoking parchment.

The instant it touched the floor, the demon disappeared, reappearing on the other side of the portal, and strolled away in the direction from which he'd come.

Silvanus wrote that he had Kitty and was willing to release her in exchange for the contract. He wanted Rake to deliver the contract in person. He also wanted "the seer, the human SPI agent, the half-elf law officer, and the demonologist."

No one else.

And if all of us didn't step through that portal, the deal was off.

"I don't like it," Ian said.

"We've just been invited to Hell by an evil wizard," Fred said. "And if we don't slam a Hellpit, demons invade and everyone dies. You'll have to be more specific, buddy."

My partner's face was set on perma-frown. "You, Mac, and Martin don't need to be anywhere near here when this goes down."

"You go, I go," Fred told him. "No arguments."

I resisted the urge to roll my eyes. "None of us want to be here, but we're on the guest list. Without Kitty, we don't stand a chance in hell . . ." I stopped. "If we live through this, that phrase is gonna have a whole new meaning."

"I have been to Hell," Martin told us. "The rest of you have not—with the possible exception of Magus Danescu. I must go as a guide, if nothing else."

Rake actually did roll his eyes. "The Hellpit isn't getting any smaller while you argue. Once the demons of Hell pass into this world, every living thing will become food—or worse. We can't help Miss Poertner, or close the Hellpit, if we don't get inside."

Rake Danescu had become the voice of reason. We didn't need Kitty to close the Hellpit. Hell itself had just frozen over.

"There were two more lines I couldn't read before it burned up," I said to Rake. "What did they say?"

"Isidor claims he cannot—or more likely, will not—guarantee our safety once we're inside. He claims to have limited influence over his hosts."

"He didn't say anything about weapons," Ian noted with grim satisfaction.

"It is likely that weapons from our dimension will not work there," Martin told us. "Particularly automatic weapons."

I couldn't believe my ears. "You've got to be kidding."

"The closer we get to the Hellpit—and therefore to Hell itself—the less effective the technology from our world will be." Martin almost looked embarrassed. "I discovered this through unpleasant personal experience during one of my excursions."

"What about your camera?"

The demonologist actually smiled. "Older technology such as this will not be affected."

"Since the Hellpit was opened by Isidor," Rake said, "and presumably that portal was his creation as well, the very air on the other side will be filled with the influence of his magic. Different rules will most definitely apply."

Ian snorted. "Silvanus's rules."

Rake shook his head. "Dark magic rules." His eyes glittered in what I could swear was anticipation. "I know this game."

"I don't know of any rules that would keep cold steel from doing its job," Ian said. "You got knives?" he asked me.

"Many," I assured him.

"Get more. Sandy?"

Sandra turned to her closest commandos and then started passing me blades in sheaths, and I put them anywhere they'd comfortably go.

"Got an extra revolver?" Ian asked the commander.

Sandra didn't say a word, just unclipped the old-fashioned six-shooter from her belt and passed it to him, along with a pouch of ammo.

Rake shook his head when Sandra offered him what I couldn't carry.

If dark magic would work, Rake should be armed for a demonic T-Rex. Hopefully we wouldn't have to find out.

"I'm fine, thank you," Martin said when one of the commandos offered him a wicked curved knife with a jagged blade.

The demonologist was smiling in gleeful anticipation.

Marty was about to see his very first Hellpit.

31

THE five of us stepped over the threshold of Bacchanalia's wine cellar and into a nightmare landscape, and we all got a good look at Isidor Silvanus's handiwork.

I had to give him credit for creativity. The other side of the portal looked like a tunnel in a prehistoric cavern complete with stalagmites and stalactites. Along one side of the rock-strewn floor was a stream of what must have been molten brimstone flowing away from us and around a curve in the cave wall. I couldn't see what was around the corner, but I could sure see the bright orange glow.

There was no way all this was on the other side of the wall from Rake's wine cellar. You couldn't fling a dead rat below street level in New York without hitting subway tunnels and/or water and sewer lines. There were a lot of things under the city streets, but a monstrous cavern complete with a brimstone creek shouldn't be one of them.

"This isn't right," was what I managed to say. "This can't be here. It's too big."

"It's a pocket dimension," Rake said. The goblin turned back to where the portal opened, and his eyes shone with intent of murder most violent. "And Isidor anchored it into the rock surrounding my cellar."

I looked around. "Jeez, how much room is on the other side of your wine cellar anyway?"

"It couldn't be this much," Fred said.

"It's not," Martin told us. "The size of the actual area outside of Bacchanalia's basement has no bearing on the size of a pocket dimension. In theory, it could be as small— or as large—as its creator wanted it to be."

I stifled a whistle at the vault of the cavern ceiling far above our heads. "Then Silvanus must be compensating for something."

"If it's a pocket dimension, then how does what's in here get out into the city when the Hellpit is fully open?" Ian asked.

"Isidor's magic made it," Rake told him. "Isidor's magic can unmake it. Once that Hellpit is completely open, he'll pop this pocket dimension like an overfilled water balloon."

"Sounds messy," Fred noted.

"If by messy you mean a cavern suddenly breaking through into our reality beneath the streets of this city, molten brimstone flowing through the sewers and subway tunnels, and demons hunting the streets—then yes, it will be extremely messy."

A swiftly flowing river of bubbling, molten brimstone ran beside a rock ledge barely wide enough for two of us to walk side by side. The altering landscape must have been a distortion of the pocket dimension—or the landscape was shifting and changing as the Hellpit somewhere farther in the cavern continued to grow. Color was apparently distorted as well. When we'd first stepped through the portal, the rocks had looked, well, rock colored. In reality they were sulfuric yellow.

And I'd always thought the Yellow Brick Road led to Oz.

That'd make Isidor the Wicked Witch of the West, Kitty would be Dorothy, and the contract Rake carried was the Ruby

Slippers. Rake wouldn't qualify as Glinda the Good on his best day, more like the Wizard of Oz. At the end of the movie, Oz had floated away in a balloon, leaving Dorothy and company to fend for themselves.

My subconscious kept replaying *that* part for me as a portent of impending doom.

Ours.

I'd only heard about Rake's power. Other than the fire door, I'd never witnessed anything big myself, and until now I'd never minded. One person I'd heard it from had been Vivienne Sagadraco. If the boss said Rake was powerful, I'd believe her without proof. However, she'd also said that he was dangerous. I'd always assumed she meant dangerous to anyone he went up against. Now was not a good time to have my assumption disproven.

I pushed those thoughts out of my head, making myself focus on what was likely to get me killed now rather than later. When in enemy territory, a little noise to cover any sounds you might make was a good thing. Usually. The sounds we were hearing wouldn't be called good in anyone's estimation. A sharp snap and crack was repeating at irregular intervals, as if something that wasn't supposed to be breakable was being broken. Like I said, not good.

We walked and walked, but didn't seem to be getting any closer to the turn in the path and the Hellpit presumably beyond.

Isidor Silvanus was playing with us.

"Does this qualify as the dark magic games you were referring to?" Ian asked.

"It would," Rake replied. "Isidor is attempting to control time here. He's trying to delay our arrival."

Fred wiped sweat from his face. "Seems to be doing a damn fine job."

There was a grouping of sharp rocks not too far down the path. "Those rocks haven't gotten any closer," I pointed out. "It's like we're walking on a freakin' treadmill."

Rake nodded once. "Exactly."

"Anything you can do about this?" Ian asked Rake.

"There is. The question then becomes are you ready for a fight?"

"Yes."

"How much of a fight?" Fred asked.

A wise man, Fred.

"I know what you're capable of," Fred told Ian. "No offense, Mac. You're feisty, but we *are* approaching Hell."

"Thanks for the vote of confidence."

"Nothing personal." The half-elf cop jerked his thumb at Martin. "Then we've got the Professor back there doing a *National Geographic* photo shoot."

The demonologist was squatting down on the very edge of the ledge, clicking off shots of a fat, pale worm-like demon that was using six caterpillar-like legs to pull itself up against the ledge like it was the edge of a swimming pool, and was curiously studying Martin with a pair of round, black eyes.

Martin must have sensed us all watching him in complete disbelief. He stopped clicking.

"Don't let me keep you. I'm fine. Merely taking advantage of a once-in-a-lifetime opportunity."

"Isidor is attempting to delay us by controlling time here," Rake told him, "so I'm going to teleport the five of us closer to the Hellpit. I need you to move closer."

Martin glanced down with concern at the chubby footlong worm. "Manipulating time can adversely affect these larvae's development. Since it's occurring, the parent must not be aware of it. Isidor Silvanus may be able to slow the passage of time, but he's still a guest here, so he really shouldn't. Would you like him to stop?"

The goblin raised one perfect eyebrow. "That was my desired solution."

"I think I can help with that."

"If so, your assistance would be much appreciated."

I didn't say a word. I couldn't. There were way too many WTFs in that exchange for me to process. Fred and Ian were likewise afflicted. This was approaching a *Twilight Zone* level of strange.

Martin reached out with his index finger and touched the larva right on top of its squishy little head. Neither moved for at least ten seconds, then Martin stood and came over to where we waited.

"The larva will relay our predicament and request to its parent." The demonologist looked back to where the worm/larva had disappeared back into the molten brimstone with a plop. "It shouldn't take long. This particular demon at this early stage of development is still telepathically linked to the parents."

"How can you be sure he . . . it will relay the message?" Ian asked.

Martin shrugged. "Demon larva like me. I guess you can say I'm good with children."

I had no response for that, either.

"Thank you, Dr. DiMatteo," Rake said. "Let's continue and pick up the pace. When Isidor realizes his efforts have been thwarted, he'll attack us in another way."

We walked faster, and after a few minutes, we began making progress.

"Let's hear it for Marty's tattle-worm," Fred muttered.

Rake and Ian had slowed, their full attention on a patch of shadow ahead of us, that, judging from Ian's hand hovering above Sandra's six-shooter, wasn't simply another harmless spot of dark.

The shadow moved and—

Wait. It *moved*?

What looked to be just another shadow started moving all by its lonesome and spread to cover the hallway from side to side. If we wanted to get past it—and we had to—we needed to go through it.

Nope.

I didn't even have to consult my lizard brain on that one. My entire brain was in agreement—no way was I stepping into that.

Fred took one step back, sharing my misgivings.

Naturally, Ian didn't budge. My partner was the poster boy for determination.

The corner of the cavern wall was visible through the apparently sentient shadow.

Rake picked up a chunk of brimstone rock and threw it through the shadow.

The rock vanished.

It went in, but it didn't come out the other side.

Nope. Definitely nope.

"Alternate route?" I asked.

No sooner were the words out of my mouth than the shadow began flowing down a narrow path, away from us, in the direction we needed to go.

Toward the Hellpit.

Fred let out the breath we'd all been holding. "And that, boys and girl, is our engraved invitation."

We'd all seen the glow of the Hellpit the entire way here. But even the glow and the overwhelming stench couldn't prepare us for what lay around that last turn.

We were hit with a wall of heat and sulfuric fumes coming off a Hellpit the size of my granddaddy's catfish pond that was bubbling with molten brimstone—and all of it irrationally located just outside of Bacchanalia's wine cellar.

"Isn't a pit more like a hole in the ground?" Fred asked.

"That's what I've always thought," I said.

"Then that's a big damn pit."

Even more disturbing was finding the source of the snapping and cracking we'd been hearing. It was the rock floor breaking and giving way under the pit's relentless expansion.

The floor trembled beneath our feet as another few inches of the cavern floor crumbled and fell into the lagoon.

There were bones lying around the shoreline. Humanoid. Meaning human, elf, goblin, or vampire. With the exception of fangs on the vampires and goblins, the only way to know for sure would be to get them in a lab.

Death was the great equalizer.

"I think we found the missing drug dealers," Ian murmured.

I had an unwanted flashback to the chicken bones in my bathtub. This was what the aftermath of baby demon mealtime looked like when they got hold of something big. I focused on the closest skeleton. That could have been me, except my remains would've been in my apartment and not on the shore of a Hellpit, but that was small comfort.

Contrary to how most humans envisioned it, the entrance to Hell wasn't in the bowels of our Earth. It was on another plane of existence. It could just as easily have opened like a door behind us, but in my opinion, nothing was a more appropriate entrance to Hell than a stinking, molten, sulfuric pit.

When we got out of here—*if* we got out of here—the clothes I was wearing were history. No amount of washing would get the rotten egg stink out.

SPI offered hazard pay to its agents. I'd been told in HSR (Human and Supernatural Resources) on my first day that since all of our work was considered dangerous, rarely did a situation arise that qualified for hazard pay. Even hunting two adult grendels and their dozens of spawn in the pitch-dark tunnels underneath Times Square didn't qualify.

Still, I had to ask.

"Does storming what's basically the gates of Hell qualify for hazard pay?"

Ian nodded. "Yeah, it does."

Oh goody.

Now we just had to live long enough to collect.

32

I scanned the opposite shore of the brimstone pond.

We'd been expecting demons throwing a beach party to celebrate their imminent invasion—at least that's what I'd expected to see. All we'd actually seen was the demon lord's mini-me, Marty's demonic toddler, and the shadow that had a mind of its own. Not that I minded reaching the Hellpit with zero attempts on our lives, but I didn't trust it. Not that I'd know what to do if one of the locals jumped out at me. Considering what the locals were, the first thing I'd do was probably wet my pants. While embarrassing, I didn't think anyone would blame me.

"Mac," Ian said.

That one word contained a world of communication.

"I'm looking. Nothing and no one yet."

I continued to scan what dry land remained that wasn't covered by brimstone. Ian didn't have to say he didn't like it. I didn't like it, either. None of us did. This setup had trap written all over it.

A stalagmite wavered.

Huh?

I blinked to clear my vision. It could be the heat. It was like a sauna in here, but nothing else around the stalagmite was wavering.

"Wavy rock formation at high noon."

Ian and Rake stepped up next to me, one on each side. Fred was a solid presence at my back. Though considering what I most wanted to do was turn and run, a solid Fred right behind me wasn't good for either one of us, unless he wanted to get trampled.

If it was a veil or shield, it was the best one I'd ever seen or heard of. I wouldn't expect anything less from an elf dark mage strong enough to have opened a catfish-pond-sized Hellpit.

Rake's hands were at his side, glowing with the bright red of a defensive spell held in check. If this had been a dirt street in the Wild West, Rake would have been the gunslinger with his hands hovering over his six-shooters.

Ian had Sandra's actual six-shooter in his hand.

An elf stepped away from the front of the stalagmite, his face and form shifting from a perfect camouflage match for the rock back to his own features.

Damn.

He'd been standing in plain sight the entire time like a chameleon. His breathing was what had made what I was seeing waver.

If Isidor Silvanus hadn't been about to release literal Hell on Earth, I would have been impressed.

And yes, I knew it was Silvanus standing on the other side of the Hellpit. I didn't need an introduction. I'd seen him before. Twice. On the other side of the portals in Sar Gedeon's apartment and in the parking garage.

Tall, dark, pale, and evil.

His hair was black, his skin alabaster, and his eyes bright blue.

Rake was right. The elf was good-looking, pretty, even. Too pretty. And too perfect. If he'd been human, I'd say he'd had work done. Since he was an elf, I'd say their highborn family tree needed to add some new branches for variety.

Silvanus had framed himself in front of an arrangement of thin stalagmites that bore an uncanny resemblance to a certain throne on Ord's favorite show.

Someone thought highly of himself.

Rake had called him obscenely powerful. Alastor had called him arrogant. I'd suggest adding vain, narcissistic, self-appointed special snowflake to that growing list.

Emerging from behind the throne to stand next to him was exactly what Bert had described to Martin.

A demon lord.

Seven-foot tall, red skin, tail as long as I was tall, smooth back, swimmer's build, horns curved and slightly tilted toward the back. Then there was the one thing Bert had left out: glowing, yellow eyes. I don't know how he missed that.

Isidor Silvanus spoke, his voice like warm honey. "I provide you with the safest passage it is in my power to grant, and what thanks do I get?"

Rake's hands glowed even brighter; now they were the color of freshly spilled blood. "More restraint than you deserve."

The elf smiled. "You took your time getting here, Rake."

"No, we took yours." The goblin met his smile and raised him two fully extended fangs. For the first time since I'd known him, Rake's fangs weren't for display only. He planned to use magic to defeat Isidor Silvanus, but if the fight got up close, I had no doubt that Rake would get personal with his incisors.

"You brought the individuals that I requested," Silvanus noted. "And I didn't think you would grant even the simplest of my requests. I was wrong." The elf turned his attention to me. "Miss Fraser."

"That would be *Agent* Fraser to you and yours." My voice didn't quaver in the least. Good for me.

"Ah yes. Agent. A member of that misguided organization that passes for supernatural law enforcement on this world. And Detective Ash. You chose to ally yourself with the mortal police." The elf mage smiled in a show of perfect teeth, a smile that actually reached his eyes. "I will enjoy watching your comrade-in-arms' feeble attempts to defend this city's citizens once brimstone—and their blood—is flowing through its streets." His sharp, blue eyes regarded Ian. "Agent Byrne I have heard about from a mutual acquaintance. He sincerely regrets that your reunion was cut short on New Year's Eve, and would very much like to—how do you humans say—'reach out' to you in the very near future."

Isidor Silvanus didn't say anything else, and he didn't need to. Ian knew exactly who the elf was referring to, and so did I.

That night, years ago, when Ian had first encountered the creature, it had taken the appearance of a ghoul. The creature had killed—and eaten—Ian's partner in the NYPD in an interrupted robbery gone wrong. Ian had joined SPI soon afterward to hunt down the thing that'd eaten his partner. When I'd seen the creature in the subway tunnels beneath Times Square last New Year's Eve, my seer vision told me that the ghoul face he'd worn then was but one of many faces and identities he'd taken over the centuries. I had seen each face, each identity, layered on top of one another, stretching back into infinity. And only last week, according to SPI surveillance, he'd been seen at the Metropolitan Museum gala.

So I believed Isidor Silvanus when he said the ghoul was still in town, waiting for the chance to get his claw-tipped hands into Ian.

Ian didn't move or show any sign that the elf's words had affected him in the least.

I knew they had, but my partner was pushing down his emotions until he could deal with them in the way he wanted. The ghoul wasn't here to be on the receiving end of those emotions, but Isidor Silvanus was. My partner was a practical man; he'd make do with what he had.

"And Dr. DiMatteo," Silvanus said. "Last, but far from least. The mortal who knows so much more about the darker realms than he should. You have been quite inconvenient."

Fred slapped the demonologist on the back. "Hear that, Doc? You're inconvenient. Way to go."

"My partners and I have been forced to accelerate our plans. I requested your presence since each of you, in your own way, is to blame for that. You will be the first to experience what your world will soon become."

"That wasn't what—" Martin began.

"That was precisely what you agreed to, Dr. DiMatteo. In exchange for the contract, I will release Miss Poertner to you. However, I have no intention of closing the Hellpit." He gazed around. "At this point, closing it would be more of a challenge than even I could overcome. Though it will be entertaining to watch the little mortal woman try."

"If you can't close this pit," Rake began, "then what is my incentive to give you the contract?"

"Give me the contract and you will not have to watch Miss Poertner die in one of the worst ways you could imagine."

Rake wasn't moved. "One life saved over the lives of millions lost. You'll have to do better than that, Isidor. Again, what is my incentive?"

"You will have a *chance*, goblin. A chance that Miss Poertner might actually succeed where I might fail—should I be inclined to attempt to close my masterpiece, which I am not. A chance was more than you had before I allowed you through that portal. Humans are such optimists, even in the face of miserable odds. It will be—how do you say—a 'win-win.' You and your companions die a noble death, and my partners gain unlimited access to this world."

"That's a crappy win," Fred muttered.

"For you, but not for Lord Danescu. This goblin has

survived every attempt to end his life, and there have been many, including my own."

Rake shrugged. "Everyone has an off day."

"But you won't be having an off day today, will you, goblin? Once again, you will fight to save your own life." The elf mage smiled. "But in the next few minutes, will you fight for the lives of your companions—even if it will mean losing your own?"

Rake's dark eyes narrowed. "You've wasted enough of our time."

"Oh, but I believe it is a fine use of time." The elf began walking around the Hellpit toward us. "Your companions should know what they have welcomed into their fold."

Ian snorted. "I wouldn't say 'welcomed.'"

"Then you are a wiser man than I would have thought, Agent Byrne. I have been observing Lord Danescu and Agent Fraser, and have noted that the goblin goes through the motions of considering her more than merely a temporary human amusement. His performance was quite impressive at the museum last week and the café a few days ago. He nearly made a believer out of me, and I know Rake far too well to be fooled. You've known him for little more than a year, Agent Fraser, and as a human, you can hardly be faulted for being deceived."

"Nice try," I said.

Truth was it was a damned fine try. It was also the oldest trick in the book. Sow doubt, weaken the enemy. There were many levels of trust, and I still didn't know which ones, if any, Rake was good for. It probably depended on which way the wind was blowing. Isidor Silvanus knew we had to rely on Rake and his magic whether we wanted to or not, and he wanted to weaken what little trust we did have.

The question "Did I trust Rake?" had two answers: yes, and not as far as I could throw him.

Both were true. Both were Rake.

Goblins were complicated.

"You and Miss Poertner are valuable commodities," Silvanus was saying. "Being a businessman, Lord Danescu is quick to identify and exploit any asset he may find. Tell me, Agent Fraser, has he offered you employment?"

Only within two minutes of meeting me.

"And when you did not accept, did his attentions turn to more of a romantic nature?"

Within two and a half minutes of meeting me.

"Our Rake can be most persistent—and patient—in acquiring the things he wants."

Not people. Things.

Every word Isidor Silvanus said was true. However, there were also grains of truth in every lie. Rake may have started out wanting me because of my seer gift, but over the past year, that had changed.

Or had it?

I knew what my gut told me, and my gut had never been wrong. But when it came to Rake, my heart was reserving judgment.

I'd never been in love. I suspected if Rake ever had been, once he'd realized what'd happened, he'd probably run in the opposite direction like he was on fire. I think Rake liked me. I know he lusted after me—and any beautiful and breathing woman. I was breathing, but I wasn't beautiful.

The only thing left was what I could do, the reason Rake had wanted to hire me the first night we'd met. The thing he lusted after.

I was a seer. A good one.

A valuable commodity, as Isidor Silvanus had put it.

Rake's motives were a mystery.

But right now, his motives didn't matter. Perhaps he truly cared what happened to our world beyond losing a strategic outpost against the elves, or he was simply too stubborn and proud to accept defeat on any level.

Rake Danescu was a goblin. He could balance motives like a plate spinner. But there was one thing that I did trust.

Rake would never hurt me. If he thought he had a good reason, he would tell me white lies, black lies, and every-color-of-the-rainbow lies, but I knew in my gut, heart, and head that Rake would never hurt me.

For now, that was enough.

Isidor Silvanus and the demon lord arrived on our side of the Hellpit.

The elf beckoned Rake to him with a wave of his hand. "The contract, if you please."

The goblin made no move. "Miss Poertner?"

Silvanus impatiently waved a hand, illuminating an area directly over the Hellpit, and dropping yet another veil.

We all looked up.

Oh my God.

Kitty was imprisoned inside a clear stalactite suspended only a few feet above the bubbling surface. Whatever it was made of, it was melting, dripping with sizzling plops into the Hellpit.

She didn't look frightened. She was furious.

Good for her. Better for her if we could get her out of there without either her or us getting flash fried in brimstone.

"As you can imagine, ice—especially hollow ice—doesn't last long in a place like this," Silvanus was saying. "I can only do so much to slow the melting." He held out his hand. "The contract, Danescu. Now."

Rake casually strolled toward them, stopping less than ten feet away. It was entirely too close for comfort. Knowing Rake, that was precisely why he did it. "I find it difficult to believe that your partner failed to put his master's copy in a safe place." He paused and smiled slowly. "Or did he put it in a place that was safe *from* his master?"

The demon lord's eyes were glowing bright yellow.

Rake hit a sore spot with that one.

"You toy with your betters, goblin," Silvanus warned. "There was another goblin dark mage who, astonishingly enough, approached my level of skill, but he recently got himself carried off by a particularly large demon. He only conjured demons to force them to do his will. I prefer networking."

"Networking? Or collusion?" Rake looked to the demon lord. "You, Lord Zagam, desired a way out of your realm and into that belonging to the humans. I say 'your realm' only in the sense that you reside there. You neither rule nor own it." The goblin smiled broadly. "I think we all know who does. And since you do not own it, you are legally ineligible to sell, lease, or rent brimstone mining rights to anyone. And you, Isidor, along with your brother, Phaon, needed access to molten brimstone. You dislike me intensely; your brother wanted to disrupt goblin intelligence, so you chose my wine cellar to anchor the pocket dimension containing your Hellpit. I am the legal owner of that property. You sought neither my permission nor offered me an owner's share in drug profits." Rake's smile was slow and confident. "Anchoring your Hellpit on my property is trespassing. Selling mining rights to a mineral you do not own is outright theft. I don't own Hell, so I have no legal recourse. I do, however, own this property. I could charge you rent, Lord Zagam. Or I could evict you." Rake glanced around with exaggerated distaste. "At the very least, I want to redecorate," he muttered. "But for now, I'll go with eviction."

The demon lord smiled as he gazed around the ever-expanding pit and cavern, ending with Kitty imprisoned in the ice. "You are welcome to try, mortal."

"As a very wise teacher well-known in this dimension once said: 'Do or do not. There is no try.' I fully intend to 'do.' Alastor Malvolia was hired and paid to draw up a contract between the two of you. You call yourself partners, but there is no trust between you, hence the contract. Alastor did as he was paid to do—and more." Rake shook his head in admiration. "To the two of you, contracts are merely words written with ink, and aren't worth the paper they're written on if you choose to go back on your word." He regarded the envelope and its contents with something close to pride. "But this little document is truly a marvel of evil magic and legal genius. Alastor not only drafted the words, he crafted the paper from both demonic and elven skin, then he mixed his own goblin blood into the ink. His words, in his blood, paper from your people, and your signatures to soul-bind you to every word on this document."

The demon lord smiled, showing even more sharp teeth than his mini-me. "This is a pocket dimension, created and owned by myself and Magus Silvanus. I am not in violation of the contract as we are not in Hell."

"Speak for yourself," Fred muttered under his breath.

"You may own the pocket dimension," Rake continued, "but you do not own the brimstone that is now flowing through it. You have misrepresented your rights of ownership to all of this brimstone. According to the contract, that means the brimstone's true and legal owner is entitled to collect damages or recompense in any manner he chooses. I don't believe His Dread Majesty will be pleased to discover that his trusted chancellor profited from the sale of his property." Rake's dark eyes landed on Isidor Silvanus, and a faint smile curled one corner of his mouth. "Or that an outsider knowingly purchased said property and exploited its use for additional gain, making you both equally guilty of grand theft. Only later did you discover Alastor's trickery in drawing up the contract—and you killed him for it."

"I should have ensured the goblin lawyer was conscious and then cooked him at a lower temperature." Isidor Silvanus smiled indulgently. "But what's done is done. Now here you are with the original—and sole remaining—copy. As usual Rake, you do far too little, too late."

The pointed base of Kitty's icicle prison ran water in a steady stream. Silvanus's concentration was wavering, and Kitty's prison was melting faster.

"You say you prefer networking," Rake continued as if Kitty had all the time in the world. Son of a bitch. "Networking has its place, but so does rendering mutually beneficial favors." He raised his voice to a ringing shout. "Have you heard enough, Dread Majesty?"

A red forearm the size of Rake's entire body emerged from the brimstone right beside the rock he was standing on. It rippled with lean muscles, and each long finger was tipped by a sharp, black nail. Thankfully we couldn't see the rest of it, but from elbow to fingertip, it looked just like the demon lord, albeit ten times his size.

If size meant higher on the power ladder in Hell, then Isidor Silvanus's demon lord pal was this big guy's bitch—or if he wasn't already, he was about to be. The thumb and forefinger extended toward Rake like he was about to pinch the goblin's head clean off his shoulders.

Rake didn't flinch, but coolly reached out and put the contract between the two fingers.

The demonic fingers pinched closed and submerged beneath the bubbling surface.

A collective, disbelieving gasp came from all of us.

Isidor Silvanus's was more on the horrified end of the spectrum.

The demon lord looked ready to faint.

Oh yeah, someone was in trouble.

"No need for concern," Rake told us. "The paper content is seventy percent demon skin, making it hellfire and brimstone proof."

Considering that Kitty was inside a melting icicle over a Hellpit, I didn't give a rat's ass that the paper was seventy-percent recycled demon.

"Dammit, Rake, hurry up!" I whispered.

"While your master is reviewing the contract," Rake said, "apparently for the first time—do be reasonable and release Miss Poertner."

The demon lord inhaled, turned to Kitty's icicle, and blew freaking fire directly at her. What was left of the ice kept Kitty from bursting into flames, but the icicle was history.

Kitty fell, screaming.

Rake caught her.

He didn't run across the surface of the brimstone and catch her as she fell—though that would have been impressive, too. He extended his arm, spread the fingers of his hand, and her fall stopped.

That would be magic.

Kitty's eyes were as wide as saucers at the sensation of dangling in midair over a pit of molten and popping brimstone.

Isidor Silvanus threw a fist full of acid-green fire at her only to have it deflected by the bubble-like shield Rake had wrapped around her.

Kitty screamed again.

I didn't blame her. Though this scream was less fear and more rage at being held in the air and used for target practice.

The elf dark mage simply chose another target.

Us.

Isidor Silvanus clenched his hands into fists, brought them sharply together, then wrenched them apart.

And the rock beneath our feet snapped apart like slabs of ice from an iceberg, putting me, Ian, and Martin each on a hula-hoop-sized personal island, surrounded by, and floating—not so well—in, boiling brimstone.

The jolt knocked me off my feet, and the sudden shift in weight tipped my slab of rock and nearly tossed me over the side. I desperately grabbed the edge, brimstone spitting like Hell's bacon grease on my hands and face.

I screamed. I didn't want to, but I couldn't help it.

This was why Isidor Silvanus wanted us here. Rake couldn't save all of us, and the elf knew—despite what he said about Rake only caring about himself—that he'd try to save some of us. More hostages, more distractions, more chance of success for Silvanus. He'd thought about what could go wrong and he'd covered all of his bases.

"This is an unwanted complication," Martin noted.

Rake quickly gave the elf a taste of his own medicine.

The ledge where Isidor Silvanus was standing suddenly broke away from the cavern floor and tilted sharply down toward the Hellpit. The elf mage had to scramble to stay on his feet. Rake used the distraction to pull his extended hand to his chest, bringing Kitty with it. This time, he did catch her in his arms. Kitty didn't look any happier now than she had while dangling.

The demon lord bellowed in rage and flicked his clawed hand at Rake and Kitty. A sickly green blur formed in the air, coalescing into a massive snake, its head rearing far above Rake's head. The snake launched itself at them.

Rake barked a single word, and a shield of shimmering red appeared between he and Kitty and the snake. The serpent's head struck the shield with a frustrated hiss. The shield buckled but held. Barely.

Even if Rake hadn't had his arms and hands full, we had a worse problem that even the most hotshot mage couldn't magic away.

I thought my eyes had to be playing tricks on me, but they weren't. The brimstone's level was going down.

The Hellpit was draining.

Into Hell.

And taking us with it.

"This is bad," Martin said. "Once the pit drains, we'll be in Hell and any demon that wants to come into this world can do so." For the first time I saw fear in Martin DiMatteo's eyes. "And the Hellpit will be permanently open."

There were only a few feet between us and the rim of the Hellpit. The newly exposed rock steamed at the contact with the cooler air, rock that only seconds before had been under molten brimstone. Martin was closest to the rim. He could make it if he jumped now.

"Dammit, Marty!" Ian roared. "Jump!"

With a defiant squeak, Marty leapt, just clearing the distance between his sinking slab and the cavern floor, both feet making a surprisingly solid landing.

Ian's slab was a few feet behind Marty's. There was no way I could make that jump, but Ian could. Both of us didn't have to die.

"Go!" I shouted over the chaos. "You can't help me from there!"

Ian jumped. One foot made it over the top. His left boot caught in the steaming rock, and the leather caught fire. Fred grabbed a double-handful of Ian's leather jacket and pulled with everything he had. He and Ian landed in a heap on the cavern floor.

The slab that was taking me down to Hell like my own personal elevator had moved too far from any shore. There wasn't any direction that was a jumpable distance. Even if I could clear the distance, any part of my body that touched that shoreline would be instantly flash fried. Once the brimstone drained, I'd be an appetizer for the demons waiting at the bottom for the feast that was New York.

We had guns, we had knives, but we didn't have a fireproof climbing rope.

My line of vision was now below the rim of the pit, but gunfire and flashes of red and acid green light accompanied by explosions and falling rock told me that everyone else was busy simply staying alive. The heat was overwhelming. I had to keep breathing, but each breath seared my mouth, throat, and lungs. I felt like I was cooking from the inside out. My grip on the slab began to slip.

"Mac!" came a shout from above.

I weakly raised my head.

Ian was on his hands and knees, leaning out over the pit. "Help's coming, Mac! Hang on!"

A moment later all I could do was stare in openmouthed horror as Rake Danescu—protected only by the red glow of his personal shields—dove into the molten brimstone surrounding me.

He surfaced seconds later next to my slab, intact and not burned to a crisp, though he was sweating.

I was beyond words, not only because I couldn't breathe for the heat, but from seeing Rake treading brimstone like water. I must have been dying *and* delirious.

Rake reached up and grabbed my forearm, his hand cool and soothing. How could . . .?

I blinked the sweat out of my eyes and looked down.

Rake's hand was glowing with his shielding spell—and now, so was my arm.

The glow spread until my entire body was encased in its protective field.

My vision began to clear, and I could breathe again.

"Let go of the rock, Makenna," Rake was saying.

What? "Are you—"

"Crazy? Kidding? Neither. I can't hold against this vortex for long. I'll swim us over to the wall."

My only other choice had me waiting to be sucked into Hell. Die in Rake's arms or be ripped apart by demons that never learned to share their food?

I let go of the slab and slid into Rake's arms.

And into the brimstone. Brimstone that amazingly felt no hotter than hot bathwater.

Rake flashed a quick grin as he held me tightly against his chest. "Like being in a hot tub, except we're not naked."

My mouth was parched. I swallowed and panted. "If that hot tub . . . was draining into Hell." I thought for a moment. "Why didn't you pull . . . me out like you did with Kitty?"

"That trick's one shot only."

The goblin was breathing heavily from keeping our heads above the brimstone and fighting the force of the whirlpool at the center of the pit that was beginning to pick up more speed.

Rake had expended an incredible amount of magical energy. Catching Kitty, fighting Silvanus, shielding the two of us—it all picked that moment to catch up with him. The current grabbed us both, sweeping us away from the walls and toward the pit's now churning center.

I couldn't think, I couldn't react, and I had no air to scream.

Rake's grip around my waist and back never lessened.

A swell of brimstone passed between us and the vortex. Something was swimming just beneath the surface. Something huge.

A white worm as big around as a pair of fifty-five-gallon drums breached the surface like a whale. The massive head swiveled and two pitch-black eyes the size of a man's fist focused on us.

It was a larger version of Marty's demon toddler.

One of the parents. Or *the* parent, depending on how demonic white worms reproduced.

I'd given up trying to make sense of anything I'd seen since stepping through that portal. I stared in dumbfounded amazement. It was all my stunned mind could do.

Rake's cough sounded like a laugh.

The giant worm submerged, and my stomach tightened at what I knew it was going to do.

Oh crap, crap, *crap*!

Rake tightened his grip on me. "Hang on, darling."

The worm surfaced again right next to us, gently but forcefully nudging us away from the vortex and toward the nearest wall. I'd heard of dolphins supporting drowning swimmers and pushing them toward shore. I never expected to experience it with a dolphin in the ocean, much less with a demon worm in a brimstone whirlpool.

The worm held us against the wall with its broad head until we could get a few much needed breaths.

"Get on my back," Rake told me.

"What—"

"I'm climbing out . . . you on my back."

"How can you—"

"Muscle . . . and magic."

At least the last part made sense.

I looked up at the jagged Hellpit wall. There were enough

hand- and footholds, but it was completely vertical. Goblins were stronger than humans, so Rake would have been able to do it if he was at full strength, but he wasn't. Plus, he'd be carrying me like a backpack and maintaining the shields that were all that was keeping both of us from bursting into flames.

I looked from the wall into Rake's eyes. The reasons why this was impossible were limitless. The other options we had were none.

I chuckled, though it sounded like some kind of vocal spasm. "Do or do not."

Rake gave me a crooked grin. "There is no try."

I got on Rake's back, wrapping my legs around his waist, my right arm around his middle, my left arm over his left shoulder, clasping my hands over the center of his chest. It wouldn't do either one of us any good if I choked him on the way out of here.

The momma worm submerged, leaving us.

With his hands and feet glowing even brighter than the rest of him, Rake Danescu actually climbed out of Hell carrying me on his back.

Ian and Fred were there along with Kitty and Martin to pull us out, but there was no sign of Isidor Silvanus or his demon lord partner.

Ian pulled me to my feet and didn't let go.

"Where's Silvanus?" I asked him.

"He ran. Rake could have either chased him down, or gone after you."

If Silvanus hadn't run, Rake would have been forced to stay and fight—and I would have been sucked down a brimstone vortex into Hell.

Thank you for being a coward, Isidor Silvanus.

I gave a little sickly grin. "I like his choice."

"It was a damned fine one." Ian's gaze searched my face. "You okay?"

"Better when we get out of here."

Ian hadn't said a word about not being able to help me. I knew he didn't like Rake Danescu, but there were times like now when personal feelings had to be tossed to the curb.

Suddenly my ears popped. Painfully. I could actually feel the hot air around us pressing down on my body. I took a quick glance around. Everyone looked similarly pained and confused.

Rake put his hands to his ears. "Isidor has used his 'back door,' as Agent Byrne called it, to leave this pocket dimension." He snarled in frustration at not having the elf's neck between those hands. "He just took the first step in collapsing it."

Fred swore. "We'll be trapped."

Rake shook his head. "It'll simply force the demons out of the Hellpit faster. They won't miss their chance to get out into the world."

I had news, neither would we.

"I have to close the pit now," Kitty said. "Quickly."

We'd all done everything we'd come to do and could do. Taking in our singed, burned, and battered selves, it was obvious that hadn't gone too well for us. Now it was Kitty's turn. Stop the worst demons that Hell could hork up from invading New York and then the world. All the little baker had to do was close a pond-sized Hellpit. A Hellpit that within minutes, if not seconds, would be drained and permanently open, with demonic hordes streaming out of it.

And she had to do it all without an anchor. Vivienne Sagadraco may have located one, but they were somewhere out there, and we were in here.

No pressure.

Rake turned back to face the Hellpit.

"Go," he told the rest of us, including Kitty.

As much as all of us would've loved to have done just that, none of us did.

Kitty quickly stepped in front of Rake and strode to the rim of the Hellpit. She extended her arms out over the pit, palms down.

The goblin was incredulous. "What are you doing?"

"My job."

"It's too big now for you to close."

Kitty's glare was withering.

"By yourself," Rake added.

Rake could be wise, too.

"Are you offering to anchor me?" she asked.

"I am."

Kitty hesitated. "What are your qualifications?"

"I'm here."

Kitty looked at me, her question there but unspoken.

Yes, Rake was here, but could she depend on him? He'd been there for me, but would he stay there for her?

The anchor mages who had worked with her in the past either didn't have the strength for the work or the balls for the danger.

Would Rake Danescu stand with her until the end—whatever that end might turn out to be—or would he bolt like all the others when she needed him most?

She needed to know if she could trust him.

She wanted to know if *I* trusted him.

Rake's eyes were on me. So were Kitty's.

I nodded to them both.

If Kitty had been able to turn the incredible power she was using now to close the Hellpit against Isidor Silvanus, the elf mage would've been a greasy spot in SPI's parking lot, she wouldn't have been kidnapped, and we never would have had to set foot inside the pocket dimension. We could have done all this from Rake's wine cellar, and then celebrated by popping open a couple of bottles. Heck, after this was over, even I wanted a drink.

The Hellpit was about half the size that it had been, when Kitty went pale and started shaking, and the sounds from below increased in volume and intensity: howls, shrieks, roars, and screams. After being kidnapped by an elf dark mage and spending who knew how long encased in an icicle, Kitty's body was only human, and it had had enough.

Rake stepped up behind her and simply placed his hands on her shoulders.

My seer vision couldn't detect what was passing between them, but I assumed Rake was boosting her power with what remained of his own.

However, as the Hellpit continued to close, the distance between us and the wine cellar portal grew.

Ian saw the same thing I did and scowled, his only reaction to possibly being trapped in a collapsing pocket dimension with an only mostly closed Hellpit. Neither of us said a word or moved, doing nothing that could distract Kitty and Rake from their task of what was the magical equivalent of world-record powerlifting.

Martin DiMatteo was fearfully looking up at the cavern ceiling.

When a man who took field trips to Hell was afraid, the time to panic had officially arrived.

"Lord Danescu," he said on the barest whisper, "the dimension is being elongated."

Kitty never took her eyes and focus off of the work in front of her, but Rake took a quick glance up, and bared his teeth in a silent hiss.

The realization of what Martin meant sank in and suddenly there wasn't nearly enough air.

Isidor Silvanus had created this pocket dimension, so he could manipulate it. The rules in here were his rules—and basic physics. The dimension was anchored in two places: Hell and Bacchanalia. Two ends of a long and narrow balloon.

As we watched, the stone ceiling of the cavern was being stretched as if the two ends of that balloon were being simultaneously pulled apart. It was what you did to make balloon animals. The balloon started off as a snake, which was the only kind of animal I'd ever been able to make. But in experienced hands, it could be twisted into a poodle. I had no doubt that Isidor Silvanus and his demon lord partner were master manipulators. Yes, they'd cut their losses and run, but if they couldn't release demons into our world, they'd cut us off from any hope of getting home, trapping us with what demons managed to escape the Hellpit before Kitty and Rake could get it closed. Or if they got it closed, the elf would be fine with trapping us in a tiny pocket dimension, forever cut off from any help, until our air ran out or we cooked from the heat, whichever came first.

Then another ugly realization hit. As badly as he wanted revenge against Rake, that just might have been his plan all along.

Lure us in, cut us off.

I didn't want to die inside of a poodle ear.

"Rake," Martin said, dropping formality and the goblin's title. "We need to run. Now."

"It's not closed," Kitty managed between clenched teeth. "They can still get out."

"It's close enough," Rake said. "And in a few moments, it won't matter."

Kitty was aghast. "I can't just let it go!"

"Just drop—" Fred began.

"The recoil," Rake said in realization. He readjusted his grip on Kitty's shoulders. "Let's ease back on it—"

Martin was still looking up. "No time."

"No choice!" Rake snapped. "All of you go. We'll be right behind you."

None of us moved.

"Stubborn humans," the goblin hissed.

"That would be us," Fred drawled. "Well, at least half of me."

I wanted to run, but I'd settle for pacing, except it might distract Kitty and Rake. So I just stood there, twitching. I couldn't get any sense that they were doing anything except standing like statues staring at a Hellpit.

"Hurry," Martin told them, his voice amazingly calm.

Rake murmured a few words in Kitty's ear as she slowly lowered her arms.

And a triumphant howl from countless demonic throats came out of the smaller—but not small enough—pit and filled the cavern.

"Run!" Rake shouted.

We all did. Rake and Kitty included.

We didn't look back. I didn't want to. If a demon was going to catch up with me, it'd happen. I couldn't run any faster, and if a demon did catch me, I'd get a good look at him while he killed me.

I had yet another in a long line of horrible thoughts. What if Isidor Silvanus had closed the portal into Bacchanalia's wine cellar? Sandra and her team were there, but if the elf wanted to slam the door in their faces, there'd have been nothing they could've done about it.

I shoved that thought aside. I'd tear into that portal with my teeth if I had to. Besides, we had Kitty. If she could close a Hellpit, there hadn't been a portal made that she couldn't rip open.

An unearthly shriek came from right behind us, immediately followed by a ground-shaking impact, Ian's shouts, and Rake's snarls. I stopped and turned.

Ian and Rake had been bringing up the rear, and now they were paying the price.

A demon had Rake on his back pinned to the path, holding the goblin down with only one massive clawed hand. The demon was blue, bald, and had biceps the size of the goblin's head.

Normally, big wouldn't have mattered with Rake. He had enough preternatural strength and speed to give that demon a run for his money.

But Rake was exhausted, physically and magically; still, he wasn't giving up.

I drew a knife. I couldn't kill it, I probably wouldn't even hurt it, but I wouldn't stand by while Rake was ripped—

Neither would Ian.

My partner had long run out of bullets for his six-shooter, but he had a pair of long knives in his hands and was moving faster than I'd ever seen him move, darting in, striking, and making each cut count. I knew what he was doing. The demon's nails were basically five-inch-long claws, and he knew how to use them. Ian couldn't get close enough for the kill, so he was trying to do enough damage to force the demon to turn and defend himself, giving us enough time to drag Rake out of there.

Then Ian would be facing the demon's full wrath.

The stone path shook, and it wasn't from the collapsing pocket dimension.

Demons, a wall of demons, were charging toward us.

And my partner had his back to them.

"Ian!" I screamed.

The blue demon half turned, and seeing his comrades bearing down on us, smiled in a show of elongated shark-like teeth.

He shouldn't have stopped to be happy.

Rake had one knife left, and he used it, slicing the demon's wrist, nearly severing it from the clawed hand still holding him down. The demon howled, and Ian dove under his guard, and with two slashing motions, hamstrung him.

The demon went down, and Ian pulled Rake to his feet.

We got Rake's arms across our shoulders and our arms around his waist, and together we dragged the goblin and ourselves through the portal Kitty was holding open for us.

No one had told us what to expect when escaping from a Hellpit inside a collapsing pocket dimension. Then again, I didn't think anyone knew.

All things considered, being in Hell's anteroom one second and stepping with a gooey plop onto the floor of

Rake's fancy wine cellar the next was a small price to pay. I could have done without being coated in exit portal ecto-goop, but I wasn't going to quibble.

Rake couldn't see through the blood that'd run into his eyes from the gash on his forehead.

"Are we out?" he asked weakly.

"You bet," Ian told him.

"How?"

"Our muscles," I told him, smiling. "No magic."

Within a minute, the goblin was more or less on his feet, insisting to us and Sandra's team medic that he was fine.

We stubborn humans had nothing on stubborn and proud goblins.

Rake leaned against the wall beside a wine rack, the front of his leather jacket and the shirt underneath hanging in shreds from the demon's claws. There was a lot of blood, but the cuts appeared to be superficial. Lucky for Rake, the demon that attacked him wanted to play with his food first.

He would have stayed on his feet if it hadn't been for the truly bad combination of ecto-goop on a marble floor.

Rake's feet slipped out from under him and he stumbled against the glass wall of one of his wine racks.

His shoulder barely bumped it, but it was enough.

Pride goeth before the fall.

He was fine. The wine? Not so much.

The bumped wine rack tilted and tapped against the first section of glass wall holding dozens of bottles of his priceless wine. That section of wall fell, triggering a domino effect until the entire cellar was a sea of wine and broken bottles.

It looked like every bottle of wine was broken, and Rake had done it himself.

The goblin started to laugh, but Fred had beat him to it.

Above it all, I could swear I heard the hissing laughter of Alastor Malvolia.

33

BACCHANALIA was still standing—at least on the outside.

When we'd all gotten out of the building, we could hear the rumblings of the club's marble floors collapsing into the hole that had opened where Rake's wine cellar used to be. Even though the pocket dimension hadn't occupied much physical space outside of the wine cellar's wall, its implosion caused enough of a disturbance to bring on a partial collapse.

"What I'm saying is that all demons aren't bad," Martin was telling Fred. "They just live in a bad place."

The Con Ed folks were calling it a sinkhole. The supernaturally clued-in Con Ed people had "discovered" the gas leak on the other side of the wall from Bacchanalia's basement in an old drainage tunnel. The line had broken as a result of the sinkhole that had opened beneath the tunnel and spread into the exclusive sex club.

Baxter Clayton was broadcasting live from a block away.

The corner of Bacchanalia's building was just visible in the background. Baxter had his cameraman keep both him and the building in the shot as he talked. The anchor was probably praying to God that Bacchanalia collapsed while he was on the air.

Baxter Clayton's prayer wasn't answered.

The Hellpit was gone, and the pocket dimension along with it, but it'd left its stench behind, which was being explained by a sewer line break.

That was one hell of a sewer line.

A few weeks later, Kitty's Confections was back in business. Same building. New kitchen equipment courtesy of Rake Danescu.

I was glad she'd stayed put.

It helped that Dr. Carey had determined in the autopsy that Alastor Malvolia hadn't died in her oven.

I was on my way to Kitty's shop. She and I were going to do a much-deserved girls' night out. I was still staying in the VIP apartment at headquarters while my apartment was being cleaned and repaired. It was almost finished, but I hadn't decided whether to accept Rake's offer of a no-strings-attached apartment, or to stay in my old place. After SPI's cleanup crew was done with it, no one would ever know that it'd been temporarily sublet by a pack of carnivorous baby demons. I would know, but I hadn't decided if knowing and remembering was enough for me to pack up and take my worldly goods elsewhere. It was a nice apartment in a good neighborhood. I liked my neighbors. It was home. But it didn't matter how much that bedroom had been scrubbed, how many coats of paint had been put on the walls, or how plush the new carpet was, if Ian hadn't been there . . .

I pushed all that out of my head. I didn't have to decide tonight. Tonight was about fun.

Rather than meet at headquarters, Kitty asked me to come over to the shop. She said she had something to show me.

I took the subway and walked the block to the shop. It had just started to snow.

When I walked around the corner onto Bleeker Street, I stopped in my tracks, not believing what I saw in Kitty's front window.

Gingerbread.

Not just one house. An entire Victorian Christmas village filled the shop-front window. The details were incredible. The houses even had tiny translucent sheets of sugar for windows.

A young family had stopped to admire Kitty's master-work. A little boy and girl, who couldn't have been more than five years old, and were just tall enough to see the village at eye level.

They were mesmerized.

While the children's attention was occupied, Kitty caught the mother's attention from inside the shop, and quickly held up two cookies with a questioning look.

The parents smiled and nodded.

When Kitty came out of the shop with two gingerbread cookies in her hand, the kids went from mesmerized to jumping-up-and-down thrilled.

Kitty was pretty thrilled herself. Actually, she was better than thrilled; she looked content, the glowing kind.

I grinned. "Gingerbread," I said when the family continued down the snowy sidewalk, the kids biting the heads off the gingerbread men.

"Gingerbread." She smiled and shrugged. "It was time."

"The perfect time."

"I'm a baker. It'll be Christmas before we know it. It needed to be done."

Truth wasn't all that could set you free. Gingerbread worked wonders, too.

Yes, her three-greats-grandmother had been *that* witch, but Kitty had faced her demons—literally—and had accepted that gingerbread baking was part of her heritage, and one bad cookie in the batch wasn't reason to abandon what you were good at.

"Come on in," she said. "I have a few things to finish up in the back, and then we can go. I'll fix you a hot chocolate while you wait."

Kitty opened the door and went inside. I paused, sensing someone watching me.

I turned to look across the street.

A tall figure in a long, dark coat stood beneath a streetlight. The young family crossing the snowy street saw a tall, dark, and absurdly handsome man. I saw a tall, dark, and absurdly handsome goblin.

"Your new partner's here," I told Kitty.

Again that mysterious smile. "He's not mine." She continued inside. "Hmm, I'd better make that *two* hot chocolates."

"Rake likes hot chocolate?"

"I found that out last week while he was helping with the installation."

"Helping?"

"Helping. And he's mad for double chocolate chip cookies."

I waited by the door as Rake crossed the street.

It wasn't his usual big cat, predatory stalking walk. Rake Danescu crossed the street like a normal man. Hands in the pockets of his coat, dark head slightly down against the snow that was coming down harder now.

After what I'd witnessed under Bacchanalia, I knew Rake was as far from normal as it was possible to be.

That knowledge didn't bother me. I smiled. Though I was going to have trouble reconciling the mage who hauled me out of a Hellpit and then helped Kitty close it, and the mage who just might know Lucifer—or at least one of his generals—with the man who loves hot chocolate and chocolate chip cookies.

"Hi," I said.

"Hi, yourself. Is Kitty inside?"

"Oh . . . um, yes." No come-ons? No bedroom eyes? If we SPI agents are anything, we're adaptable. Just go with it, Mac. "She said she had some things to do in the back." I opened the door. "She was going to fix us some . . ."

Two steaming mugs of hot chocolate were waiting at a small corner table with a plate of chocolate chip cookies. The store lights were off. The window lights were on, illuminating the gingerbread village, and one of those tiny lamps that you'd find in those romantic restaurants glowed beside the plate of cookies.

Kitty was fixing things, all right.

Rake's dark eyes gleamed in the dim light. "You think it's a trap?"

"Oh, I know it's a trap."

"Shall we trip it?"

"If Kitty went to all this trouble, we'd better. Besides, I want that hot chocolate."

Rake didn't say what he wanted, but his eyes were doing a fine job of saying it for him.

Now *that* was the Rake I knew.

I took an exploratory sip of the hot chocolate. Too hot. I blew on it. "Thank you for taking care of Kitty's kitchen."

Rake nodded. "I offered another store location, but she wanted to stay here."

"I'm glad she did. Don't let anyone run you out of a place you love."

"Have you decided what to do about your apartment yet?"

"I figure I'll wait until the work's finished, then go over and see what kind of vibes I get. Homey vibes or *Amityville Horror* 'Get Out' vibes."

"My offer still stands."

I reached for a cookie. "I know. And I appreciate it."

"But you won't accept it."

"Probably not."

"Why?"

He seemed genuinely confused. Maybe a goblin woman wouldn't feel odd about accepting an apartment from the playboy owner of a sex club. Then again, I didn't have any evidence about Rake's playboy status. I'd always just assumed. Maybe I should ask.

I felt suddenly awkward. "I think I'm still a small-town girl. Old-fashioned. At least when it comes to accepting a luxury apartment from a mysterious goblin billionaire."

The edge of a smile appeared. "I'm mysterious?"

"And that's putting it nicely."

"What if I told you that deep down I'm an old-fashioned guy."

"Don't make me choke on my cookie. You're a spymaster. I'm sure you've had practice being just about everything."

"What if I told you I wanted to have more practice being someone your grandmother would approve of?"

"You couldn't practice enough to fool her. Advance warning: her favorite weapons are a shotgun, a cast-iron skillet, and a butcher knife. Usually two at the same time."

He didn't even bat an eye. "Duly noted."

It didn't look like Rake was afraid of Grandma Fraser. He should be. Passing a contract to the devil himself for his reading enjoyment was one thing, ticking off Grandma Fraser was just plain dangerous.

I smiled. If that ever happened, I wanted a front-row seat.

"I've had plenty of experience persuading women not to kill me," Rake said.

"I'm sure you have." I took a sip of hot chocolate. "What about Bacchanalia?"

Rake shrugged. "It'll go down as another New York club that had its time in the spotlight and then faded away."

"Or in this case was swallowed by a Hellpit." Then I snorted a laugh. "I'm sorry; I can't help it."

"You're not in the least bit sorry. Yes, I know. The irony is priceless. A den of sin gets swallowed by Hell itself."

"So you're taking that as a sign and aren't rebuilding?"

"No, I'm taking it as what you would call 'a blessing in disguise.'"

"Pardon?"

"The reason that Hellpit wasn't found until it was nearly too late was because I hadn't been to the club in over a week. Businesses like Bacchanalia require hands-on management."

"Pun intended?"

"Actually, no. If I had been there like I should have been, I would have known the moment that pit first started to open. But I wasn't, so I couldn't, and as a result . . ."

"Hell ate your building."

"Quite so."

"So what are you going to do now?"

"After my lawyers and I fight with the insurance company over a settlement, I'll take my money and invest it in a business or a building that I don't have to be personally involved in with day-to-day operations."

"How about your employees?"

"Those who need assistance, I'll see to it that they find alternate employment, but most of them have already been offered well-paying jobs. I spent a good deal of time while running Bacchanalia fending off other nightclub owners who were constantly trying to steal my staff." He shrugged. "Now, they have what they wanted."

"I think you also gave Alastor Malvolia what he wanted."

I hadn't been the only one who'd heard the goblin lawyer laugh in Rake's late, great wine cellar.

"Isidor got away."

"For now. And thanks to you and Al, he's got bigger trouble than you hunting him down."

"I want confirmation."

"So call up His Dread Majesty again and ask." I hesitated, suddenly uneasy. "Do I want to know how you contacted him to let him know to eavesdrop?"

"It didn't involve a virgin sacrifice, if that's what you're asking."

"You'd have never made it to Bacchanalia in time if you'd had to run around looking for one of those."

"Probably true. Let's just say I have a few highly placed connections in warm climates, and leave it at that."

"Fine with me."

"Though I'm going to be busy enough with all of Alastor's other instructions."

I gave him a questioning look.

"In addition to seeing to it that his copy of Silvanus's contract was brought to me, Alastor named me the executor of his estate—and then left me most of it."

I barked a laugh. "Not bad from a guy who didn't like you when he was alive."

Rake wearily leaned back in his chair. "I haven't put a dint in wading through Alastor's corporate holdings."

"A lot?"

"Oh yes. I'm certain I'll find things he willed to me that would be the last thing I would want to own. A man who hated you will leave you some nasty surprises."

"Do you really think he hated you?"

"I may have had his respect on occasion—"

"That wasn't what I asked. Did he have any family?"

That earned me a puzzled look. "None that were referenced in the will."

"No family, no children. He had a lot but no one to leave it to." I smiled. "We can't pick our family, but we can pick our friends. I think Al Malvolia just might have considered you a friend, or perhaps even the son he never had. He obviously respected you. That's one small step from admiration. You're just as sneaky as he was, maybe even more so. He had to admire that. It's something to think about."

Rake's lip curled. "I'd really rather not."

He said it, but I didn't think he really meant it. I was certain

Rake had done plenty of thinking since last Wednesday, about a lot of things.

"I think Al's fixed it so you won't have any choice. Sneaky and manipulative from beyond the grave. But deep down, he knew he could depend on you to do what needed to be done. So did Kitty."

"Once you told her."

"What do you mean, once I—"

"I have sisters. I know all about nonverbal communication between women. Kitty wanted to know if she could trust me. That nod of yours assured her that she could."

"Kitty was looking for trust, but she needed bravery. You dove headfirst into a Hellpit of brimstone, and then carried me out like a backpack. I'd call that brave."

Rake gave me a sheepish grin. "Or insane. I'd used that shielding spell before for fire, but brimstone isn't exactly something you get an opportunity to practice with."

I blinked. "You didn't know if it would work?"

"I suspected it would. Strongly suspected."

"Maybe that makes you insanely brave. Either way, any man who'd dive into a Hellpit is certainly up for a little Hellpit slamming."

Rake's sheepishness spread into a full grin. "I didn't slam that Hellpit, either. That was all Kitty."

"But you—"

"Didn't give her a power infusion. For one, by then I didn't have it in me to give. I barely had enough to stay on my feet. Kitty needed to do as much by herself, unaided, as possible. Magic takes strength, but it also takes confidence. You have to believe that you can do it. Kitty had had too many anchor mages fail her. That affected her confidence in her own ability. Soon thoughts began to run through her mind. Maybe she hadn't been good enough. Or if she'd been stronger, her anchor would have survived. Doubt is like poison. Once it gets in, unless stopped, it will run its course and kill you. In

Kitty's case, it wasn't her body that was in danger, but her spirit. I gave her just enough of a boost to make her feel secure and confident in her own power. To let her know that I was there and that I wouldn't leave." He glanced toward the kitchen door. "Kitty has enough power of her own, a truly astounding amount." Then he leaned forward. "You say you trust me, but you don't."

"I trust you." I paused. "Your motives, not so much. On the other hand, you could say that I do trust your motives. I trust them to be devious. That is on those rare opportunities when I even know what the hell they are."

"I'm a goblin. It's how *we* are. Though I promise you, I swear to you, that I have no ulterior motive when it comes to you. What Isidor said—"

"What Isidor said doesn't matter," I lied.

"Oh, yes, it does. It's what you've thought since we met. I am being honest with you. I need you to be honest with me."

"I have been."

"No, you haven't. You've been avoiding me."

I folded my hands on the table in front of me. "Okay, then. I'm here. No avoiding. Why are you interested in me? I'm a small-town girl. I clean up well, but I'm not beautiful."

Rake started to interrupt.

I held up a hand. "Let me finish. You could have any woman you wanted, and you probably have. Yet you want me. The one thing I am that they aren't is a seer. You tried to hire me that first night."

"And you said no."

"And you've been after me ever since. I want to know why."

"Do I have to have a reason?"

"Goblins always have a reason."

I reached for another cookie. Rake's hand arrived at the same time. He let go of the cookie and took my hand. He started to cover it with his other hand, and then stopped.

He was giving me the option to pull away.

I didn't.

"Makenna, I don't know what it is that we have, or what I feel. Believe that, believe *me*. What I really want is a chance, a chance to get to know you, to find out what we do have, what we *could* have. And I promise not to ravish you." He gave me a slow, wicked-sexy smile. "Unless you want me to."

I gave him a flat look. "Rake."

"Sorry. Old habits, hard to break and all that." Rake gazed at me a moment across that small table, his expression unreadable. "I jumped into a pit of brimstone wearing a shield that might have failed. If that had happened, we wouldn't be here having this conversation. I wouldn't jump into a pit of fire for a potential employee."

If that shield had failed, Rake would have been burned to death, and I would have been . . . well, whatever would have happened to me in Hell. He was right; we most definitely wouldn't be talking now.

"The only reason I dove into that pit was because you were there," he said. "I had a chance to save you and I took it." He gave me an exaggerated frown. "I was really glad it worked. I wasn't keen on being vaporized. It would have only hurt for an instant, but still. I'm not ready to die yet. I have things to do."

I couldn't help it. I felt a smile coming on. "And seers to acquire for mysterious reasons?"

"There are other seers. Who knows? Maybe even better seers." His eyes lit with mischief. "And I only hire the very best."

"I probably wouldn't even make the final interview."

Rake raised my hand to his lips, his eyes solemn. "There are other seers. There is only one Makenna Fraser."

ABOUT THE AUTHOR

Lisa Shearin is the *New York Times* bestselling author of the Raine Benares novels, a comedic fantasy adventure series, as well as the SPI Files novels, an urban fantasy series best described as *Men in Black* with supernaturals instead of aliens. Lisa is a voracious collector of fountain pens, teapots, and teacups, both vintage and modern. She lives on a small farm in North Carolina with her husband, three spoiled-rotten retired racing greyhounds, and enough deer and woodland creatures to fill a Disney movie.

Visit her online at lisashearin.com, facebook.com /LisaShearinAuthor, and twitter.com/LisaShearin.

Explore the outer reaches
of imagination—don't miss these authors
of dark fantasy and urban noir who take you
to the edge and beyond . . .

Patricia Briggs	Anne Bishop
Simon R. Green	Marjorie M. Liu
Jim Butcher	Jeanne C. Stein
Kat Richardson	Christopher Golden
Karen Chance	Ilona Andrews
Rachel Caine	Anton Strout